DOUBLE DOWN

*Gambling High
Stakes Deals
Creates Deadly
Rip Currents*

NATALIE NEWTON

MasterLit
GOOD READS FOR A GOOD CAUSE

For Jesse and Linda

Special thanks to
Frank Green and Regula Noetzli

In memory of Buddy

While this novel is inspired by real events, it is a work of fiction and is not intended to be an accurate representation of specific people, places, or events.

ONE

*Dreamtime quiets souls screaming
in Walkabout revelations.*

December 27, 1987
Eden, New South Wales, Australia

SAILING SOLO IS a rare choice among well-bred Southern women. The educated and charming Ava Marks remains massaged into that sentiment. The Sydney-to-Hobart Yacht Race is no exception. Not just because Bassie is the cemetery of the Bight, but because the moments of joy in life are for sharing. *Oz Rox* has no chance of winning the race. She isn't entered to win. She sails in the tradition of the Sydney Yacht Club, in the tradition of shared moments of salty dreams and steeled nerves, and as a memorial. A damn memorial.

Ava is no gambler. Only a month from the "bell tolling thirty," as she refers to it. Never needs gambling in her world. She'll sit this one out. Heroes and oceans double down. She is not a hero, either. Eden is the final safe harbor before Bass Strait. Besides, it is that lazy time between Christmas and New Year's Eve. No need troubling the authorities by drowning at sea. She doesn't need or desire to know Bassie's strength. She enjoys that special social refuge afforded beautiful young women of charming character. Her refuge is so stalwart that, until these events, the existence of it remains unrecognized by her. As does her inability to transfer analytical skills from work to life. Her mama warned her the devil hides in a charming package. That description sums up her relationship with men. And now she is here. Because of a charming package and a promise.

"And good for her, Skip," she says aloud, her soft Southern accent whispering through the empty room at the inn. "Okay, so I sailed solo to the hot tub and stationary bed. I know you're smiling about the race . . . and my jumping ship."

No answer. Sometimes she anticipates one. A thought she keeps quiet.

Skip Dubbledon. Their meeting seems so long ago. Not even two years. A lifetime in two years. She had a call from a friend of a friend, someone who sounded fun and self-confident. Powerful. He introduced himself as Skip Dubbledon. She recognized the name straight away. Ava talked to her friend Nathan, a critic and writing coach, about Skip less than two weeks prior. Skip talked on the phone for 45 minutes from Sydney, Australia, to Morehead City, North Carolina. Chatted like it didn't cost a cent. *Hell, my boyfriends never talked that long from down the street,* she remembers thinking. Nathan told her that Skip was the president of a big oil company. The fact that Skip never mentioned this fact made her like him immediately. He telephoned her as soon as he received a letter from Nathan. Said the letter mentioned that Ava would be in Sydney. Nathan asked Skip to be a contact for her. She didn't know what else Nathan's letter said, but Skip called her immediately—for 45 minutes. They laughed through most of the telephone time.

She had no idea what was so funny. Never remembered any of it. Just remembered that Skip sounded charming. More engaging than the typical businessman she met. She sidled right up to the offer they meet for dinner in Sydney. Finally, she might have met a gentleman who leaves behind his change. And makes her laugh.

I was right, she tells herself. Her nose stings at the memory. She sniffles. *Stiff upper lip, Old Girl.*

Five Years Earlier
Northern Territory, AUS,
February 1982

THE PUNCH OF sharp steel jolts Skip backward. His stocky six-foot-one frame goes cold then hot then cold. The American executive veneer cracks. His primitive brain breaks free of convention. Flashing back in time. Fanged by an Outback viper a year earlier. Lived through two strikes in this Dreamtime desert. Warm blood. His superego grasp of problem-solving rapid-heartbeats back to him. Going into shock. Muted pub noise. Battle fatigued from university football. War-worn from a decade of oil deals. Good instincts. Imprinted reflexes. His left hand yanks at the short drunk's dusty paw. Knife exits Skip with a sick, slippery squirt. Right arm elbows the swearing miner with the power of a tidal wave. Skip turns as the miner's jaw rises to the ceiling like a pilgrim come home to the Lord.

The drunk thumps the floor, releasing an orange dust cloud that fogs his dry riverbed features. His calloused paw still grasps the leather-handled knife.

Blood slides a warm, red glove over Skip's left hand as he applies pressure to his wound.

A lanky, black-haired man of six feet pushes past Skip. The man is wearing the only grey pinstripe suit in the Territory. Walked out of the pub only moments ago, his Samurai-style gate catching Skip's attention. Thought he looked Indonesian and something—maybe Egyptian. That is the moment the scruffy miner set his eye on the man left alone—the definite Indonesian sidled up to the bar. Skip is good with body language. Sees a pending tackle as easily as a bluff. These Territory miners don't bluff.

The pinstriped Samurai starts flinging the drunk miner toward the door in seven-foot tosses. One hundred eighty pounds heaved as easily as a sack of coward's feathers.

The Indonesian man in the aviator sunglasses and black Armani tie remains motionless. True to the buffed nails and recently clipped black hair. Skip had heard him order two fingers of Black Jack and Coke as if trying to look like a Yank. "Two fingers of Black Jack" in a bar of XXXX beer. That alone would bring out a viper. The pub was crowded with men two hours into slamming back after a month in the open-cut mines. That and looking "far'n."

Yep, Skip noticed. Sizing up Black Jack before the miner drew on him. Guessed Black Jack was probably in his mid-thirties, like himself. And comfortable due to the protection of others—*money and paid others*, he mused. *Must be a mining investor or investment banker.* A lamb for the taking in the outlying pubs of the Northern Territory.

Skip feels a tug on his shoulder. He leans into the Black Jack and Coke Indonesian—the shorter stranger he just saved from the knife. Skip's blood is making mainsail stains on the side of the man's white, raw-silk jacket. He can handle himself in a boardroom and a brawl. And he sometimes cares for others more out of instinct than goodwill. Probably comes from growing up in a house full of sisters. Good-looking sisters who needed some looking after.

The man Skip ran down the bar to save is now saving him. Sound pulses louder. Men yelling. Heart boom-boom-booming in his head and abdomen.

Just push the Indonesian away from the drunk Aussie before something happens. That's all Skip thought. And now something has happened to him. Consciousness wanes.

The Indonesian grips Skip's right arm and walks him to the door. "You come with me. You come now."

Knife! Was I knifed? Son-of-a-bitch. Skip's chest has the cold feel of a cherry icy treat eaten too quickly as a child. The musty room is the orange mist of sailors' nightmares. Rapid blinking won't bring focus. Everything smells like soured towels left in the ship's hold. His white dress shirt is wet red below the waist. Hard to concentrate. Looks like one of his sisters spilled nail polish all over him. Like the high school letterman jacket—ruined the first day home by peach nail polish. *Fucking peaches. Never ate them again. Never dated a woman in peach nail polish. Mostly never.* No pain the moment he smirks at the memory. Then it is gone—the memory, the lack of pain. But not the struggle for focus.

He sees the miner lying by the car park. The man's tan work shirt is splattered with blood. His canvas hat rings his right arm, knife still secured in the fist thrusting through its crown. He is rocking on the ground. Not much. Just enough that Skip knows the miner is alive.

The lanky man helps the Indonesian into the waiting black Mercedes.

Skip sees his blood blotted on the man's linen shirt and silk jacket and pants, like a white map marked for drilling leases. *Black Jack is red Jack,* Skip muses in a woozy-headed fog. Doesn't feel much now. The desert sun squints his eyes. The lanky man is talking fast. *Must be apologizing. Red Jack* slides across the back seat and motions Skip to follow. "Skip Dubbledon," he says to the Hong Kong tailored Indonesian. Skip knows a good suit when he sees it. He also knows a ruined suit. He offers his bloodied right hand. "Shorry about the shoot." The Outback glare goes as black as the car.

The young medic in khaki shorts and a brown cotton jumper peers inside Skip's open shirt. "Mr. Dubbledon? Mr. Dubbledon? . . . Get t' canvas so we can-a take him inside. Someone a-call the oil company. No, call t' Host Department. They'll know what t' do." The medic's shoulder-length, surfer's blond hair is stiff from too much ocean water. It brushes Skip's face as he adjusts the makeshift bandage.

"What the hell?" Skip alerts with a jolt. "What? Where am I?"

"I'm t' medic, Mr. Dubbledon. We . . . tumm . . . need t' get you a'side. I'll dress t' stab wound. She's a beaut. Lucky twasn't two inches to the . . . Hell of a way to start me shift."

"Fucking Kiwi. . . What are you, twelve? Mum's a Cockney, I'll wager." Skip takes a hard look at the tanned young man and weakly brushes him aside. "Christ. You go to med school in Bali? Long way from t' surf, aren't you?" He still stung from the New Zealand oil deal gone bad. After that, any Kiwi was a target.

The New Zealander sets his jaw and breathes deeply. "I'm t' fuckin' Kiwi who a-goin' to give you a transfusion afore you bleed t' death." He grips Skip under his arms and slides him out of the car as two other men hoist him onto a stretcher.

Can't see the other men. Black as the Mercedes again.

The white-suited Indonesian removes his mirrored

sunglasses. "He stops the knife for me. Great tiger. We stay with him. You know him, yes? Any needs. Anything. You know him?"

The medic walks beside the stretcher, keeping pressure on Skip's wound. "Dubbledon. Damn Yank. President of SpearCo Petrol."

The lanky Samurai-type sidekick grabs the medic's left arm so tightly that the medic stops without a word. The stretcher enters the Quonset hut medical building.

"Prince Kanjeng. You address Prince Kanjeng with respect!"

The prince taps the Samurai's gripping hand. It releases immediately. The prince smiles and offers his hand to the stunned medic. "You *will* take care, yes?"

The medic accepts the firm handshake. "So sorry, Sir. Ya Highness Sir. I mean, yes. I will take good care of him."

"We wait with him. Adjul, tell my uncle what has happened. Find out what you can about this SpearCo. What he does here today." The prince speaks in English so the "fucking Kiwi" will be concerned with his job rather than figuring out what they are saying.

Kanjeng's English is considered excellent in his small principality near Sumatra—a principality surviving the Dutch colonization and the Japanese enslavement of most of Indonesia and now even surviving its own form of democracy. Kanjeng had the advantage of a year at Cambridge, then a year traveling through Western Europe. He took more advantage of the year traveling. He skipped the Netherlands. Then came the two years in New York dealing with family investments. New York is where he discovered Jack Daniel's. And many other forbidden things. He did not have the best head for business. He did have a good sense for character. And for this trait he was most useful to his uncle who, behind the scenes, still ruled their principality. And for his *worldly* nature and ideas, he was much publicly criticized and privately liked by his uncle. For all his travels, the prince still had the sheltered experience of one who is preceded by rumors of wealth. He knew the sting of being patronized. He did not know the sting of the viper.

Prince Kanjeng expects his bodyguards to protect him, die for him if necessary. *Why would this stranger help me?* People cater to all the royal family, protect them, befriend them. He does not trust the idea that Western strangers would help someone just because it is right. Never witnessed that trait in London or New York. Never had the comfort of friends he knew liked him rather than what he could do for them. *Here is a man of courage. A tiger. A true heart. Saving a man's life is no small thing. Saving a prince's life requires thought on the reward.* And such a man, he knows, will not expect or accept a reward. It must be subtle. It must come with time so the debt is settled.

Skip stirs on the rough sheet. His shirt is missing. His side is fanged again when he moves. "Dammit!"

Prince Kanjeng offers Skip his hand. "Good. You will be well. . . . I say 'Thank you.'"

Skip is barely alert enough to remember the brawl. *Oh yeah, Black Jack and Pinstripe.* "Would have done it for anyone. You're welcome. . . Skip Dubbledon." He attempts a firm business handshake. "And you are?" He pulls back in pain. "Where's that fucking Kiwi?"

"I am Pr-. . . Ken. I'll get the fucking Kiwi." The prince smiles and nods. "Adjul . . ."

Skip hears Adjul in the hallway: "Prince Kanjeng says come now." Through the nausea and punching pain, Skip recognizes the Indonesian name. Recognizes that the prince is offering friendship. The hand is played and he has won a friend—the hard way, but he won.

Four Years Later
Sydney, AUS, September 1986

WITH FINE BLONDE hair and hazel eyes, Ava Marks wore the all-American girl look as casually as a Saturday morning jogging suit. Her pretty face, wreathed by golden tresses, was not what men noticed first. It was her thin, suntanned, five-ten frame that elevated her to an object of desire. She knew it and carried it with a confidence gained from a decade of flirtations and flowers. Her only flaw, B-cup breasts, made some men lose interest immediately. She continued naively unaware of this shortcoming, thinking any man not attracted to her must be truly in love with another or gay or perhaps just intimidated. Most of the time she was right. Quick to laugh, even at her own expense, she projects Mimosas in the morning while inwardly thinking more like a double shot at midnight. She truly had just enough experience to be dangerous—to herself and others. Fate—and men—had guided her through many an unnoticed minefield.

The first time she heard, "Loose lips sink ships," was in one of those World War II movies her history-buff father watched incessantly. Both the saying and the sentiment stayed with her. And the love of her adoring father, whose standards were so beyond reproach that no man would ever equal him in her heart. This was one of the few things she knew for certain. And like other deeply held notions, she told no one. She held her thoughts with what she decided must be the definition of the British stiff upper lip. Though she was a Southern girl without doubt. With equal conviction, she simply expected the attention of most men she encountered. The combination would be her making and her undoing more than once. She adds to these attributes a gift of intelligence that she employs sparingly, as if afraid its total release might explode her sheltered world. And indeed she would prove this fear correct—in the sheltered epiphany of one smart enough to shut up.

Ava lifts her tanned face to the orange sun gliding beneath the far upward curve of the street. "So what is the deal with Jakarta? Did you have a productive trip?"

Skip had to park a couple of blocks from the restaurant. Fine with him. He enjoys a leisurely walk in the early spring evening air. Still hard to feel comfortable with the seasons reversed from his "before life." The "before life" was everything "before money" as far as he was concerned. The muted traffic noise is no match for the click-click-click of Ava's green, high-heeled sandals on the cement sidewalk. She is wearing a knee-length, print dress, in greens and yellows and oranges of a summer garden. He thinks she belongs there amidst the flowers. They are early this season, and he is ready for beauty, ready to escape the endless offices and drilling sites. In this land of Oz, spring comes at year's end. He is from Texas. Spring is supposed to be the respite in a continuous summer. Like he thought of Australia the first time he learned SpearCo was sending him here. Not the sleet and cold that is the real southeast Australia weather throughout the middle of the year. The side street in Sydney is surprisingly quiet for a Friday night. Mingled scents of grilled steak and marinara sauce hang in the air.

"Sure. Sure. So, everything good with you?" Skip is walking with a youthful sway to and fro. He is comfortable in the cloned three-piece suit he has been wearing since 7 a.m. "Always take time to stop and smell the steak!" He winks at Ava.

The first time Ava met Philip "Skip" Dubbledon he described himself as "two hundred pounds of driving sex machine." From that moment forward, he enjoyed shocking her, which she enjoyed making difficult.

Cresting forty, he is six-one and definitely a little over two hundred pounds. From his anecdotes, Ava decides he is no doubt a sex machine. His dark brown hair is innocent of grey and he keeps a rakish mustache cropped just above the lip. She easily pictures him in his university football uniform. Only his neatly trimmed brows show the grey of wearing years. He is a graduate of a university in Texas with a BS in geology and an MBA, but he says he majored in football. Played fullback on a full-ride athletic scholarship. No dumb jock, he drove straight into the Texas oil industry. Twenty years and two wives later he holds the title of President and CEO of SpearCo Petroleum Australia and Pacific Rim.

Skip attributes his success to years of team experience playing football. After getting to know him, Ava attributes it to his mastery of chess. And his willingness to gamble with the house. He has that quiet, methodical quality of planning business relationships and deals years into the future. Unfortunately, this intensity is equally offset by the man whose quest is to remain "two hundred pounds of driving sex machine."

She'll remember that line the rest of her life. She will remember it in his low voice that he uses for emphasis, not in the inner voice that talks back to her in the night. Even now, she knows it will always be remembered in his voice. He will always be talking to her. He is the only orca in her dream world. She enjoys these times close to him.

His suits are all so similar that Ava can't tell them apart. She remembers them lined up on neat wooden hangers, looking more like a department store rack than a personal closet—little soldier uniforms waiting to make a deal. She sighs with pleasure. The air is so rich she can taste it. And Skip is happy—with her. She enjoys his quips. And that he is smiling for no apparent reason.

"The shows are in the can. Patricia has already flown back to New York, and I go on Monday, so I'm really glad I got to see you tonight." Ava reaches out, and he takes her hand as they walk. She is happy. She loves the slower life-style of Oz and Sydney's friendly people. Nothing like New York. More like her cherished North Carolina. Though people in North Carolina stopped leaving doors unlocked two decades ago.

"I haven't done this since high school." Skip smiles and swings their hands back and forth. "Fiona, my secretary, doesn't approve of us, but she told me that she likes you and you seem to like me, so she guesses our friendship is ok." He chuckles in breaks, like a man who doesn't laugh often.

"Well, just as long as Fiona approves . . . You know she treats you more like her son than her boss. And I bet she knows almost as much about that office as you do. She was a good find." Ava squeezes his hand just a little.

"She was here when I came. I inherited her with the office, and I'm glad I did."

"You should be. I think you can trust her."

"I think I can trust you, too." He turns to the restaurant door. "Well, here we are."

"Thank you. That was a nice thing to say. So where the hell are we?" Ava enjoys hearing him laugh again.

To her, this place is like entering a speakeasy with a doorman—make that door-woman. And it doesn't get better. Turning the inside corner, the hostess greets only Skip, makes eye contact with only him, and leads them through a dining room of red-on-red damask flocked wallpaper and several booths shrouded by red tie-back velveteen drapes.

Ava feels as if she's in a French brothel turned restaurant. "Hmmm. The steak smells good: meat-market fresh and mesquite earthy, charcoal-sizzling good."

Skip chuckles and nods to a man revealed by a tied-back side curtain. "New geo from the office," Skip whispers to Ava. "He's fitting in fast." No stop. No handshake. Not appropriate here.

Skip reserved a nice table along the wall. No curtain.

Ava doesn't know where to look first. "And what the hell is this place?" She is on display. Men around the room glance at her while their dining partners vie for their attention.

Skip's eyes water from holding back his glee at her shock. "This is where all the business executives bring their mistresses."

"What?"

"See, you're already having fun. And the food is very good." He takes a big gulp of his water, cooled by the Aussie limit of two ice cubes.

"And you know that how?"

Whether it was the question or the look on her face, this was the first of only two times she ever saw Skip snort liquid out his nose. And the only time she ever saw him knock his fork to the floor, grabbing for his napkin—red, of course. She raises her hand to the waitress.

"I'll bay rot ova to tike yaw awdah, Mademmozel," the waitress says, mixing Eastern States Aussie and something with what sounded like an attempt at a French accent.

The affected accent almost comes across as Southern.

Please. Ava is not amused at the comparison she notices. "Would you bring him a bourbon on the rocks and me a pink champagne, please."

"Cert'ly, Miss." The curly-headed brunette prances off in her French-maid-takes-a-holiday costume that is at least one size too small.

Skip finishes wiping his nose. He is stifling a laugh. "I didn't know you drink pink champagne." He clears his throat and takes another gulp of water to help.

Ava unbuttons two more buttons on her dress. "I thought I should blend."

This is the second time she ever saw Skip snort water out of his nose.

"So who is the guy hiding behind the curtain," Ava asks. "Who?"

"The one you recognized on the way to the table."

"Ohhh," he leans in closer to whisper. "New bloke at the office. Finished a contract for some German company. The Texas office says he called looking for work, so they sent him to me. Knows somebody in the home office. All kinds of experience. Poor guy has a limp from falling down the stairs on a rig years back. This business can be dangerous. Seems to be working out. Good guy. Surprised to see him here. He's probably the only one here who is not married. More power to him."

"The only one?"

"Well, besides me, of course."

They order steaks, both medium-rare. They joke and gossip. A government official sits two tables away accompanied by a woman not his wife. Dinner is fun. They're mid-way through it when Skip calls over the waitress and orders chocolate soufflé.

"No need to rush it. I'm enjoying myself. Aren't you?" Skip is relaxed. He had unbuttoned his worsted-wool vest and loosened his Armani tie. These are the nights he enjoys: *good food, good whiskey, beautiful woman.* Figures he isn't getting sex, though. Ava never gave a sign and he knew all the signs. *May as well have chocolate soufflé,* he decides.

"I've seen three executives who know me by first name yet pretended not to see me. And two politicians out with women not their wives nor secretaries nor daughters. A baron out with someone I'm guessing will never be on the house-party list. I'm having a great time. Does that make me terrible?" She gives him a slight wink.

"You know if you tell anyone, I'll be paying for it for years." He takes the last sip of his second whiskey.

"Hey, this place is about as off the record as it gets. What fun."

"Do you know the baron?" Skip looks up from his plate, eyes staring through just graying, barber-clipped brows.

"No. I'm not on that house-party list, either. I work for a living."

Now Skip winks, not the normal flutter of eyelashes, but more squinching the whole left side of his face. "He worked for it, too. Made his money in dry goods and bought the barony."

"No. Really?" Ava knew nothing about the creation of titles and passage of land-grant titles and *all that peerage stuff*, as she thought of it. She met a few peers in Western Australia as well as some deposed royals, and then there was the whole group of knighted titles. Way too complicated. She decided long ago to listen for the name used by everyone else. Who could remember all that title plus first name or title plus last name protocol that now flitted around her mind at hummingbird pace?

Skip leaned closer to her over the table. "Really. I've been thinking I might just make myself a fortune and buy one of those estates in England. Skip, Baron of Whatsitbury. How does that sound?"

"Oh, hah, hah. I thought you were serious. You know, I wasn't sure how that worked with the manor . . . oh never mind." *Don't sound stupid.*

"Actually, I am serious. At least about the money. And maybe the barony. Wouldn't you like to be a baroness?"

Ava turns on her best Southern accent honed during her North Carolina upbringing. "W'y Mister Dub'don, are you proposin'?"

"If you think that, two glasses of champagne are waaaay over your limit. No, really, I've worked all these years for SpearCo and made connections all over the world for their benefit." Skip lowers his voice so much that she leans forward to hear him. "Why shouldn't I do that for myself? I've got a partner I've been seriously talking to for over a year. We're going to start our own company. He's on a huge project in Egypt right now. We've been waiting for the right opportunity, and now we have it. Funny how things work out. Years ago, four I think, I rescue this guy in a bar fight in the Northern Territory. Turns out he's up there on a mining investment for his uncle. You see his uncle runs this principality that we know is prime oil country, but has never let anyone lease drilling rights."

"And now his uncle is going to let you do that because of something that happened four years ago? Who has been at the bar too long?"

"No, now *he* is going to let me do it. The uncle passed away a few months ago and guess who moved into power? I just met with the guy in Jakarta." Skip sits staring at Ava, eyebrows raised smugly. His left forefinger raised slightly to signal the waitress for another whiskey.

"I don't know. This sounds dangerous to me. At the least, very risky. How do you know you can trust this guy . . . or your partner?" Ava is stone cold sober now.

"I've known my partner for years. Good guy and a smart driller. Has his own roughneck crew. We can't do it without each other. That's why we can trust each other. As for the other one, let's just say that is the luckiest stabbing that ever happened."

"What stabbing?"

"That's right, you haven't seen the scar on my side. I could pull up my shirt and show you," he says as he pretends to reach for his shirttail.

"No, no. When were you stabbed?"

"Oh, in the bar fight. I took a knife for him. Took several stitches at the clinic up there. Good job. Scar could have been much worse. Kiwi doc' did okay."

"You must have been nice to him," Ava says nodding. "I've liked every New Zealander I've met. Most Aussies, too, for that matter."

Skip shifts in his seat. "Yeah, sure. Have to be nice to someone stitching you up, right? So anyway, this guy's bodyguard—that's a joke—took us to the clinic, and we have kept in touch ever since. We see each other occasionally when we're in the same cities, but no more bar fights. I think he had enough of seeing the real world."

"I don't think you should be telling people about this, Skip. I mean, are you leaving SpearCo tomorrow?"

"No, no. Probably be another year before we're set up."

"Then don't tell anybody."

"I think I can trust you."

"I understand the lure. Just don't understand the need to keep having more . . . more money, more excitement, more power. SpearCo is very good to you. Made you rather wealthy, I imagine, and given you a taste of power."

"Where is your sense of adventure? You never get anywhere without taking chances."

"Please don't tell anyone. I have a bad feeling. Not about you. No doubt you can pull it off. I just have a bad feeling. I'm a journalist. We usually don't see people because things are going well. I may be young, but I know you don't show your hand at poker."

"You and Fiona, you are both worriers. I'm too much a public figure for anyone to touch me."

"Oh, god. You told Fiona? She works for SpearCo."

"Of course I didn't tell her. But I did ask her if she would follow me anywhere."

"What did she say?"

Skip laughs and raises his voice back to normal levels. "She said, 'Of course not. I'm not leaving Australia to go to Texas or some other SpearCo office because you want another challenge.' She's got spunk. I told her I was just messing with her."

"Don't *mess with* anyone else, ok?"

Skip twirls the large dessert spoon the waitress set at the top of his plate. "When I get my barony you can teach me what all the forks are for, and I'll make sure you're on the house-party list," he says matter-of-factly, just like a successful business man who could not imagine anything failing. He takes the whiskey before it touches the table, nods to the waitress, and gulps a big sip before planting it firmly in front of his plate.

Ava reaches across the table. "Deal. And you will make sure the bloody English servants put ice in the cold drinks. You would think they still hand chip it from a block."

They shake on it. They both know the other is good for a handshake deal on anything.

"Yaw soufflé, Munsur."

Skip looks at the waitress. "Perfect timing. I just told her," he nods in Ava's direction, "that my wife found out about her, and I can't see her anymore."

"Uh, yes Suh," the waitress stammers and hurries away.

"You are terrible. You are really divorced, right?" Ava inhales the velvet, cocooning aroma that is warm chocolate and grabs her spoon. "Who cares?"

Skip instinctively holds his scar as he gives a full belly laugh. "You make me feel young. . . On that note, I need to change my will. You know that bitch gets everything because she offered to help write my will the first year we were married. I had forgotten that little item until I was in my safety deposit box the other day."

"You should take care of that, Skip. Who would you want to get everything?"

"I guess I'll leave it to my mother. That seems the right thing to do. She's alone now. My ex has the house on the hillside in Sydney that she always wanted. That is enough of a million-dollar blood-let. There's really nothing else. Well, money and the *Oz*." He plays with the soufflé in front of him and avoids eye contact. Talk about death makes him nervous.

"Maybe leave the *Oz* to your twin daughters. You'll need to leave them money for college." Ava takes a bite of the steaming chocolate delight. "Oh, yum! They do decadence well here."

He makes eye contact, but there is no smile. "I'll leave them enough for college. That's it. They don't even return my calls. And the *Oz*, they spent our last cruise in the front cabin reading or whatever they do. Did it just to spite me."

"Okay, so leave me the *Oz* and leave the twins a wad of cash. That way, if anything happens to you, they can feel guilty the rest of their lives." Another bite of fluffy yumminess.

"Yeah. Let them feel guilty. Do you want the *Oz*?"

"I was joking. By the time a bear like you is ready to go, the girls will be way past their teens and into being Daddy's girls again. Then they'll want it."

"So, you really enjoy sailing on her?"

Ava can tell that she needs to stop the daughter talk for now. "Of course. Who wouldn't enjoy sailing, well, except teenage girls who just want to be with their friends?"

"Have you heard about the Sydney-to-Hobart race?" He finally removes that pinstriped suit coat and squirms into comfort. His eyes follow a freshly charcoaled steak passing the table, the smoky fullness of it making them deep breathe in unison. "You can never get enough charcoaled steak . . . or ice. Would someone come put some bloody ice in my ice water?"

"Of course I know about the race. All the rich crazies tackle Bass Strait to get to Hobart for New Year's and have a rage."

He laughs softly and nods. "Not how I would describe it, but yes. It's too late for me to move things around this year to make it. Do you want to go next year? The yachts sail on Boxing Day." He is gobbling his dessert a big spoonful at the time.

"I would love to go. Count me in!" She enjoys her final sip of a Barossa Valley Cab, sarcastically savors the last sip of the pink champagne, and grabs a generous dollop of his soufflé with her spoon. After all, her soufflé is finished and what man would deny her his dessert?

"You really have to make a commitment. I had plans to go last year and the crew backed out on me at the last minute. Both of them. . . . You'll have to help crew. You know, make sandwiches and stuff. . . . You can have the front cabin. Are you sure you want to go?"

She reaches across the table once again.

He extends a firm handshake without letting go. "1987 Sydney-to-Hobart. We depart Boxing Day, so you'll have to be at the dock by 5 p.m. on Christmas Day at the latest. I'll take care of everything. You're sure," he says, his head tilted down as he looks at her through narrowed brown eyes. He finally releases her hand, leaving his hand resting half-way across the table as if waiting for the right moment to touch her again.

"Hell or high water, married to a prince, you sporting a barony . . . or baroness, pregnant with triplets, I'll be there. But you have to pick up a take-out order of this soufflé." They shake again. She notices his hand is large and unusually rough for an executive. For a moment, she pictures him dressed for battle in a football helmet and a polyester football uniform instead of a wool, three-piece one.

He releases her hand. "Damn, you *are* fun. I'm used to seeing women just for sex. Here, we aren't even having a roll, and I'm having fun. Of course, some of them are really good—"

"Too much information. Too much information." She holds up her hand to silence him.

"So, you don't like sex or what?" he asks matter-of-factly, as if he were inquiring about tomorrow's weather report.

"I can't believe you just asked me that. Let's just say I truly enjoy making love, but I am not a notch on the bedpost." She realizes she is squirming in her chair. Truth is, she wanted to have sex with him long ago, maybe two days after she met him. Not having sex was a calculated move. Everyone has sex with him, so her strategy was to make him wait for it. Be his friend. Flirt shamelessly. Give him the slow kisses of his life. Make him wait. In the end, she would nab his heart or settle for friendship. Better friends than losing him altogether, which is exactly what she knew would happen if the sex came too easily. Men like Skip enjoy a challenge.

He quickly looks at his dessert and gives a little "umm-huh." He fidgets with the suit coat hanging next to him. Starts to say something, catches himself, and leans back in his seat. "I've done the white picket fence twice already. Women turn into bitches after you marry them. I'm not sailing into that harbor again. So maybe you don't want to go after all." He takes his last bite of dessert, but seems not to enjoy it.

"Oh, I'll be there. You don't get out of an invite that easily. Besides, we shook on it."

She sees his mouth curl into a smile, but he still stares at his plate. "Damn, this is good. The take-out is a good idea. Think it will keep?"

"Oh, it will keep, all right."

AND KEEP IT does. Ava and Skip maintain contact with a few telephone calls. Both of them keep it light. Pretend nothing is between them. Not really. They are too busy for relationships. Instead of "catch you later," he now ended all calls with "still in for Hobart." Even when Skip catches her out of town and makes an offer that seems out of character, she doesn't think much about it. She can't accept his offer due to work obligations. Doesn't really give it a second thought until she learns he met a woman in Melbourne the next week—a woman who then visited him in Sydney. Ava feels the flush of jealousy. And competition. She has to know more. So she makes a quick trip, but fails to find the competition.

A month later Ava is back in Sydney. Skip graciously offers her his condo while he takes out the *Oz* for a fishing trip. Even though the gesture surprises her, the meaning is not discussed. She accepts. She already knows turning down the first offer caused a rift. But nothing else about last month's *Sheila* from Melbourne. Good riddance. Maybe she was just the flavor of the month.

Ava brings along her unit producer, Patricia, to the condo. They deserve some luxury. November in Sydney means the onset of summer. Hard to note seasons changing from studios and tiny network apartments.

The Sydney business district is a dark ghost town on Saturday night. Abandoned grids of streets and office towers sit in silent judgment of the frenetic week. Deals made and lost. People made and broken. Land orcas swimming cold streets. Sometimes made. Seldom lost. Never broken. But a riptide of arrogance can drown intelligence. Ava breathes a bit more rapidly as she drives Patricia through the dark streets to the condo. Dimly lit parking lot. Dimly lit lobby. Dimly lit elevator. There at last.

THE LARGE WINDOWS covering the north wall of Skip's eighth-floor condo frame the entire Sydney skyline. Patricia gazes over the twinkling downtown in the early evening. She takes a big bite of her salad and ham on a roll. "This is the life. If I was in like Flynn like you are with Mr. Dubbledon, I'd be up here every night."

Ava ignores the comment. "I'll open the Shiraz. Would you like a glass?"

Patricia walks along the windows, studying the scene. "You really need to ask? Say, how far are we from Sydney Harbour?"

"I have no idea. Keep looking." Ava yanks the cork and sets the bottle on the coffee table. "There you go."

"So you two living in sin up here, or what? I'd be tempted but the nuns are too loud in my head. I think I've been ruined for life."

"Guess there are advantages to Catholic school. No. Nothing like that. We're just friends."

"But you like him, right? I mean you want it to be more, right?"

"Drink your wine." Ava pours a glass nearly to the rim and hands it to Patricia.

"You're right. That'll shut me up." Patricia unwraps the towel from her wet hair, letting it fall to her shoulders. One long, eyes-closed sip of the wine. "Mmm."

The two friends share a laugh and plop simultaneously onto the suede couch facing the view. Co-workers for four years, they have grown into the comfort of familiarity and shared adventures. And inside jokes. Once they had inside jokes, they were family. Now, they sit munching milk bar sandwiches and clink their glasses in a silent toast.

Patricia finishes the last of her roll. "Leave it to you

to find an oil baron with an empty condo *with* a sauna. I could've sat in there half the night. . . . I'm still hungry."

"Let me rest a few minutes and eat *my* sandwich and I'll go back—"

"Halloo!" Skip peers into the half-open door. "Here you are, snuggled in all nice and comfy."

Ava instinctively touches her wet hair then her face with no makeup. "The sauna was great. We're just having sandwiches and some wine. Let me pour you a glass. I thought you were fishing on the *Oz* through the night."

Skip smiles at her. "Well look at you beautiful ladies. Yeah. Made it a couple of hours and turned her around. Must be crazy. Why would I go fishing with some hairy bloke when I have a beautiful woman—two beautiful women in my condo? Left him on the boat. Told him to call a friend and have a good time. I had to get home."

"Did you bring more wine?" Patricia asks, looking over the back of the couch.

Skip chuckles. "You ladies shouldn't be eating sandwiches. I'll change and we'll go out for steaks." He disappears into the hallway going to his master bedroom. Before the women can discuss the situation, he is back in a white dress shirt and blue jeans. "Well, let's go."

Ava points to her head. "We have wet hair. Can't we wait till it dries a little?"

"I swear, Ava, you could look in my bathroom for a blow-dryer. You are so . . . standoffish." Skip disappears back down the hallway and within seconds returns with a blow-dryer.

"Me first," Patricia says as she starts around the couch reaching for the dryer.

"Oh, no." Skip holds the dryer up in the air. He pulls two side chairs from the dining table and places them side-by-side. "I know women. It'll take forever. You two sit here and I'll do the drying."

Patricia pours herself another glass of wine and sits. "Well, come on, Ava."

"Really?" Ava pours herself a glass of wine and smirks at Skip.

He pats the empty chair. "You're wasting time. I want steak. Don't you, Pat?"

"Yeah. We want steak, Ava." She pats the chair next to her.

Ava reluctantly sits. "Okay, but—"

The loud HMMMMMMMM of the blow dryer drowns her out. Skip stands behind the women, blowing Pat's brunette hair into her face as she laughs. Then he finger-combs Ava's hair HMMMMMMM while she squirms in the chair. Pat holds her hands to shield her face when it's her turn again.

Patricia jumps from the chair. "Be right back. Need to get my brush."

"Yeah. Brush. That's a good idea." Skip grasps Ava's hair like a bunched ponytail and blows the ends. "I think this is the most you ever let me touch you."

Ava slides out of the chair. "All right. All right. I think it's dry enough. We'll change."

"I'M TAKING US to that ah, ah, new place near Darlington Harbour. Heard they have Kobe beef." Skip whips the BMW around the corner of an empty street and opts to ignore the stop sign. The effect of too much alcohol on the *Oz Rox* and no food is beginning to show. "Beauty. Got her last smunth," he slurs. "She does hug the road."

"It's a beautiful car," Ava says nervously. "Don't want to scratch that shiny black paint. Love that new luggage smell," she adds, so he won't think she's criticizing.

In an instant, a flashing light looms from behind and quickly gains on them.

"Oh, shit. I'll fix this." He zips down a side street and dashes for the business district. The flashing light fades. He squeals around the corner by a large bank and ends up going the wrong way up a one-way street. "Don't worry. Nobody round here on a weekend night. We'll just—oh shit."

The flashing light speeds out of a side street and screeches to a stop some yards ahead. It blocks both lanes and the next turn.

Skip jerks the BMW to a stop. He slams into reverse.

Patricia yells from the back seat. "Mr. Dubbledon!"

"Right. Better not." He puts the car in park and turns off the ignition. "Don't sworry, Ava. I negate for a living." He climbs out of the car and sets out toward the police car.

Ava turns to Patricia, who is leaning over the driver's seat for a better view. "Oh, shit."

"Oh, don't sworry," Patricia sneers, "he negates for a living."

Ava laughs lightly. "Stop that. This could be serious."

Ahead, the policeman is walking down the street to meet Skip. Ava sees Skip take out his wallet and show something. Then he hands the policeman what looks like a business card. The policeman grabs Skip by the arm.

Ava opens the passenger door and gets out of the car. "I'll see what's going on."

Interior lights dimly shine through the open driver's door of the city police car. Parked mid-intersection, it blocks both lanes of the one-way street. The business card offered to the city cop moments earlier flutters across the sidewalk. The cop yanks Skip toward the car. Big catch for a Saturday night. Police car headlights flood a side alley, where cat eyes glow from a doorway. Swaying left, Skip throws his weight against the lanky officer. The circular yellow glow of a single streetlamp spotlights the scene. Ava hears her high heels as she runs toward them click-click—-click—click—click-click against the pavement.

Skip pulls free. "Now wait a minute. Wait a minute," he says as he tosses the keys of his new BMW into the street.

She hears muffled voices, then silence as Skip is jerked into the back seat of the police car. "Damn shoes," she says under her breath as the three-inch heels click-click—-click-click along, slowing her down.

"Take the car," Skip yells from the police car as the door slams shut.

Ava stops when the cop sights her.

He waves toward the keys lying in the street. "We let you people come over hay fa business and you act like you a' on a thud wud 'oliday. He's goin' with me." The policeman gets in the car and speeds off, leaving Ava to fetch the keys from the street.

She walks slowly back to the BMW, less concerned about Skip than about the blisters forming on her feet. She realizes she has no idea where they are located. Nothing looks familiar.

"Well, we'll remember this night." Patricia is looking through the tome known as the *Sydney Street Directory.* "Wonder where the station is?"

Ava sits in the driver's seat and slips out of her heels. "I wonder where we are. Get up here. You're navigating."

TWO

One Year Later
Kirribilli Neighborhood, Sydney,
December 1987

THE MIDDLE-AGED SUPERINTENDENT, a "contri bah" as they say in New South Wales of men reared in rural areas, is inside the Kirribilli apartment when Ava arrives. "Bloody mess," he mumbles as he bangs on the hot-water heater below the sink. "Ya flat mate been fixin' her agaaan," he says sarcastically. "Not comin' bock this time. No wurrees. Triple two empty cupple wayks." He stands and throws his wrench into the wooden toolbox on the floor. "Get ya' things. See ya' down thay. Might lucky catchin' me ha on the Christmas day."

Ava shrugs in frustration, twirling her long blonde hair nervously around her right hand. Fortunately, she is packed. Boarding the *Oz Rox* tomorrow for the Sydney-to-Hobart Yacht Race. But she doesn't like inconveniences and really doesn't like last-minute changes. *Be nice. Can't complain when the Network lets you use their apartment for free. Just be nice. At least the crashing videographer is gone and can't break anything else.* She grabs her two bags from the second bedroom and scoops the bathroom toiletries into a plastic bag she finds in the vanity. She pauses at the metal stairs at the end of the breezeway. *Triple two. Two-two-two. Why can't they just say that? This double and triple shit sounds like two or three. Triple two should mean three-two.* She walks down one flight, struggling to carry her large pocketbook, two leather bags, and plastic bag. She is tired from a busy day of errands. Colloquialisms aren't helping. Well brought-up Carolina girls are encouraged to speak in the correct accent—Southern, never use slang, and politely tolerate the less well schooled. Moving for one night tests the toleration lesson. The Aussie *contri bah* screech no longer explodes her nerves. Numb deciphering is her reaction. *But they are so nice,* her coping mantra.

The tarnished brass numbers on the open door read 222.

The super hands her a key as she enters. "Jus' retun with ta othe' one on the morrow." He closes the front door behind him.

"Okay," she sighs aloud in frustration.

The generic Kirribilli apartment is identical to the last one. New carpet in this one. Front living room with a mottled polyester wool sofa faded from brown to beige. Over-polished coffee table. Round wood dining table with four side chairs newly covered in a tartan damask. Rotary phone on the counter in the kitchenette. Dial tone. Bleach smell. She goes to the main bedroom, the one with the bath adjacent, and drops everything on the unmade mattress. She kicks her alligator heels aside. Just as she is pulling bedding from the cupboard, there is a knock at the front door.

"What now?" She almost ignores the super, but remembers the door is still unlocked. *Better go see what he wants.* She walks to the living room barefoot and sees the door opening. "Forget something?"

A man in his early twenties stops in the doorway, his hand still on the doorknob.

Ava is startled. She feels her face flush. *Nice suit. Short clipped hair. Something not quite right.* "Wrong apartment," she says firmly as she walks toward him.

"Tummm . . . hoping I might have use of your phone. Ad in the paper for an apartment to let and no one there." He looks at the phone on the kitchen counter. *Western states Aussie, probably Perth*, she deduces from the accent.

Nice Southern girls usually agree to requests like this one. He has a newspaper in his hand. But there is something. Years on the road have put her survival instincts on autopilot.

Don't ring! she shouts internally to the phone and pushes past him onto the breezeway. The cement scrapes her feet. *Don't get caught inside.* "Sorry, just moved in here and the phone isn't turned on yet. The super should be in the office."

The man stays in the doorway. "Who? Oh, no one there. If I could just check—"

Ava yells to the breezeway above her. "Hello up there! Hello . . . Try upstairs. I could hear someone walking around up there." She looks over the railing to the parking lot. No super. "Oh, there he is. Hello down there. This man is looking for an apartment."

The young man leaves the doorway and crosses to the railing. "You don't need to—"

"There you are. He just went in the office." She takes three quick steps past him and closes and locks her door. *You are so suspicious.* Checks the deadbolt again. Pushing back the curtain from the front window, she comes eye-to-eye with the man. She waves and smiles and steps back out of view. A few long seconds pass. Finally, he walks past the window toward the stairs. Ava catches her breath. *Probably nothing.* Sailing the Bass Strait in *Oz Rox* feels safer by the day. *Everything triple checked. Trust the crew. Skip picked them. Get some sleep*, she tells herself.

Eden, AUS

FOR THIS 1987 Sydney-to-Hobart Yacht Race, Bassie brought her full temper, gusting winds churning sky and sea like a grey Aussie Rules football match—fists and feet of foam fighting for wood or fiberglass prizes, some yachts are claimed as trophies as others are tossed homeward. Just the way Skip warned her. The Safe Anchor Inn is one of those places where players of pastel hearts sit out the remainder of the race. Staccato radio reports offer a backdrop to wine and seaport.

Cautiously stepping onto Eden's anchored planks, a maze of low, narrow, aged grey board walkways, she grabs for the cold, metal rail. Without looking back, she shouts a goodbye. Her crew member on the dinghy, tossing like a rocking chair on a patched porch, sends a muffled reply. She ignores him. She is trying to identify the olive Thomas Cook drover coat running toward her. *Iain Miller.* She recognizes his deep voice even through the horizontal sheets of pin-pricking rain. Iain is a Sydney-based AP journalist. He keeps telling her it's "journo" here. He is smart waiting in Eden for the less crazy sailors to come ashore. She is indifferent greeting an old acquaintance. For Ava, everyone is in a category. There are strict rules separating acquaintance from friend. Greeting a friend in the stinging rain is fine. Acquaintances should wait for a dry room.

She quickly nods an agreement to meet Iain at the Safe Anchor in two hours, "Yes," she shouts abruptly, waving her left hand toward the inn as her right hand holds the hood of her yellow slicker. She just wants to keep moving toward her dry room.

Brown leather Topsiders squish with every running step. The torrents thundering against the dock boards drown the sound. Her soaked hairline sheds a curtain of rain rushing her forehead and forming river rapids down her stinging nose. Just yesterday it was swimsuit weather on a serenading sea. Today the sea is angry and crying icy downpours on the land too far for pounding. Shivering inside her yellow squall jacket and soaked white leggings, she feels numbness in her fingers and toes.

Head lowered, she concentrates on her hurried steps across grey planks to grey-yellow sand to grey-red slippery rocks. *Careful. Careful. Not the glassy one. Slow down. Take the puddle, not the slippery rocks.* Finally, she reaches grass then—*yes!*—two porch steps. She doesn't know the origin of her fear of slipping and falling, just that the fear is there. *Shelter.* She grabs one of the white towels stacked just inside the front door of the inn. Warm, baby-blanket soft. *Civilized.* Stepping out of the inch of cold water in her Topsiders, she notices most of the dozen or more people gathered in the room are wearing UGGs. She flings the water from her shoes onto the porch. How wimpy the Topsiders look compared to the chunky, Aussie shoes. The Aussies do cozy well, but she can't imagine anyone in the States wearing shoes that ugly—even with the comfy factor. In fact, she can't imagine herself ever wearing something that ugly. Three of the men in navy windbreakers nod greetings to her as she gathers her shoes. The fourth one turns away. Something familiar. She can't place him, but she is good with faces. She'll think of it. Her Topsiders leave two fine lines trailing water all the way to the young woman at the desk. Ava doesn't recognize anyone and doesn't bother to look back just in case. She is used to being noticed.

The young, strawberry blonde woman at the desk is wearing a maid's apron. She nervously hands Ava a key tied with a rose-colored, satin ribbon.

Probably Irish, Ava thinks, *always so frail and pretty.*

The maid manages a nervous "Baroness . . ."

Ava flashes an insincere smile and heads for the room. Her backpack feels suddenly heavy as she slowly navigates her way up the two steep staircases.

"The ocean's mirror distorts reflections as it clarifies life lessons. Love the dolphin. Bet the great white," she started one of her articles. For some reason, the words repeat in her head.

The stair rail reminds her of the one in her grandmother's house. Ava's favorite childhood spot was the upstairs front bedroom window of her grandmother's farmhouse on the Neuse River in North Carolina. She spent two weeks there every summer until age twenty-one. Cocooned in heart pine, she watched the dolphins return in the moonlight. The Neuse River, about five miles wide at that point, was their safe harbor. She regarded them as the people of the sea, just as she regarded people as the dolphins of the land. Musings of childhood that became her happy memory through many stressful times. She hears the gentle tide, smells the salt breeze, and once again is the innocent child exhausted from swimming and sandcastle building and washing dishes after garden-fresh meals. She strokes the aged stair rail and remembers.

Lately, she imagines herself as the spotted dolphin. She is a kind beauty endangered by the slow onset of survival skills. Though she never considers the slow onset part. Not before now. She has the ocean's grace and endless resources. And she has the pod's safety. To her, Iain is the bottlenose dolphin, his endearing stretches of playfulness punctuated by lapses into aggression. His epiphanies are full-throated. *And he will prey on his grey-pearled counterpart when other hunts prove dissatisfying,* she reminds herself. She doesn't worry about the orcas. *Always see them coming.*

Simply a seaside musing to her. The subconscious is usually disregarded that way. These travelers little know that great whites touch their lives on land and in the seas of their minds. This voyage sinks them into an emotional hurricane so stirring land and sea and sand and seaweed that sharks easily hide. For this survival lesson, they must learn to calm the distortions. Learn that trust built on knowledge buoys life. Land masks predatory fish as complex mammals, the condemned hunting in a school of naïve souls. And our gliding porpoises are learning to bet the great white.

But for this quiet interlude, she is again that sheltered girl from North Carolina. *Dry feels good. Still ground will feel good when I recognize it. I wish my legs would stop wobbling. Odd I can't tell them to stop.*

Off to her period room with the jarrah four-poster bed, overstuffed goose feather pillows, and an adult-size bathroom with a tub—*a real tub*, she thinks as she enters the room. Everything seems huge after her ketch accommodations. She notices all of it. These moments are the ones she remembers. Fingertips gliding over well-polished furniture. The slightly salty scent mixed with years of baking apples. The tea-stained lace sheers, gently waving to her from the two windows left open an inch at the bottom. The window-sills shiny with rain and needing a new coat of white paint. Bassie churns in the distance. No dolphins.

The inn breathes with the sigh of many a weary traveler. It greets all with the aged wood smell of worn floors smoothed by a thousand boots before being coddled with meadow-fresh wool rugs. *Evening campfire rich*, she thinks. Many a tense traveler is lulled by these floorboards eek-eek-eeking like a front porch swing.

Steam rising from the chipped slipper tub warms her with anticipation. She pours in a pouch of lavender bath salts. *Always travel with a quality corkscrew and bath salts.* She smiles at herself and the life lesson learned from her sister-in-law. Stepping into the tub so eagerly that she nearly slips, Ava grabs the cold metal curve at the top. "Ahhh." Warm water shocks her feet then spills over her cold legs as she lowers herself into the steam, making her flinch as it covers her clammy stomach. Her sigh of pleasure fills the room. A sigh of many miles navigated. A sigh of a moment's respite from facing facts. From facing deceit and death and other dramas she keeps pushed deep beneath the wavy surface.

Eden is a new stopover for her, but she's seen it before. Small towns in Australia are very similar to her: a John Wayne Western-style hotel doing extra duty as the local post office and pub and restaurant. The board lunch offering means you eat what the owner chalks on the blackboard that morning or you don't eat. She remembers the warning of a Sydney friend about tipping at establishments: "They'll think you're coming back to steal the chooks." At least the Safe Anchor Inn looks more Outback Oz than Hollywood Wild-West saloon. Not that she is averse to saloon hotels. Ava flashes back to The Bushranger Hotel in the village of

Collector in New South Wales. *That was real Australian flavor. What was the story I covered there?* The places usually make more of an impression. *Skip would have liked it. Hubbie, never.*

All writers are blessed with curiosity, but some also have an addiction: wanderlust. Ava falls into this category to the dismay of her conservative family, nestled in North Carolina for centuries. For her, the memory priority is the journey then the destination and then the story . . . and, of course, the next journey. In another month, she will be a jaded thirty years old. She will have wandered through fifteen countries and a couple of marriages, the first to a man with a wandering eye. Naturally, she assumes that he must have been in love with another, or gay, or intimidated. The second time "took" as she describes it. Now, snuggling alone in this room, she thinks of both *hubbies*, as she calls them. *I hope I've finally reached my destination. Something is taunting me. Withdrawals or intuition?* She tries not to think about Skip. No energy for tears.

For her, rules are not made for following or breaking. They are simply assessed for justness. She lives by karma, comforted by the belief that whatever she does will come back to her though she usually disagrees with the timetable. She is in Eden because of karma . . . because keeping a promise is just and will come back to her. She shook on it with Skip. That's not to say that she will like the truth karma sees fit to reveal, only that she will know it in her heart. Karma promises truth, not humanly flawed facts. It's blind to what one desires that truth to be.

CRISP AS GRANNY Smith apples air, the kind you get in southeastern Australia just after a spring downpour, waves past the lace-curtain sheers, refreshing Ava's face. Dry clothes and dry hair, the warm breeze lures her outside to relish the ancient aroma of wet grasses pushing through wet stone. She is unsure if she hears the surf or just wants to hear it. One last check of the room. She likes leaving things tidy.

She misses coastal North Carolina, where scents of salt and wet sand and fish intermingle within a medley of seagull cries, waves endlessly shushing against the Atlantic Beach sand. Tiny shells massage bare feet. She is eternally a Carolina girl. Carolina stock for hundreds of years. Making one of her lost causes explaining to Aussies why someone from the Carolinas does not like being called a "Yank." She settled on the benign "It's like a Yank saying 'ossies' instead of 'ozzies.'" This explanation had some success. The one she really wants to give but keeps to herself is, "It's like someone from Ireland being called a POM." That one would make the real point. *Loose lips . . .*

Kirribilli. That man looks like the one in Kirribilli. She stops for a moment to reclaim the face in her memory. *That's who he looked like.* She remembers the man in the navy windbreaker. *Can't be. You're seeing ghosts, Ava.*

The *Condor* from Bermuda took the Sydney-to-Hobart race last year in just two days and twenty-three hours. That is when Skip reminded her that this race needs more "Take your time. Tame the sea. And touch the dock for New Year's entries." Three years ago, Skip built the seventy-foot ketch *Oz Rox,* which she just abandoned. This is her first Sydney-to-Hobart. Just as she promised him over a year ago in Sydney. She smiles remembering the "bordello dinner," as she refers to it.

At the Safe Anchor, the *Sovereign* is this year's favorite

to win, mainly because she is a New South Wales entry. *Oz Rox* is a Morehead City, North Carolina, entry docked in Sydney since she splashed. Skip splurged for the computerized helm so the ketch can sail solo. Though why anyone would want to sail alone Ava couldn't fathom. He also splurged for the upgraded cabins. Varnished mahogany and brass glisten everywhere.

She thinks of the luxury yacht thundering forward. *Beautiful berths for her crew. Too bad I never learned the computerized helm. Just as well. I am through sailing solo,* she reminds herself. Most importantly, Skip splurged for a seagoing vessel. *You can trust her.*

Ava abandoned ship to save herself from seasickness rather than a fear of sinking. *Oz Rox* can be trusted. The ketch continues to Hobart cocooning the crew as she charges the Bass Strait. *Three crew . . . Skip is with them,* she reminds herself.

The aged metal doorknob screeches as she turns it to leave the room. *No need to lock doors here.* Eek-eek-eek resonates beneath the mottled wool runner, cushioning her dry to the point of itchy feet, slightly swollen and scraping the leather seams of the wet Topsiders. *When I get back to Sydney, I am buying UGGs. But they are so . . . nope, I am buying a pair. May a baroness wear UGGS? Good god, I'm a baroness.*

The local parrots have softer cries than Carolina gulls. Waves of pale grey and soft blue and light pink fluff balls fly through the last drizzle to perch in the inn's open kitchen window. The extra-wide window ledge, whitewash slowly worn away by tiny feet and thousands of cooling pies over the years, is the perfect landing.

Smells of cinnamon-spiced baking apples and sizzling

lamb on the barbie push Ava's hunger button. She can taste the smoky crunch of the fatty lamb. Chirpy cries of joy mean some apple peel or bread crust just flew through the window. Ava's spiritual sea settles into the soft landing of Mother Earth.

No doubt this scene has repeated itself almost daily since the 1840s when this inn opened in Eden, New South Wales. *The Safe Anchor Inn. I doubt those wayfarers and seafarers ever imagined this place of creaky floors and covered porches would host well-heeled aristocrats and artists and business executives taking refuge from the Bass Strait. Somehow, I manage to sit in the anteroom of all three categories.*

She likes words like "anteroom" but reserves them for mental conversation. Though she says she doesn't care what others think, the truth is she greatly fears being thought pretentious. Most of her clothes have designer labels because she likes them and because it's hard to buy off the rack for a nearly six-foot female frame. Even so, she's a little self-conscious about it. Generally, most women don't like her very much, even without Chanel or Hermes or Armani. She doesn't feel the loss as she has little in common with them. She doesn't like babies and never plans to have one. She has a graduate degree when most women she meets never finished or even started undergraduate degrees. She is a journalist, a "man's profession" she was told when selecting a major in the 1970s. She often travels alone to foreign destinations and, yes, even eats alone in restaurants. Of course she usually ends up accompanied by some interested party within the hour. Sometimes she feels as if she's living the scene in *Gone with the Wind* when it was gossiped that Scarlett had "taken to driving her own buggy."

She walks into the sitting room. Four men in yellow Macs turn and smile at her. The same maid is still at the desk.

Ava pauses. She catches the maid's eye. "Miss, the men who were here earlier. Four of them in navy jackets. I think I know them. Do you know what room they're in?"

"Oh, yes, Baroness." The maid thumbs through a box of index cards. "T'aren't here. Mistress checked them out."

"I see." Ava stares at the box. "Mr. Andrews and Mr. Pollock, right?"

The maid looks at the card. "Sorry, Miss. Just says *Pinyup crew*. Be glad to look at the charge but they paid in cash."

"You have a good memory."

"Yes. Ta. They added a nice tip. For me 'oliday, they said."

"I imagine it's just because you're so pretty." Ava gives her a quick wink.

The young girl blushes and curtsies slightly. "Ta, Miss . . . Baroness."

Ava nods to the men, who are talking low and still eyeing her. Gossip or admiration. Not sure which, but she'll go with admiration.

Men like Ava for all the reasons women dislike her. One of her few outlets for female friends are other educated, well-traveled women. They are seldom alone. She is confident this division of roles will diminish one day. Confident the next round of daughters will not be told women are "too emotional" to be physicians and "too shallow" to be journalists and "too delicate" to do, well, anything men are uncomfortable with them doing. Hopeful there will no longer be "male professions." Today is not that day. So Ava has male friends. Mostly, she has male acquaintances. Now, she heads out to meet with one. She prefers a good nap, but *one must not neglect people who are always nice to you.* And Iain is always nice to her. Sometimes patronizing. Sometimes needling. Always nice.

The damp breeze blow-dries Iain's matted hair as he waits solo on the front porch. He is early. Ava knows he likes being early, first, prepared. "All the better for watching everyone else," he once told her. The oilskin coat is gone. One of his signature white shirts with pinstripes helps Ava recognize him from behind. Today's stripe choice is azure blue. His sleeves are rolled up to his elbows. The sassy slouch leaves no doubt it is Iain Miller.

Ava pauses for a breath of the rocky-scented breeze, lightly caressing her face like a soft cotton ball. *I had to wear my azure sweater. God, people are going to think we're here together. That's all I need.*

Iain is perched on the back legs of his porch chair, a glass of Cricket Pitch in his hand and two bottles of the pale wine already opened on the small wooden table. A neat plate of sliced kiwi fruit and cheeses appears untouched.

Iain and Ava casually know one another through a Sydney rowing club. Ava made a respectable name for herself conducting and producing on-air interviews. She has a way with stuffed shirts. She also published a few short stories and some poetry which, as she says, "with fifty cents will get me tea." Nevertheless, one night after several tinnies at the Club, Iain told her that these accomplishments make her a writer, while he is "merely" a journo. She doesn't know if he continues to make this distinction out of respect or to make fun of her. Iain is one of those men apparently not attracted to her. He is not gay as far as she can tell. That leaves deep love or intimidation as the only remaining possibilities in her mind. But she does like him even though she doesn't want to like him. After all, he is always nice to her. It's the rake thing.

You like them as acquaintances. Just don't want your friends dating them, she reminds herself as she stops for a moment out of his view. She is also distant because he doesn't seem all that enamored of her. *Not knowing Thomas Cook from Coco Chanel is a plus,* she muses. She heaves a sigh and continues to his table.

Word at the rowing club is that Iain amazingly just made it to his fiftieth birthday. He is definitely one of the boys and held quite the party, "a Bob's yer Uncle rage," according to the twenty-something bartender at the Club. Iain played soccer, "football" to the locals, well into his thirties. He had a couple of marriages, both a source of endless amusement to his friends thanks to his penchant for tackling women who relished public displays of anger. No one knew much about the first marriage. Iain chose country living in those days. His follies with women and football were capped by a some-what failed two-year career as a foreign correspondent.

Then Iain returned to Sydney, rising above it all, and made a name reporting the illegal dealings of some of Australia's top businessmen. Lately, his sights are on Alan Bond. Bondi brought the America's Cup to Western Australia nearly a year ago, so the country is in that love-hate relationship known here as "tall poppy syndrome." A local hero like Iain needs a nickname, so Iain was dubbed "Feenie," short for Phoenix, by the Club regulars. It stuck. He's lucky that's the name that stuck. And here he is.

Ava doubts his bird nest of salt and pepper hair has seen a brush today. Somehow, that makes him more likable—as an acquaintance. She proceeds. *One last deep breath. Smile.*

He is onto something. The more disheveled Iain looks, the more the crooks better run. "Hello, Iain." She can't bring herself to call him Feenie. Ava is not one of the boys.

"Baroness, have a seat." He slightly rises from his chair, sending it banging to the porch floor. Iain's ridged, puffy face shows the years of alcohol and tobacco, making him ruggedly handsome and ruggedly sad. *Hell of a start. She'll be laughing about that graceful move with her mates. Damn! She does look apples. Even in this weather.*

Ava quickly takes the other seat before he can assist her. No need to send her chair toppling to the floor as well. "*Ava,* Iain . . . *Ava.* We knew each other long before I became a baroness." *Lady, Iain, Lady Shropley. Even journos should know to call a baroness Lady So-and-So in social situations. Shut up!* She suddenly realizes that a mistake she could have made a year ago is now a pet peeve. *A year ago. . . . Now it's the end of 1987. A lifetime. A girl from the Carolinas can't be expected to have etiquette training in addressing peers. Was that really me?* Her breath stops at the thought of whom her ignorance may have amused or tormented in the past. *A journo from Australia should know better. After all, they are still enmeshed with the monarchy and certainly Western Australia is no stranger to deposed and ex-pat royals and peers.* Ava takes the barrette from her seersucker trouser pocket and captures the wave of flying hair into a ponytail. *I'll worry about it later.* "On glass number two, are we?" she forces a smile.

The tease puts Iain back at ease, but not enough to lean onto those back chair legs again. "Sure is breezy," Iain says. "Heard you booked a room here three months ago." *That tidbit will make her forget the chair.* "Does that mean you never intended to make the sail to Hobart . . . *Ava?*" His facial ridges deepen as he struggles to get comfortable in the conversation.

Ava notices that Iain is using his arrogant voice. A month into knowing him she recognized that tone as his tell that he does not *really* like you, not really. *He is making small talk. Iain doesn't make small talk. Iain also doesn't stand on ceremony. He wants something to do to pass his time here, and I don't want to tell my "What it feels like to be a baroness" story again. Smile. Be pleasant.* "Just means I was a Girl Scout," she says shrugging. She casually pops a dripping kiwi slice into her mouth and enjoys the exotic smush, like tart sea breeze mixing with heavy whipped cream—Tahiti in a fuzzy ball. She grabs another one. Smush. She sees Iain smiling at her as she wipes a sugary green trickle from her chin. *Great. Now he'll be joking at the Club about the slurping Baroness. Forget it. He's never going to want to be friends with someone like me. Or any woman. The thought would never cross his Neanderthal mind.* "Did you luck into a room?"

He empties his glass with a savory sip. *So the Baroness isn't so perfect. Maybe we can be mates.* The ridges soften as does the tone. "Nice finish, that. I'm no Boy Scout, but I booked mine early, too. I like a captive audience of wankers avoiding my calls, and you can find them here every year. Begging your pardon." He hopes the use of "wankers" will startle her. If it does, he can't tell. He'll try again.

Ava gives one of those forced half-laughs that tosses back the head. *Wankers? That's your best Iain? Good. It's just a social drink.* "Who's your lucky target? The Pinyup crew?"

He finger-brushes a matted pouf from his hair. "Who?" Iain takes a crumpled paper from his trouser pocket. "No

Pinyup crew this year. Friends of yours? Guess they didn't make it. . . Anyway, got the quotes I need. That means the pitch is to you, so to speak." He looks at her as he pours her a drink and is rewarded with her obvious catch of the pun. Iain likes feeling pleased with himself. It doesn't happen often with women.

"Ah, Cricket Pitch. You knew I would appreciate the pun. And what do I know that is so interesting? Or did you finally pull a full pisser and end up on the social desk at the Sydney paper?" She didn't look him in the eye. *He thinks he is such a ladies' man. Always so pleased with himself.* Poker is not Ava's game. She needs to know where he's leading. Needs the security of predictability. The sea returns. She feels herself climbing onto that tightrope between the wankers and the fools. *I'm no fool, though playing one often gets you interesting information.* "Most interesting thing in my life was a garden party for the New South Wales premier a couple of weeks ago." Ava pretends to examine a kiwi slice.

Iain pours himself another glass. "That right?" He leans back slowly on his chair legs, pointing his toes like a stretching panther. "We can start with how your name was included on the report when the good ol' President of SpearCo Petrol was arrested September last year. And now, here you are, Baroness . . . *Ava*, with that same president's yacht entered in this race under your name. I don't know most of the story between you two, but—"

Bizarre that it was only last year when it seems a lifetime. "But you think I'm willing to fill in the missing pieces." Ava blows the South wind from her lungs, sounding much like the mainsail flapping limp. "Skip isn't easy for anyone to know. To start, the title is President, SpearCo Petroleum Australia and Pacific Rim. Yes, he was driving drunk that night. Yes, I was in the car with him as was Patricia, my location producer. I'm sure you saw her name, too. Our names were included because we tried to pay bail that night, but no, Skip was such a menace to society that he had to stay in jail until his hearing the next day. You don't really think I would be part of an expose or whatever you have in mind. Old news, Iain, and the tabloids did it to death." She thuds the wine glass on the table for emphasis, liquid sunlight splashing over the edges. Shush-boom. She wipes the wine from her hand with a single swipe of the stiff cotton serviette and stands to leave.

Iain lets his front chair legs fall to the floor. The small table catches his nervous tension. "I am thinking you will want to be part of justice," he says, jutting his chin like a man in a stiff collar. "I know there is more to good ol' President Skip's story: the arrest, break-in, the suspicious death, all of it. And I know that you know there is more to it as well." Iain gives her an arrogant smirk he reserves for women just before patronizing them to get what he wants.

His apparent lack of respect for women doesn't anger her as much as his ability to patronize them void of guilt.

"Keeping quiet won't help anyone." Iain lowers his voice for emphasis. "And it is less dangerous to tell a secret others want kept quiet. Besides, you are one of those *honest* Sheilas. Telling things just right and expecting that from everyone else. Some of you Sheilas have a rich fantasy life. You're different, Baroness. You get the real shake of it. When billions of dollars are at stake, truth gets very cheap, hey? Bloody hell, life gets very cheap." Iain leans on those back chair legs again. He knows Ava isn't going anywhere. They're both creatures of curiosity. "I know you want to do the right thing." The panther stretch. The predatory eye.

The bottlenose pointing right at her.

There it is. He's right, but his tone strikes a shrill note in her nerves. "How gracious, Iain, to believe any woman would want to do the right thing, that any woman values honesty."

The smirk becomes a grimace as he looks away, rolling his eyes. He turns back to face her with a knowing smile. He remembers she is not one to test, not one to suffer his patronizing gladly. He levels his chair.

She sinks back into the slatted chair like it's a battered lifeboat. She sips the light wine, savoring oak and apple and something. . . . *For all of Skip's faults, he was as honest as anyone could be and still work as an oil executive.* "I guess we could start with that night and see where we go. After all, what better place to eat of the Tree of Knowledge of Good and Evil than Eden? But not here."

A couple of fellow castaways in yellow Macs breeze into nearby chairs on the porch. A solo sailor, his face obscured by a navy baseball cap, takes the far table and pores over a map. Noisy young men tussle and laugh as they trot up the path from the dock.

Ava stands up in slow-motion jerks. "Let's take a walk. The sun's finally shining." Suddenly tired arms lift her from the sinking lifeboat to the rolling porch. Shush-boom. *Walking with sea legs, but I am walking, and it feels good. Move forward, Old Girl.*

She wobbles along the path like a child on her first push-bike. Training-wheel memories push her forward motion. She remembers thinking Skip's joking was just that. Remembers the three life lessons she quickly learned. She repeats them in her mind in her own voice just as she had contemplated them: *a) an oil company president can bed endless gold diggers, and b) there is an endless supply of gold diggers, and c) oil company presidents like a challenge.* She remembers the conclusion she made the first time she threw *Oz Rox*'s lines to the dock. *If he gets sex whenever he wants, he just won't get it at all from me. I can play chess, too.* And she had. But her pawns were falling before he fell. And the house always finds twenty-one. His private life seemed more like Black Jack than chess. Gambling was rapid-fire sexier.

She flinches from a cold touch to the back of her neck. Just the wind. But at that moment she wonders if Skip is in Purgatory. *Odd thing to wonder about.* Everyone always says their friends are in Heaven. She doesn't think he made it. *Great success here. Not so impressive up there*, she muses. *He'll get his do-over. He'll like that.*

Silence is welcome as they put some distance between themselves and the front porch. Iain knows when to keep quiet. He has broken enough stories. Eventually, the subject feels compelled to fill the silence.

The cool gusts remind Ava of Margaret River in Western Australia. She loves watching the dolphins ride the waves there with the surfers. She sips the Cricket Pitch she had forgotten she was carrying, pale as a Golden Delicious apple. Somehow she feels she just plucked it from the biblical tree. The Cricket Pitch is as crisp as the gusts. In her mind, she hears the two twenty-something men aboard the *Oz Rox* yelling as they come about, her fiberglass hull thundering against the sea in a shushhh-boom, shushhh-boom. Salt spray moistens their voices. Skip built a good boat. *I don't need to worry about them. But I do need to stay alert with Iain. Why is he so damn quiet? May as well get on with it. Don't think too much about Skip. Stop it! Buck up, Ol' Girl.*

"That night started with Kip," Ava clears her throat, "*Skip* . . . onboard the *Oz Rox* fishing with one of his mates. I had the keys, so Patricia and I were enjoying a sauna at his condo in Sydney. His building had this great sauna room. Actually, I also went over that afternoon. It was the first time I was alone in his condo. Sooo . . ."

"So you snooped." Iain gulps back the last of his wine like swigging a shot. *Every Sheila snoops.*

"So I snooped . . . a little. Let me tell you. His 'house specialty' lasagna he made for me on previous nights—take-out box in the kitchen trash. His closet . . . spiffy as a rack in Hermes . . . His drawers, all messy jock. I don't think that's too personal to tell you. Besides, it may be relevant. You see, the weekly maid straightens the closet. Total guy—the kitchen was bare. I mean four glasses, all highball glasses, three mismatched plates that I later noticed matched some in the SpearCo break room, one soiled dishcloth, and one perfect set of flatware no doubt just opened from the store. No paper towels; no tea towels; no napkins—serviettes, no food, no milk. Nothing. Just three bottles of liquor in the cabinet—make that bourbon. The refrigerator is empty. Not even mustard. Guys always have mustard. Ok, maybe not in Oz. But at least Vegemite—right? Of course, the ice trays are full—no doubt to accompany the bourbon into the high-ball glass." She sighs deeply, exhaling the ghost of memory. Shushhh-boom, shushhh-boom. "That's when I really fell for him. That moment." Ava nods in recognition to herself and is quiet.

Iain first thinks the pause is for effect. Then he sees her face as he slides past her on the bramble-sided, sandy path. She is staring. The kind of stare that time travels to a memory and resurrects it. For just a moment he allows himself to feel the weight of the tale—the story of real lives. To see Ava, if for only a second, as a mate that life punched when she wasn't looking. He knows that feeling. Seems he is never looking.

THREE

"WHO WAS THE mate on the *Oz*?" Iain looks behind them.

"Oh, that night . . . I never asked," Ava says as she starts along the trail again. "He needed a weekend on the water, and I'm not much for personal prying."

Iain breaks a smirk, that kind where the left corner of the mouth talks in silence.

They both stop and turn for a moment at the sound of someone approaching. Just the man in the navy baseball cap out for a walk. He seems to notice them and turns back toward the inn.

She appreciates the gesture of privacy. "Aussies are good like that," she comments, gesturing toward the departing figure. "They don't like to pry. And I save the prying for my job, okay?" Ahh-choo! "Excuse me. Guess the weather is getting to me. . . ."

"Or something," Iain says.

"Skip and I were friends for over a year, you know—talking on the phone, dinner here and there when we were in the same cities. Even innocent kisses. He liked me because I wasn't after him. . . . Well, not overtly, anyway." She gives Iain a little wink. "I was probably the only single woman he knew that *wasn't* after him. But I just couldn't resist a project. I felt sorry for him." She mistakes Iain's dark expression for a sarcastic response to her feeling sorry for an oil baron.

"No really, I did. I knew his indiscretions and probably his wife's ruined their marriage. That's not for repeating, by the way. And now here he was, professionally successful and no one around who cared about him and, it would seem, not really caring about himself."

"Are we talking about the same Dubbledon?" Iain asks.

"Okay, so you probably see a narcissist. But all those women. I think he wanted to feel needed. He was afraid to need, so they had to be casual. For whatever reason, I wasn't casual. Maybe because I genuinely liked him. And I asked for nothing." She catches Iain looking at the sky and thinks he doesn't believe her. "I did. I genuinely liked him. And no, I didn't ask for anything. And he liked me way past his comfort zone. . . . Now I sound like the narcissist."

She feels uncomfortable. Nauseous. Talking about it makes it seem like decades ago. That is a good feeling. Remembering how it really felt. That makes it a minute ago. That is like $500 riding on nineteen and the house turns over twenty-one. She gulps back her shot of wine mocking Iain's swig. She gets the laugh she wants. The nervous unspoken agreement to leave ghosts asleep. *Shut up, Ava! You always talk too much when you drink wine. No more wine.*

Iain finger-combs his windswept mat of hair. "I bet he didn't like having *that* talk with you." Iain watches a small wallaby meander through the nearby bush. The animal seems unaware that humans are predators.

"Imagine telling Dubbledon that he doesn't care about himself," Iain says. "That's a crook. I mean, if you say so, no worries. You knew him."

"We never discussed it." Ava pauses along the trail pretending she wants a better look at the innocent creature. *Am I just realizing that we never mentioned it? Neither Skip nor I ever mentioned it.*

The wind calms, but she suddenly smells the saltiness of the sea. Shushhh-boom goes the *Oz*. Ocean spray salts her mouth as surely as if it were real. Her knees give instinctively to cushion her from the waves. She is a Carolina girl.

"You know me well enough to guess that I can't leave anything alone." She shakes the ghost from her head. "So, I went to the Super Kmart and bought everything: tea towels to deli boxes of pasta salads. I filled the cabinets: put matching plates on the shelf, tomato paste and mustard—or what passes for it here—in the refrigerator, ice cream and extra bread in the freezer, and, of course, a coffee machine. No one should live without a coffee machine. He could eat out of my shopping for two weeks without leaving home. I stocked well, cupboards and freezer."

"And he didn't say anything when he cashed his get out of jail free card?"

"Nope. And I didn't either because I felt guilty for snooping."

Even the wallaby could notice Iain's eye-roll.

Ava thinks changing the subject is a good idea. "Did you know he is from a family of sisters, five or six of them? A Freudian analyst's dream. Actually, our hair looked pretty good after he dried it. Guess he handled a blow-dryer in his past. I could just see all those sisters lined up in chairs getting their hair dried while he coerced them to introduce their pretty girlfriends."

"Right-o." Iain nods and chuckles heartily. He had done some sister-coercing in his day. No clue what she meant about the hair drying and not about to stop her talking.

"His bourbon reasoning thought that trying to outrun Sydney cops was a good idea. A shiny, big-ass BMW attracts attention in Sydney. Yes, Skip did go the wrong—yes, the wrong way down three streets. I know he denied that later. But, yes he did"

"Brilliant." Iain smiles and nods, enjoying the scene. "Oh, Skipper . . ."

"Yeah, oh Skipper." Ava can't help laughing. "I knew we were in real trouble when Skip said, 'Don't shorry, I negate for a living.'"

Keeping the conversation light helps when she remembers. But ghosts are everywhere.

Iain shakes his head as he stares at the ghost trail of the wallaby. Now he pauses along the path. "So those reports of Skip having a wild rage on the town that night were all false. I guess you can't believe everything you read. So you handled costs?"

"No, his secretary did. Have you met Fiona?"

Iain nods negatively, but doesn't dare interrupt again. He knows when a Sheila is on a roll.

"Well, she's great. I wonder where she works now. Never really thought about it." Ava feels odd realizing that her analytical mind can skip past the obvious. "No one at the police station would tell me anything. I didn't know when Skip had his hearing. They didn't even tell me that Skip was already gone when I called later. He took a taxi home and called me the next day to get his car. That SOB called from the condo and never said a word about the kitchen. Can you believe it? He did say he was enjoying his first cup of coffee of the day. Never thought about it. He was trying to get me to say something, and I never caught it till now," she muses. "I guess that was his way of telling me he found the kitchen goodies. All he said was, 'Thank you for taking care of the car.' Now that I think about it, when I met him at his office that afternoon, I returned his car keys and his condo keys, and he hesitated; just for a moment, but he hesitated. That few seconds that he held my hand with the keys between us, when we were both too proud to be the first one to say something, that moment was the first time I knew that he cared something for me." She shakes her head, trying to rid her thoughts of the shushhh-boom spray of the sea and the salty drops escaping her eyes. "Let's sit over here on the bench for a minute. My sea legs need a rest." *My emotions need a rest, too.* Indeed her emotions came as full as the waves of the tide, but much less predictably.

The two sit quietly. Sounds of distant voices make good company. Ava thinks ahead to the events of the week after Skip was in jail. She recalls her meeting in Melbourne. Iain seems far away. *Perhaps he is remembering a time when he was too proud to say something, when the right words might have kept one of those fiery women by his side,* she thinks. The sun warms her face. She closes her eyes to enjoy the distant parrot-cries and softening song of the sea.

"The way you talk about Dubbledon, I want to like him," Iain finally says, pulling his thoughts back to the present. "Heck, nearly every bloke I know could or should've been caught driving after too many tinnies. The world sees this Yank oil man out with two women ten years his junior and thinking he is above the law . . . well, tummm . . ." Nodding in empathy, Iain finger-combs that thick hair. His tone is different. He is talking to an equal.

"Yes, I know. All our stories have real people behind them, Iain. They may be drilling for oil, so to speak, but we're drilling just as much for that story to make our careers. We're drilling for oil, too. Then he was unlucky enough for it to be a slow news week. He actually got a call from the Texas office about it. Fiona told me with that look of disapproval she would flash my way at times. I guess she thought I had him out partying on the town."

"You certainly were good at keeping out of the headlines in the local rag the next few days," Iain said. He didn't want to conjure any ghost of a conscience at this point. He almost likes Skip right now. He almost believes Ava's story, Ava's view of this enigmatic character. Almost.

"Well, I was in Melbourne. I was already set to film my interview with Bob Ansett regarding his expansion of Ansett Airlines and, of course, sponsoring the marathon in Melbourne. It was in the report that Skip was with two women and in the police record that Patricia and I went by the station, but no one could really place us in the car. Because it was all speculation, I was spared the brunt of it. And Mr. Ansett was a total gentleman. He never mentioned a word of it, though I saw a copy of that gossipy pulp fiction on his desk. One of his eager-beaver helpers was no doubt delighted to run over to the newsstand and update the info on me. We did the interview without a hitch. You may have seen it on the ABC. We were scheduled to have dinner with his Marathon Race Director at a local hot spot, but I spared them the possible gossip by bowing out. I used the excuse that I had to get to Adelaide to prep for the Grand Prix." Ava stops for a moment, realizing that Iain managed to get her talking without thinking first. *Slow down, Old Girl. Slow down.*

Iain is remembering every word and quickly looks out over the brush when Ava pauses. A glance can stop a story mid-sentence.

"I was already scheduled to stay with a lovely family in Adelaide," she continues. "The husband did business with SpearCo and was a friend of Skip's for several years. Did you ever notice how people in Adelaide seem to think Yanks are great fun, while many in Melbourne seem to hate us? I mean the adults are all stuffed-shirt polite and everything. It's more the uni age that feels threatened or superior or something," she says. "Maybe they think that's how the Londoners would behave. Been my experience that Londoners are the very breath of polite hospitality. Couple of scary close encounters with the oddballs, but they are everywhere. Then, again, thinking about it, I suppose the only Yanks the Aussies see are the ones with new money and/or the ones from California, so I get the assumptions. And my view is tainted by my Sydney friends," Ava says. "I hear there's a long-standing rivalry between Sydney and Melbourne. Both cities have positive traits, but I have to say, I've always felt welcome in Sydney and rarely in Melbourne. Funny... Never mind." *Loose lips. Loose lips. That's enough. You are a Yank second in their minds now, Old Girl. Must be some nice people in Melbourne, but ol' Feenie has a hard on for them... Of all the things to pick up from Skip, it has to be those crass expressions. Anyway, people like people who think the same. Best to let Feenie assume we are of like minds.*

Iain chuckles a little about the California comment. *I like her even if she is lazin' the day. She'll see I don't change subjects so easily and she's right about Melbourne. Stuffed shirts the lot of them.* "So, when did you see Skip again?" Iain asks. The ridges are back and so is the tone. He can tell Ava is holding back. *She knows something. Thinks she can sidetrack me with some Melbourne bashing. Everyone knows I don't care for those Prisoners of Mother England.*

"I actually saw him in Adelaide. That's when I first

faltered with Skip." She pauses for emphasis. And she wants the satisfaction of making Iain confirm that women can admit they are not perfect. She surmises by his tone that he likes her more after her astute observations about Melbourne rudeness. She knew that opinion would make him an ally. She can use one. She still doesn't know where he's going with this conversation.

Ava waits nearly a minute for Iain to look at her in recognition. "That's right. I faltered. Skip had two tickets purchased on a cruise to Antarctica. We sat alone in the living room of his Adelaide friends and Skip asked me to go to Antarctica. You have to understand. There was no relationship with us past a few dinners and a couple of kisses." She sees that smirk again. "Really. He had women with whom he was regularly intimate. Didn't mind at all mentioning it to me. It was like he was talking to one of the boys. I don't know how much of it was true. He always enjoyed startling people. I think some of the stories were for shock value because I refused to react. Anyway, here he is, out of the blue, telling me how he always wanted to go to Antarctica and he finally decided to take the time to do it. He booked two cabins and had my ticket with him. The trip was not until January this year. I was already booked to cover the America's Cup. I told him I couldn't go because of the Cup. Skip stuffed those tickets back inside his suit coat pocket and started talking about my work schedule for the following month. Just like that. I knew he was angry. I told him it wasn't that I wouldn't consider going another time, but he wouldn't even discuss it. Honestly, when he left about ten minutes later, I didn't know if I would ever hear from him again. I guess in his world no one ever said 'no.'"

After a good hands-reaching-for-the-sky stretch, Ava

stands and starts back for the inn.*Start walking and that will end the story. You need to think before you say too much. Iain knows something. He doesn't fish for the sake of it. He doesn't stay in without nineteen. He is steering you to it. But what? What does he know?*

"But you obviously did hear from him again." Iain follows Ava. "An oil executive going to Antarctica would attract a lot of attention, but maybe not if it were under the guise of a pleasure trip. Are you leading up to telling me Skip had his eye on drilling rights in Antarctica?" *She knew. Don't let her stop talking. She knew about Antarctica and SpearCo. She has talked her way right to it. She was trying to steer away from something—maybe protect a reputation. Maybe protect her reputation. She's a journo and she sat on a story like that—unbelievable.*

Ava stops. Right there. Not another step. Her mind races. It was just a trip to her—a gesture from a friend wanting to take their relationship to the next level. Could she be that naïve?

"Iain, do you think so?" she asks, her voice in a whisper. "That angle never crossed my mind, but I can see how someone else could think . . . It makes sense when you know . . . Let me just tell you what I do know. We can speculate later. And, honestly? Skip didn't call. I called him. A week passed without a word. He knew where I was. Finally, I left a message with his secretary. No call. Two days. No call. So, I called him at home. You have to understand that he would tell me when other women came over for what he referred to as 'a roll in the hay.' I'm a horse person. Even I would prefer he just said 'a shag.' Sounds less personal. I don't know if he was bragging or thought I would be jealous or was just being a cad."

"A cad," Iain says without hesitating. "Know that one well as I have played it myself. My therapist calls it passive-aggressive." He realizes he has mentioned therapy and quickly holds up his right hand to prevent comment. "Yes, my therapist. Hell, nothing else has worked. So, Dubbledon is being passive-aggressive and . . ." *And he told you about the drilling rights, didn't he, innocent little Ava. Bloody hell, Iain, she might know who is paid, who is blackmailed, bloody hell, no wonder a Yank scored a title.*

Ava doesn't need Iain to tell her that Skip could be a cad. Maybe learning she had been on the receiving end made Iain more sympathetic to her. She wants him more sympathetic. Iain worries her. He can be one of those loose cannons that ruins reputations on page one and prints a retraction post-apocalypse on page thirteen. *He's sharing about therapy. He must be identifying with me.* The thought relaxes her and makes her feel a touch of friendship for Iain. *Maybe he could be moved from the Acquaintance category to the Friend category.*

"Yep, Skip tells me that he can only talk a few minutes. This woman he met in Melbourne a month before has shown up at his door and is going to stay the night. She had just gone to the parking lot to get her overnight case when I called. The week before he's inviting me on a cruise with my own cabin and now what? Well, women everywhere would be proud of me. I calmly asked where he met her and some basic info, tell him to have a good night and that I just called to say hello and update him on my schedule. He's a little stunned. I guess passive-aggressive expects aggressive in return. Anyway, he tells me how her showing up is a 'complete surprise' and asks if there is any reason he should tell her not to stay. 'You should do what you want,' I said and hung up the phone. I was insulted, all right. Seems he met her the month before while in Melbourne overnight. She was the band singer at his hotel. So, now he's picking up lounge singers. Knew I should let it go. I hoped she would see those tickets lying around."

"Aren't you the forgiving sort?" Iain grins broadly, more in doubt than amusement at her version of events. "All of this lover's quarrel stuff is interesting, but I'm after the business issues. I don't think a lounge singer is the person he would need to worry about seeing those tickets." As if his comment weren't condescending enough, Iain flashes her a look of irritated boredom.

The bottlenose dolphin is on the prey and unwavering. He wants the full story on Antarctica, not on ol' Skipper's sex life.

Ava's emotional tide is rising, but not because of Iain's attitude. She feels inept, all right. Not inept at relating the story, but rather inept in her ability to save people from themselves, to save even herself.

"But you see. This is when it all started to get . . . odd. This is when I should have done something." Ava's eyes begin to pool. "I'm a writer, Iain. You know I checked out the competition. I should've sensed something. Now I understand that saying about 'not seeing the forest for the trees.' I had the information running barely a block ahead of me. You see, I left Adelaide and went back to Melbourne. My god, was that only fourteen months ago? Had to be late October because the Adelaide Grand Prix was about to start. Drove from Adelaide to Melbourne chasing a ghost. I was following a trail that I totally misinterpreted."

4 Months Earlier
Melbourne, Victoria, AUS,
October 1986

"SURE. I REMEMBER that Sheila," the twenty-something
bartender is polishing glasses, each one clanging as he hangs
it too close to the last. With his black, prickly hair of dried
gel, he's like a trimmed porcupine.

Ava immediately decides his "G' day" greeting makes
him a better fit for Sydney. Melbourne is newly polished.
Most executives she meets here are first- or second-generation Australians and first- or second-generation management. They did not ship over from Knightsbridge: Brooklyn
to Park Avenue in a generation, so to speak. In Ava's mind,
the polish is a thin veneer. They would never say "G' day."
Never have the confidence to let loose. She tilts her head to
the right. Her tell that she's feeling smug.

She usually interprets haughtiness as insecurity. And
she meets it on every visit to Melbourne—probably because
she looks for it, keeping up with how long it takes. Three
hours ten minutes is the record. She doesn't know why the
locals dislike Yanks. Only that most of them don't hide it.

*Making people feel welcome is the sign of a good up-
bringing,* she reminds herself. *What is it the Aussies say?
'Putting one at ease is a sign of royalty.'* Head still tilted,
she purses her lips at the thought.

In fact, Ava is very welcomed by the Melbournites
with status or position, be it wealth or political position.
Unfortunately, her encounters with the "second rung normal people," as she calls them, are very warm everywhere in
Oz except Melbourne. The contrast makes her resentment
all the more heartfelt. And makes her wonder if some of the

acceptance is really just patronizing. She can't decide if they simply dislike Americans or snub her in anticipation of being snubbed themselves. Of course, there are nice people. Just have to ferret them out once they hear her Southern accent. And her Sydney and Adelaide and Perth and Broome friends gladly reinforce her opinion. So she bristles and keeps to herself whenever entering the lion's den. The bartender is not what she expected. A needed surprise.

Feenie always says that the acceptable Melbourne accent is more affected royal POM than Eastern States Aussie. Who knows? Maybe an accent really can change in two generations of higher education. Ava shakes her head to expel the musings. She needs to focus on this out-of-place fellow. *I'm really angry at Skip . . . and at myself. Won't help to project that anger onto Melbournites,* she reminds herself.

"She was in here for open mike night," continues the bartender. "The hotel holds open mike Wednesdays and Fridays to bring in the business crowd. Works out three Patsy Cline songs with the band, then decides to wait at the bar, says she's building up her nerve."

"Well, don't you have a good memory?" Ava's sarcasm accomplishes her goal. He stops polishing glasses and gives her his full attention.

He scratches his pale cheek on his left shoulder. The hair doesn't budge. "Yeah, yeah. Okay, so I'm thinking I have a shot at a shag. A man remembers those nights. She's all talkative like she's me best mate and all. Said she just moved here from Sydney, but sounded more like those Sheilas that spend time in Bangkok. Asked her, but she claimed she'd never been there. Then this old guy in a three-piecer takes a table near the door. Suddenly, she's ready to sing. And she was good, too. Comes back to the bar and says g' night like we're best mates again. So, I'm thinking I've got a real shot here, but the Sheila just turns around and goes over to the old guy. Pretended she wanted a light, but she didn't have no fag at the bar. I'd have given her a light, I would. . . Can't trust Sheilas."

"And . . ." Ava waits for him to fill the void.

"And she leaves with him. Yeah, yeah. Leaves in right on ten minutes. She's a looker, too: brown hair to her . . . arse, and some bumper tits out front. Manager doesn't like that type in here. I say live and let live. Probably makes more in a night than I do all week. Is she in trouble or something? That why all the questions?" He starts chopping fruit for the night.

"Just asking. A friend heard her sing and thought she was good. Did you happen to get her name?"

Usually the singers come twice a week until they get a gig. Usually, the, ah, *ladies* come in until they get something regular, too. Maybe the ol' three-piecer made her a good offer. Was one odd thing. When she said g' night she sounded like a local, you know, that accent the nobs put on down here in Melbourne."

Ava couldn't help smiling at the comment. "Maybe she'll be back. . . Hey, you probably attract some attention yourself." She gives him a quick wink. Tossing her YSL tote bag onto her shoulder, she lists leeward under pounds of change and notebooks and three city map books and an appointment book and makeup. One quick look back. *Always leave on a positive note.* "Better luck tonight."

"Yeah, yeah," he says sarcastically, but with a smile.

Good, I can return if I need more information.

The fifty feet to the door are too far. Her eyes sting from the daytime lounge mix of settled cigarette smoke dampened by ammonia cleaner. She wonders how these places seem so appealing after dark? CLANG! The heavy glass-and-metal door slams behind her, sounding of cheap thrills. She walks into the midday sunlight and street noises of the crowded Melbourne business district. Cold and alone on a busy, warm street. The Melbourne chill is internal.

Could be on a side street of London . . . which is exactly what a local would want to hear, she thinks. *Safe here, and I need a good walk. Okay, so she is a looker, but so am I. She might be a little younger, but that's okay. I'm definitely more interesting and probably much smarter. Of course, with Skip I have to face the fact that boobs would trump smarts every night of the week.* In fact, this so-called singer sounds like a young version of Skip's ex. A fact not lost on Ava. *And Patsy Cline songs, what was that all about? What young Aussie, male or female, even knows Patsy Cline songs? Skip is a Patsy Cline fan, so he must've been caught up in the moment,* she decides. *Was his bout of food poisoning about the same time? Serves him right. I would like to think it was a nervous stomach from his conscience, but probably just from gobbling a sandwich after shagging. Glad I turned down his cruise! . . . I hope he won't ask her to go.*

Ava sits on the empty, covered bench at the bus stop. Needs a moment to rest. Compose herself. Stare at the sidewalk and keep from crying. The urge to cry sweeps her like a rogue wave—with an origin just as mysterious. A young woman with textbooks takes a seat on the twin bench facing Ava. Without looking up, the bobbed brunette re-arranges her three textbooks and crosses her ankles.

Ava shakes back her tears. "Hello. Beautiful day," she says, more to interrupt her musings than be polite.

The woman glances at Ava, looks down at the YSL tote,

half rolls her eyes and busies herself adjusting her books.

Ava checks her watch as she stands. "Twenty-three minutes," she says, hoping the woman will ask for an explanation. Flinging her bag over her left shoulder, Ava stands facing the woman she guesses is a student at the University of Melbourne. Ava waits. She's just angry enough to wait. Twenty long seconds. Finally, eye contact. "You'll do well here in uni," Ava says. "The entire environment is such a finishing school of good manners. Enjoy your day, Dear." She smiles broadly but doesn't wait for a response. Doesn't expect a twenty-year-old first- or second-generation college student in Melbourne will have one worth hearing.

Ava's hurt morphs into anger. She's glad of the encounter. Anger is more comfortable. Her brisk, determined strides feel as if she is moving in slow motion. Only two more blocks to the car. A twenty-something man in a grey, wool pinstriped suit waits next to her for the pedestrian light. She gives him a quick smile when he glances her way. She is used to men glancing her way. She's smiling because she thinks he must be trying to look older in that suit, maybe old enough to have learned some manners. He returns the smile and checks his watch. She wants to ask him something—the time, directions, anything to reveal her accent just so she can be cuttingly clear about his ensuing rudeness. The signal to cross blinks, saving her from a scene.

Adelaide, South Australia,
late October 1986

AVA DRIVES TO Adelaide with her second sight. It's a long seven hours. She makes it in less than six. Knows the roads by subconscious autopilot. Scary. A car horn startles her, urging her to move. The light is green. Her hard head-shake breaks the trance. One more block. A lucky parking space is within twenty feet of the hotel entrance. Back to where she left long before sunrise. "Rode hard and put up wet," she says aloud, vacillating between anger and hurt.

Street bands play 1950s music while the city preps for the 1986 Australian Grand Prix. Too tired for rational thought, the sounds lure her down the sidewalk. The annual Formula One race puts the entire city on party alert. Locals say it is always the "rage of the year."

I am sooo ready to get lost in a league of poodle skirts and rolled T-shirt sleeves holding packs of cigarettes. Ava shifts her heavy pocketbook to her right shoulder. Exaggerated impersonations of Buddy Holly and Jerry Lee Lewis compete on a side street. "Goodness gracious great balls of fire!" she says aloud. *Yum!* Turning the corner reveals a street vendor with a huge red box, pop-pop-popping hot buttery popcorn into a large plexiglass box. "Large, please." Her oily fingers pop the salty crunch puffs into her mouth at wood-chipper pace. She weaves through the quiet business suits on the way home. Smiles at the chatting jeans and ponytails as she wends her way out.

The popcorn only makes her hungrier, realizing she has not eaten all day. Calmed by the street scene and comfort food, Ava heads back to her hotel to order room service. She is glad that privacy waits at the hotel. Yesterday she chose to stay with Patricia at the Downtowner Hotel in Adelaide, not feeling quite right about staying with Skip's friends again. A quick phone call from the hotel to thank them was all that was required. They were not expecting her until tomorrow. The hotel entryway is freshly washed, wetting the soles of her alligator pumps. She notices the strange tracks they make through the glass doorway. If only other women were tracked so easily.

Ava stops down the hallway from her room to see Patricia. From a room-service tray on the floor across the hall, waft lingering scents of garlic and butter. *Definitely room service*, she decides. *Nothing like Italian food for comfort.* The hotel room door opens with the first knock. "I'm back from Melbourne. Whew! That's a long drive in one day."

Patricia is a curvy five-four with shoulder-length brunette hair as thick as a Quarter Horse tail. She is a couple of years younger than Ava and much less jaded. And tonight she looks very animated. Not her usual stressed, no make-up, and a hair barrette look she dons as she manages everything on the road plus helps produce Ava's interviews for the ABC and other outlets. Patricia is naïve for a native New Yorker, having grown up in the bosom of a close-knit, middle-class Brooklyn family. Tonight, she is wearing a black knit dress that shows off her figure and makes her look like a true New Yorker.

"Glad you caught me. I'm just on my way over to the race grounds." Patricia walks back into the room to check her huge, purple satchel. "So how was your favorite place? Surprised you didn't want to stay longer." She pulls back her wavy mane into a purple scrunchie and turns to Ava with a broad smile. "Sooo, did you find out what Dubbledon was up to? Come on. Give me the goods." She buckles the strap on her satchel and picks up her room key.

"Nothing to tell. Found the place where he stayed. They have a small band. The singer wasn't there. Really nothing to it." Ava regretted telling Patricia about the woman Skip met in Melbourne, but it was too late now. *Don't make a big deal and she'll forget it.*

"Too bad. Be nice to get a look at the competition. Not that you have any. I don't know why you don't just go all in. You know he likes you." Patricia lets the room door close behind her. "Want to ride along?"

"Nope. Worn out. Headed down the hall for room service and a hot shower. And don't call me when you return. Hopefully, I'll be dreaming of sailing. See you tomorrow." Ava wants to get to her room and call Skip. And she has learned her lesson about involving Patricia. *I'm not taking advice from someone who thinks a long-term boyfriend is someone you dated over a month.*

Ava calls Skip before calling room service. Even though it's almost 7 p.m., she tries the office first. Not unusual for him to keep strange hours during his deals. Fiona, his secretary, answers at the office.

"Hello, Ava. Mr. Dubbledon left early today. I'm here faxing some papers to the States," Fiona says, sounding out of breath. "Try him at home. I think he might not be feeling well. He looked a little worn. I'm sure you can make him feel better."

Ava is incredulous. *Hah! I imagine Miss Melbourne is still there for night two. He never skipped work for me.* She decides to wait and call in a couple of days. *I wish I had more popcorn.* She grabs a mildly cool Perrier from the mini-fridge. *Probably twenty bucks.* The green bottle fizzes as she loosens the cap. *Who cares? Should have called room service first. Screw him!*

THE NEXT DAY Ava blurs through her interview preps while Patricia sets the schedule and coordinates with the film crew. Tonight is the obligatory round of parties. Something they feel obligated to complain about, though they both enjoy the whole scene.

Ava stands under the hot shower, steam filling the bathroom until she can't see the billowing white shower curtain. She spent all day not thinking about Skip. Not thinking about the brunette from Melbourne. Not thinking about sailing with him. Not thinking about him with that woman. In fact, most of what she remembers about the day is reminding herself not to think about them.

A red button on the hotel room phone is flashing when she flip-flops her way out of the bathroom. She is wearing an XXL Grand Prix T-shirt with the tag hanging from the neck. A white towel tightly turbans her shampooed hair. *Skip?* She rushes to the phone. It's Patricia. She met "a hot English guy" working for a local television station and he just called and invited her out for the evening. Ava gently hangs up. Her hand stays on the receiver. *No, no, no. Don't you dare call him. Fiona must have told him where you are. Don't think about it.*

Ava sets out solo to see Adelaide. Tonight demands her best party dress. Tomorrow is the Grand Prix. There are a couple of A-list parties happening for the Formula One race crowd. She is more in the mood for local flavor. And she doesn't want to answer questions about Skip. Even more, she doesn't want to be tempted by some "hot guy" at a party. She knows she's vulnerable and in no condition to match wits or ignore promising advances. She checks off the party list like viewing location shots. A quick walk-through with air kisses and distant greetings glides her through the annual chore. Activities are fun or trying, depending on emotion more than entertainment. Busy disco. Check. Snooty cocktails in a ballroom. Check. Bands of guys in matching leather logoed jackets. Check. Live fifties band with the twenty-something "too cool to wear kitsch" set. Check. Done! She gladly drives back to her hotel and follows a couple all around the parking lot to grab their spot as they depart. Time to decompress.

Young women with Rapunzel perm-waved hair and either long skirts with bobby socks or leather mini-skirts crowd the streets. All that hair looks awkward pulled back into scarf-tied ponytails for the occasion. Ava is blessed with the kind of wispy, straight hair that hangs like pale yellow silk on a rack. And that is all it will do. It defies the strongest perm, the stickiest hair spray, the teasing of an angry beautician. It looks great for what it is, and it will never be anything else. Every twenty years, it will be in style. She figures she is halfway there already And she is jealous of the Rapunzel hair. Poodle skirts—keep them. They could only have a comeback in Japan, where fashion decades compress into a merry-go-round seasonal rotation . . . and once a year in Adelaide.

A long avenue is blocked off for the festivities. Makeshift stages dot the sidewalks, raising "fifties for a night" cover bands to their cheekiest heights. Blonde wigs pulled into ponytails sway like wagging dog tails as backup singers doo-wop through America's fifties tunes. Women in leather skirts and Nina heels try to twist with their jeans-clad escorts. Everyone's smiling and laughing as if in some backdrop for a Sandra Dee movie. Ava stops to catch her breath. Compared to reserved Ava and more reserved Melbourne, it's a lightheaded experience.

Yes! She smells the buttery aroma of the popcorn vendor. Pop . . . pop-pop-pop. . pop-pop . . .goes the street siren. The siren changes from seductive melody to haunting song. The sound is from 100 paces down the block, but she hears it as clearly as a shutter banging deep into a starless night.

"Crazy, crazy for thinking my love could . . ."

A group of joking uni students, all laughing and talking over one another, pass by, drowning out the Patsy Cline message, and saving Ava from fear of the dark. She ignores the attraction of the salty, buttery crunch. Back to the hotel to give Skip another call. The spring night feels much warmer, but something in her is chilled. Restaurants filled with charcoaling steaks now only emit the stench of souring beer. She is through not thinking about it.

She autopilots back to her single hotel room. Auto-dials the code for an outside line. Auto-dials Skip's number. Auto-greets him and sits quietly as he fills the line with explanation.

Ava twirls her hair with her right hand trying not to interrupt Skip's sleepover story. "So she only stayed one night," she says. "Well, better luck next time." Ava wonders if Skip hears the irritation in her voice. "At least you have your trip to the Outback. Maybe find the exploration company located a good field for you. Have you visited that Aboriginal tribe in the past?"

"That trip will have to wait," he says. "Trip to Jakarta just came up. Be headed there maybe February. Trip to the States now. That will take at least a week. The captain can only leave the ship so often. Besides, I think I should get home for Christmas this year. The girls are going snow skiing with their mother's family. Think I'll go to Texas and see my mom. She's not getting any younger. Going to miss camping with the Aborigines, though they won't miss it. Aborigines don't like whites. Have to turn on the charm. Maybe after Christmas. Be surprised if there's oil out there. Worth a look all the same." Pause. Silence from Ava. "Probably see Bev in a month . . . unless I'm surprised with a better offer." Pause.

Still no comment from Ava. "Bev only gets a couple days off from the band at the time. Are you on your way back to Sydney?"

Skip sounds stilted to Ava. She's used to his joking around on the phone, but she can tell something is different. "Can I catch Bev's show in Sydney?"

"No, no. I thought she told me they were still playing Melbourne. My flight goes through there tomorrow on the way to Texas, but when I told her that, she reminded me they'll be playing in Adelaide then."

"Is that right? Where in Adelaide?" Ava suppresses her sarcasm.

"I didn't ask. What is the sudden interest? If I didn't know you better, I'd think you're jeal-l-l-lous." Skip drags out the last word with a light laugh.

Ava wants to tell him that "Bev" is a fraud. Wants to tell him Bev was not with the band in Melbourne. Wants to tell him Bev is probably marking him for a "loan" for some sick grandmother. Problem is, Ava doesn't want Skip discovering she checked on Bev's story.

Ava pauses, carefully weighing her words. *He is a big boy. If he can run an oil company, he can see a con coming down the road, even one with enormous bumpers.* "You know me," she says. "Just trying to show an interest in your life. You need to be more careful, giving out your home address to women you meet on the road. I'll be in Sydney for the editing on the Melbourne Cup doc and the Grand Prix doc, should take a couple of weeks. You know, loops and voiceovers. Want to make sure the Minister of Suntan is happy. I hear the network got big bucks from the Ministry of Tourism for putting together this tourism package disguised as documentaries."

"Minister of Suntan," Skip laughs. "Can I use that? Let's meet for dinner a week from Friday. I'll pick you up in Kirribilli about eight. And you're right. I must've been in the bar too long, because I don't even remember giving Bev my address, and I've taken great pains to be sure it's unlisted. Can't say I'm sorry she remembered it."

"Ok. Ok. I don't need details. Eight is fine. Have a good trip."

"You, too. See you in a couple of weeks."

She sits on the tan, polyester bedspread in the hotel room, noting how many petroleum products are in the room. For nearly five minutes, her hand rests on the molded plastic telephone receiver as if it still connects her to him. *Telephone. Petroleum. Hotel pen. Petroleum. Shower curtain. Drapes. Petroleum products. Aboriginal land. Petroleum?* She wants to see some of the Outback. Needs a break.

Maybe she'll check on the crazy American women running and cycling across the country. They are always just steps ahead of her. She missed them at the Melbourne Cup and the Grand Prix. Maybe she'll take time to catch them on the way to Perth. Maybe she'll drive the Outback. Take her time. Think. *Need to run it past the powers that be.*

Bev's good, Ava decides. *If that is her real name! Where did she get his address? I guess Skip has too much on his mind to worry about such a detail, but he didn't forget. I've seen Skip way past "Go" at the bar and have never known him to forget anything.*

She notices a ghostly presence of Old Spice in the room. Skip wears it. Brings it back from stateside by the gallon. Her late grandfather wore Old Spice. He was a gentle giant who made everyone feel safe and loved. He gave her a love of the sea and of a good yarn. Old Spice makes men smell like the sea. To her, it also makes them smell of love and protection. Skip and her grandfather have little more in common than Ava and a love of the sea. And a penchant for Old Spice.

"Hi, Pop," she says aloud to the empty room. "Thanks for visiting if you are here. This is a fine mess, huh?"

Truth is known in the world of our souls while facts are limited to man's faulty memory and interpretations of his physical world.

She muses over these words, first written in one of her university philosophy papers. It was not well received. She didn't care then and doesn't care now. She still believes it, and repeats it to herself once again, so settled in her mind that not a single word of the sentence has changed in eleven years. For some reason, thinking of the men in her life always results in repeating this sentence to herself. Over the past year, she has found herself traveling between these worlds of truth and men's facts too often. And wondering about her foolish choices.

FOUR

Eden, December 1987

IAIN AND AVA jog back to the Safe Anchor Inn as the drizzle picks up once again.

"So, this trip was planned before last year's event." Iain asks the question like a statement, knowing he needs to keep the conversation flowing.

"Yeah. I guess so. I wonder if the afterworld views us with amusement or pity." Ava wipes her wet brow with the back of her hand.

"Here it comes," he yells as buckets of water are bailed from the heavens. They both run for the porch. "Pity, I think!"

Her Topsiders easily pass his UGGs on the uneven trail. Bounding up the porch stairs, she turns to wait for him. "I feel like I just showered fully dressed."

Iain clomps three steps onto the porch. "Tea anyone?"

"Not me. I'm headed for a hot shower and room service. I need some rest."

"But the story is just getting started. Brekkie, tomorrow? My shout." He shakes his soaked hair like a shaggy dog, spraying a six-foot radius, including Ava.

"You're on, Iain. I'll remember you said it's your treat,

um, shout. You tend to forget that at the pub, sometimes."
She uses both hands to wipe away the water trails down her
face.

"Hey, don't start bashing me balls, now. Oh, Ava, I
mean—" He sounds sincerely apologetic.

"It's all right. Go on. Get out of those wet clothes, or I'll
have to buy my own brekkie."

The aged door latch clicks behind her. Promise made.
Promise kept. *Oz* is on her way, and Ava decides that she
did sail as far as prudence allowed. The entire conversation
with Skip was little more than a year ago, but it seems so
long that it's like remembering a movie with other actors. If
only she knew then what she knows now, maybe something
would be very different. She knows that she made the right
decisions. No regretting the commitments.

*If we just could have seen even a little farther down the
road*, she thinks as she peels off her soaked shirt. If I had
tracked down that damn, fake lounge singer. If I could identify Mate X. If the ex-wife had just stayed in her house on
the hill.

Over a year later and even more questions than they had
unspoken that night. She tries smelling the Old Spice, but
the memory is gone. The eek-eek-eek is her sole companion.

After a hard sleep of dreams she can't quite capture, Ava
dresses and heads down to breakfast. It's early, and the resi-
dent rooster is still announcing daybreak. The empty hallway is cool and comforting. The dining room ahead is quiet.
Turning the corner to the doorway, she's surprised Iain is
sitting there, solo in the room, with a pot of tea.

"Can't sleep much anymore," he says in anticipation of
her comment. "Join me." He motions to the plump mistress
of the house, peeping from the kitchen, for another pot of

◆ 78 ◆

tea. "So, where were we?" His eyes are puffy either from too much alcohol or not enough sleep. His voice is weary and hoarse as if it yelled over a Bassie storm all night.

"Your shout or not, I answer no questions before tea," Ava says, unsuccessful in removing the grumpiness from her voice.

"So, Ava, not a morning person. Ann . . .," he clears the catch in his throat. "Annelisa wasn't a morning person."

Ava doesn't ask. He obviously wants to talk about it, but, again, not a morning person.

"She was my first wife." The hoarse voice catches on the last word. He pauses, waiting again for Ava to swim after the bait.

The sixty-something mistress of the house shuffles to their table, Australian-map tea towel over her left arm and her matching apron splashed with flour. Uncomfortably out of shape Mary Janes scrape along the wooden floor. She's short, making her wide hips look even squattier. She has let her hair and her temperament go grey. She sets a steaming pot and matching teacup on the table. They are the cutesy, flowered kind made as poor knockoffs of Dalton china. The black tea is real Earl Grey. No mistaking that turned-earth aroma in the morning.

"G'morn, Bar'ness." Slight curtsey. "Is m' Lady ready for suvvice?"

Ava stifles a smile. "Give us a few minutes? Oh, and serviettes, please." She busies herself by dropping two sugar cubes into her cup. Her morning voice is silently asking, *does this country have a napkin shortage or what? Either I am still fuzzy or Iain really does want to talk about Annelisa.* She surrenders. "Can't fault anyone for not being a morning person. I'm sure she was extra great the rest of the day."

"Oh yeah, that's why we divorced."

Ava remembers the gossip that the divorce followed Iain's forgetting their marriage vows. *She must have found out in the morning,* she muses, her head tilted to the right in smug recognition.

The shuffling woman's arthritic hand daintily places two cloth napkins in the middle of the square table. "The bawd's there, m' Lady." Slight curtsey. She makes a half-point gesture toward a chalkboard listing "2 eggs scrambled, scone, 1 slice ham."

In the back kitchen, Ava hears the first of the morning ham pop onto the grill with a sizzle. All the willpower in the world won't stop her from eating that entire board breakfast once that sizzling fatty smell evolves into the promise of a rich, salty taste.

"She didn't bring you a radio message, so the *Oz* must be through the Strait." Iain employs the old journo trick of starting on another topic to get the subject talking. He coughs the catch out of his throat and sips his steaming tea.

"Pot of tea, Iain. Pot of tea." Ava holds up her left hand as if to shake off the attempt. Shushhh-boom. The *Oz* visits again.

He leans onto the back legs of his chair. "Sheilas."

Despite his protest, he is obviously comfortable waiting. He knows that she requires talking through this story as much as he requires hearing it. What he doesn't know is that she is still figuring out the story. Time has a way of sliding back the filtering sheers that soften truth. Sometimes, we just can't take the full sunlight. He slept on her telling of events yesterday and wonders at the accuracy. No time to talk about it. He saved the talking for today. Never interrupt a subject unless you want the information flow to come full stop.

A quiet five minutes pass between them. Iain slowly lowers his chair. "Off to the men's. Can you get my breakfast if she checks on us?" He takes his Akubra, a cowboy-style rabbit felt hat, from the table and sets it on the extra chair.

Before Ava responds, the shuffling woman is back. "Service now, m' Lady?"

Ava waves Iain towards the men's room. He may as well keep going. Their hostess seems oblivious to his presence.

"Yes, we'll both have the board breakfast, please." The tea eases the grumpiness from her voice.

The woman nods affirmatively and disappears in the kitchen doorway. Ava hears eggs being scraped around an iron skillet. Muffled talking. In less than two minutes the hostess shuffles back with plates in hand. The ham still has sizzling bubbles on top. The salty aroma is heavy in Ava's nose.

"More tea?"

"Please, for both of us." Ava cuts the tender ham. Only needs her fork. The slightly seared, sizzling saltiness melts across her tongue. Just that right temperature between praising taste buds and scalded tongue. She closes her eyes. *That woman may be the only cook in Australia who doesn't overcook ham.* She is enjoying a full mouth of firm eggs, fresh from the chooks out back, when Iain returns.

"Looks good." He also goes first for the ham.

"We may as well talk about the America's Cup this January. My stories must have been all over the place yesterday." Ava takes a sip of the steaming tea that makes the smell of turned earth and warm sugar appealing. "Skip and I talked at least every couple of weeks and had near misses a couple of times as we traveled for business. He said several times that he would 'try' to make the America's Cup Ball with me, but in early January he told me he had a business trip and had arranged for a guy in Perth to show me around. You know that part. Patricia and I hit Sydney running. We had several cross-country spots set up to shoot en route to Perth, so Skip suggested I leave my jewelry with him. I did have a few pricey items in tow for the Cup and thought that was a good idea. I realize now that getting a courier delivery from the SpearCo CEO may have alerted the wrong people. And that woman still haunts me. Anyway, there are things I'm still figuring out about all of it—like being snapped into a water spout and helplessly spun and dropped. Maybe my talking about it can help both of us sort out the puzzle."

Iain is eating quickly and nodding intently. She knows his feeling. That thought of don't say anything or they might stop talking. Suddenly, there are screams in the distance.

Seconds later, the innkeeper runs through the dining room to the kitchen. "Keep your seats. Keep your seats," he yells as he passes.

Iain jumps up. "Never keep your seat when that's what you're told. I'll check it out." He grabs his hat, offering Ava a quick wink as he plops it onto his head.

Ava does keep her seat. None of her concern and nosey onlookers aggravate her when she's trying to work. She'll leave the innkeeper to his duties. Muffled voices emanate from the inn's front yard. Heavy footsteps are heard running upstairs.

Iain returns short of breath and takes his seat. "Bloody business. . . . Looks like some bloke fell off the docks and drowned." Iain removes the broad-brimmed Akubra from his head and looks at it. "Poor bloke still wearing his Akubra. Suspect they'll identify him soon enough. Probably out drunk on the dock last night. Wearing his Thomas Cook."

"How dreadful." Ava pushes back from the table. Her appetite is gone.

Iain dons his hat. "Let's get out of here."

They walk quietly around the grounds. Neither notices the kangaroo and her joey plucking an apple across the orchard fence. No need to fill the silence. The drowned man's ghost opens a portal to submerged caves of repressed memories. They cope in silence comforted by the presence of a peripheral friend. Without a word, they slowly sit side-by-side as they dispel the conjured ghosts. Still and silent. Their thoughts like lighthouse beacons alerting every mystery in the dark. Distorted time passing without notice.

Iain finally rises from the bench behind the inn. "So ol' Skipper was marked by a gold digger. The Sheila in Melbourne, I mean. Kind of ironic." He chuckles. "I feel better. You okay?"

"Maybe it's karma. You mark enough deals and somebody marks you. Dare we head back inside?" Ava stands, following Iain's lead. She is free of the waterspout and exhausted from her spinning struggle.

"Been quiet for a while now. Poor bloke probably identified by his shipmates. Guess they're wishing they had stayed at sea about now. Come on. It's cooling off. You look tired." Iain avoids eye contact as he talks. His emotions are too raw. A sympathetic look might draw them from the well.

Ava stretches toward the sky. "Thanks, Iain. You look crappy, too."

He chuckles again. "Well *eff* you, Baroness. Come on, now."

The friends walk quietly back through the scene of two lingering policemen staring at the discovery site, their car in front of the inn emitting the muffled sounds of a police radio. Several strangers huddle on the front porch. Nothing like tragedy to draw a crowd. Ava and Iain keep to themselves. None of their concern.

She walks to her room in the dark hallway. In the bustle, the maid must have forgotten the lights. The damp wool rug scent reminds Ava of the Aboriginal houses she visited. Dirt floors blanketed with rough woolen rugs and kangaroo hides. Not all Aborigines live that way. Or so she is told. But she saw it near Yalata. She drove through the Nullarbor Plain and was, as legend says, never the same after crossing the Outback. After her Melbourne hunt, she needed the respite. Aussie lore says that spirits draw you into the Outback. They are drawing her places now. The heart beat in her ears begins the rhythm of the bush beating of the hunt. Safe in her room. Safe asleep. Transported by mind or spirit or portal to the Outback.

One Year Earlier
Yalata, South Australia,
December 1986

AVA TAKES THE network chopper from Sydney to Ceduna, South Australia. The tourism docs are in the can. She can breathe. Not due in Perth for three weeks. The low flight over the countryside is a beautiful ride. Just Ava and the young pilot. He buzzes some kangaroo herds along the way and points out huge flocks of parrots looking like pink and blue cotton candy topping the green canopy. Blue eyed Aboriginal girls swarm her when she walks to the car rental. Just enough for an ice cream. She is glad to hand over her Aussie coins. The tiny car rental building is stuffy and dusty. No air conditioning. Screen door. She hands over her credit card for her Mitsubishi sedan rental. One way to Perth. Quick photocopy of her international driver's license. The rental agent reminds her that she can take the train across the Nullarbor Plain.

The clerk in his mid-twenties hands her a map and her keys. "The blue one that bloke just pulled around front. Sure you want to drive it? Not much out there. They say you're never the same after you cross the Nullie."

Ava is busy untangling her chopper blown hair. "I'll take my chances. Besides, I want to see some of the real Australia. Can you help me load the camera in the car?" She grabs her large pocketbook and carry bag. "Is there a ladies?"

"Just through there." He points to a door behind the counter. "No worries. I'll get the trunk," he says nodding towards her large suitcase. "Need the keys back to open the boot."

"Sure thing." Ava hands him the car keys. "How long to Yalata?"

"That'll take about two hours plus. Make sure you fill the petrol at the Roadhouse. Nowhere to stop for a distance. Going to film the crazy wildlife?"

"Something like that. Four American girls are crossing Australia. Two of them are trying to be the first ones to run across and cycle across the country. The ABC wants an update and I need a good adventure and some time to myself."

"I met those Yanks. Came through here some time back. Nice girls. Raising money for hunger relief. One of them seemed quite the rager. Good on 'em. I couldn't do it."

"Thanks, again." Ava pulls onto the empty street. *Stay left*, she reminds herself. Driving on the left is always hardest for her when there is no traffic for a visual or at those "damn roundabouts," their official title as far as she is concerned.

The drive is a pleasant one. She passes Penong. Stops to photograph a herd of kangaroos resting in the afternoon sun. They ignore her. Farther down the Eyre Highway she meets two huge tractor trailer trucks pulling extra trailers. The Aussies refer to them as road trains. They speed towards Ceduna buffeting her car with tidal waves of wind. Past Nundroo. A grey-bearded elderly man sits high on his bench seat. His huge, rickety wagon is piled with weathered blankets, haphazardly loaded boxes, and a couple of chickens as it lumbers towards her on the right hand side of the Highway. He has four camels in hand. Three goats run along behind them. She stops for a photo and is met with his waving hand and shouts of profanities. He turns the camels onto the Plain and creaks into the wavy orange-red heat. She takes extra photos of the surreal image as it grows smaller against the open desert. Some visions even require proof for the witness.

Finally, Ava spots the sign for the Yalata Roadhouse on the right. As she approaches, she can see the two Budget crew vans for the American team. They are parked in the only shaded area off the lot. The vans are impossible to miss covered in bright corporate sponsor stickers. A young woman with short blonde hair pops out of the smaller van. She has a beer in hand and is wearing red nylon running shorts and a white T-shirt. Ava recognizes her as the one jogging across the country. The one always stepping forward in interviews. Ava parks on the opposite side of the car lot and watches for a moment. Three other women emerge from the large camper van. Ava recognizes the six foot blonde. The cyclist and journalist. The one hanging back in the spotlight. Ava watches as three young Aboriginal children with two middle aged Aboriginal women in tow approach the cyclist.

They seem to be thanking her for something.

So much for the Aborigines disliking whites and not speaking to them, Ava thinks.

She gets out of the car and locks it out of habit. Aussies never lock cars. "Natalie! Natalie Newton," she yells towards the cyclist.

Natalie says a couple of words to the Aborigines and walks towards Ava. Natalie's deep tan is set off by two feet of flowing pale blonde hair. She is very thin. No makeup. Pink silk shorts are topped by a white Hawaiian Tropic T-shirt. Flip-flops. "Hello. How are you?"

Ava recognizes the Southern accent mixed with . . . something. "Ava Marks. The ABC asked me to stop and check on you ladies since I'm driving to Perth. I think you're a mascot for the America's Cup. Right?" Ava offers her hand.

"That's what they tell me. Sure look glamorous right now, huh?" Natalie jokes. "Mary, our road manager, told me you might catch us on the road. We just finished for the day. Let's go inside out of the sun."

Ava likes her immediately. *We could be sisters, we look so much alike*, she thinks. "I need to get my camera out of the trunk."

"That can wait. The locals are wary of tourists. Best to let them have a look at you first. Come on. You can buy me a Pepsi." Natalie smiles and walks to the front door of the roadhouse.

Ava follows Natalie to a table in the corner. Two tables away are the Aboriginal women who were just outside. They look at Natalie but look away when Ava smiles at them. A middle aged white man in a cobalt blue "Surf Hawaii" T-shirt stands at the counter. Behind him are packages of cookies and other goodies for sale. A small basket of red apples has a hand written sign saying "$3 each." A glass-front, refrigerated case behind the counter holds soft drinks and iced coffee.

"I'll get us both a drink," Ava says as Natalie takes a seat. She asks the man for two bottles of Pepsi.

"Another Yank. Five in one day. A record." He pops the bottle top, hands her the drinks, and takes her money. "Hey, I know you. Ellen Marks, right?"

"Ava, Ava Marks."

"That's right. Have to tell the Missus. She'll be sorry she missed all the excitement."

"Thanks for the drinks." Ava returns to the table where Natalie is waiting. "Thanks for making time to see me. You must be exhausted. You cycled all the way from Bondi Beach in Sydney, right?"

"Actually, Sarah ran all the way from Bondi. We had to get her through city traffic, so my cycling was very haphazard until we made it to Canberra. After that, I cycled and she ran down to Melbourne then up to Adelaide then over to Port Augusta then Ceduna then here. I was in Ceduna twice because my bicycle was run over by our cook."

"Really?" Ava starts laughing.

"I know." Natalie laughs. "Make it over half-way across the country and your own team member runs over your bike. It was an accident, of course. Anyway, Mary, that's our road manager, drove me back to Ceduna. The bicycle shop owner there is repairing my bike while I ride his loaner. I'll show you outside. I have lovingly named it The Hulk. My bike should be here on the mail truck today or tomorrow. That is the great thing about Australians. Can you imagine someone in the States giving a stranger a loaner bike and arranging to switch them back through the mail truck? Never happen. So, I guess you want the usual funny stories about our adventures and what wildlife we have seen and so forth."

"I was thinking just that on the way here. May I ask you something?"

"That's why you're here. Of course, I may not answer." Natalie smiles.

"When I pulled into the car park, I saw you talking with a group of Aborigines. They won't usually talk to us, the press I mean. And I've been told they don't like whites."

"You want to know how I make friends so quickly."

"Yes. I guess that's it."

"My secret weapon is a Polaroid camera."

"Really?"

"Yep. I had one with me in the Soviet Union to shoot proofs before I set up for my slides. It drew a crowd every time I used it. Started taking photos for the locals and giving them the photos. I was invited everywhere. Everyone talked to me. Drank with a wedding party. It's a magic box."

"So you took their photos."

"First I took a photo of the roadhouse. Then I showed the children and asked if they wanted a photo of them. Gave them a couple of shots and they ran home and came back with women I think are their grandmothers. People are people. You offer friendship and they will likely return it." Natalie takes a long drink from her icy Pepsi. "Invented in North Carolina. Did you know?"

"Of course, I'm from Morehead City."

"It really is a small world. I was born in New Bern. Birthplace of Pepsi."

"So you and Pepsi have been all around the world." Ava says, hoping to impress Natalie that she did some homework.

"I guess that's right. Actually brushed my teeth with it in the Soviet Union. Can't drink the water. That's funny. Never thought about it. Here we are, three products of North Carolina in the Outback."

The women share a laugh and clink together the necks of their Pepsi bottles.

Natalie closes her eyes for a moment at the cool refreshment. "Maybe they'll let you film me walking through their village. I guess you know we are on Aboriginal land here. They own the roadhouse. Their village is just behind here. More down the road. Probably more interesting than filming me answering the same questions I've already answered a hundred times."

"You think they would let us go back there?"

"They were inviting me when you arrived. Get your camera. I'll talk to them and go get the magic box."

Ava doesn't ask twice. Private insights into the Aboriginal communities are rare. She likes Natalie and, for a moment, Ava is very homesick.

The women and children are from a second village down the road. They park Ava's car on the roadside. The dirt track back to the village is only distinguishable by tire tracks covering a twenty foot wide trail. Looks too sandy for driving a sedan. Good way to get stuck. About a half-mile down the dirt track, small frame houses line one side of the tire tracks. A couple of rusty Holdens sit next to the first house. One of the cars has the roof and doors removed. Between the houses, children play a game of tag. Clothes hang on lines strung between the houses. At the end of the homes, a group of men sit cross legged on the ground around a campfire. As the women enter the village, the children and mother and grandmothers come out for a better view. Many of the children are touching Ava's and Natalie's blonde hair. Natalie offers photo shots and quickly goes through nearly two packages of Polaroid film. Ava is invited into a home where she films the dirt floor covered by blankets and hides. The next home has remnants of a campfire inside on the dirt floor.

Natalie speaks to Ava in a low voice. "My understanding is that the government built them the houses. They remove the floors because they think they are supposed to be next to the earth. They have a kind of sixth sense that allows them to see lines, maybe magnetic, I don't know, on the earth. That is how they walkabout without getting lost. They fear removing themselves from the earth will remove this sense. I'm sure an expert could better explain it." Natalie thanks the woman at the house and they move on down the track. A young boy takes Natalie's hand and drags her toward the group of men sitting cross legged around a campfire.

"Hunt. We hunt," the boy says with a broad grin.

Beside the men is a pile of boomerangs and a few knives and some spears carved from gum tree branches. Some of the boomerangs have beautiful carvings of wildlife.

Natalie turns to one of the original grandmothers that talked to her. "Is it okay to pick up a boomerang?"

The woman motions to the young boy who grabs a boomerang from the center of the pile and hands it to Natalie.

The boy is pointing to the carving. "I do this one. My emu. I kill him."

The boomerang has a carving of an emu and the circle sign for watering holes.

"Very nice." Natalie says. "You did this all by yourself? And you brought home an emu for your family? You must be a special boy." Natalie hands the boomerang back to the boy who runs with it to a sitting man. Maybe his father. The man takes the boomerang and hugs the boy.

Ava turns to the two grandmothers still with them. "Thank you very much. You are very kind. We'll go back to the roadhouse now. Thank you."

Natalie takes a last photo of the men sitting around the campfire and hands it to the father of the young boy. "Thank you," she says to all the men.

Ava and Natalie are almost back to the car when the young boy catches up with them.

"You come hunt. You come on hunt with us tonight?"

Natalie turns to the young boy. "That's very nice. But I don't think that would be okay."

"Yes. Yes. You come if you want. Only watch. No kill. No boomerang." He tugs on Natalie's T-shirt.

Natalie turns to Ava. "Well, what do you think? Not likely to get that offer again in a lifetime. Want to go?"

Ava is hesitant. Most Australians she met have not spoken well of the Aborigines. "I don't know."

Natalie looks at the boy. "Are you hunting tonight?"

"Yes. Yes. But you no hunt."

Ava looks at the boy then at Natalie. If you're in, I'm in."

Natalie claps her hands. "Good. We have to change our clothes. How long before you leave to hunt?"

The boy looks at the lowering sun. "When the sun is there," he says pointing at the gum trees low on the horizon.

"We'll hurry. Tell them yes we will come. We are very honored. Thank you." Natalie watches the boy run toward home. "Better wear long pants. We'll probably be in the bushes. And long sleeves. It gets chilly fast when the sun goes down."

AVA CAN'T BELIEVE her luck. She changes clothes in the camper van while Natalie tells Mary where they are going and asks her to keep it quiet until they are gone. Unlikely that bringing along someone not invited would be acceptable.

The fire sparks in the dusk. The men are standing now. Several boys from the village have joined them. Each one has two differently shaped boomerangs and a short spear. Knives are tied at their pant-waists. They ignore Ava and Natalie when they arrive as if the women are regulars in the hunting party. One of the grandmothers from earlier in the day is there. She smears some kind of tree resin type mixture on the sleeves of Ava and Natalie.

The woman holds their arms tight while she smears the mixture on both sleeves. "Need to smell like 'roo," she explains in a deep voice.

"Having fun yet?" Natalie jokes with Ava.

Ava is too nervous to respond. She figures Natalie has had a month of Outback shock therapy. *That's why she's so calm. Skip is going to say I'm a frickin' idiot*, is all Ava can think.

They walk silently into the dusk. The desert is dreamily lit by thousands of sparkling stars. Bushes and short, leaning gum trees dot the landscape. The men break off into groups without a word. Ava and Natalie turn up their palms in a questioning gesture to one another then quickly follow the group with the boy. Half-hour out. Don't want to get lost. They look back as if with the same thought, but the glow of the village fire is gone. They instinctively walk closer together.

Crumple—crumple—crumple go the spears against the brush.

Ten more minutes of walking.

Then a rustling. Everyone stops.

Thump. Thump, thump. Thump, thump, thump thump . . .

The 'roo herd is running along with a flock of emus. Swooshing sounds of boomerangs and spears. Two cries as animals go down. Whoooosh—whoosh—whoosh—squeal! A smaller animal down. The sound of twenty bare feet running across the hard desert floor. The air is pungent with the scent of the gamey animals and fresh blood. The stirred earth releases an ancient, almost peat smell. Ava grabs Natalie's shoulder to lean on it.

"Welcome to Oz," Natalie says to her. "They are right, you know. Never the same after a crossing."

The young boy offers to take the women back to the village while the men gather the animals. They gladly agree and double-time it back to the car.

Natalie heads for the camper van. "You're welcome to bunk in with us tonight. We have two extra berths in the camper."

"That would be great."

"Come on. We have beer in the 'frig. Even in the dark I can tell you need one."

Ava laughs nervously. Not really a beer person. Until tonight. She starts toward her car and sees a man peering through the car window. "Can I help you?" she yells across the car park. She catches a good look at his face as he turns to go around her car. *Clean cut. Nice clothes. Unlikely a thief. Very out of place.*

"Sorry, wrong car," the English-Aussie accent yells back. He leaves in a similar rental parked a few spaces away.

The car park is poorly lit and her car is the only one remaining. Normally, this situation would make her nervous. No longer. Ancient earth shields her. She'll take her time driving to Perth. Maybe a couple of weeks at El Caballo Blanco. She'll call the trainer from the Roadhouse tomorrow. He'll remember her. "The Yank Sheila who charms stallions," he called her after she finished his interview for the doc on the horses of Australia. He let her ride an Andalusian in training. Power and grace. And the horse nuzzled her after the ride. She never mentioned the sugar cube gleaned from breakfast and pulled from her pocket. The trainer thought she charmed the horse known for head butting and nipping. But she had charmed him. Scratched that little place low on the withers that says, "Hello, friend." She could tell at the time that he needed a friend. Rode him on a loose rein. No spurs. Gentle words telling him what a good boy he is. He lived up to it. Good breeding usually does.

FIVE

Perth, Western Australia, AUS,
January 1987

"HELLO, FIONA. IT'S Ava Marks. I'm in Perth two days early. Fabulous time at El Caballo Blanco. I'm a new woman. Is Skip, Mr. Dubbledon, in his office?"

"Oh, hello Miss Marks. Mr. Dubbledon isn't in at the moment. I don't know how you do it. Those giant horses scare me. Glad you had a good holiday. Is there a message?"

"First, please call me Ava. I think we know each other at least that well. Just ask Mr. Dubbledon if he can send my jewelry to the Orchard Hotel tomorrow. Okay?"

"Well, he is out of town for two more days. Would three or four days be all right?"

"Sure, no hurry. I didn't realize he was out of town. What is the number? I'll be glad to ring him myself."

Silence. Silence. Silence. "I don't . . . Ava, he's in Tahiti. He took that stopover for the trip back from the States."

"Oh, that *is* a great layover. I've done that one myself. Do you have the hotel number? What am I saying? Of course, you do. You probably know what he had for dinner yesterday. Have the number handy?" She starts searching her purse for a pen as they talk. *What luck,* she thinks, *he'll be in a great mood in Tahiti.*

Silence. Silence. "Ava, I don't believe he's there alone. I mean, he wouldn't want me to say that. If you could not mention that I told you . . ."

The purse searching stops. Her heart stops. Her brain stops. Deep breath. "Oh. Ummm, that's okay. You know we're just friends. It's none of my business what he does. But don't worry. I won't say anything. I'll call back in three days. Thanks, Fiona." She hangs up in slow motion. *We are just friends. It isn't any of my business. Why do I keep thinking this thing between us is more than it is? Why does he keep making me think it's more? I know he isn't going to change. Why don't I just get out? But I'm not in; how do you get out when you're not in, not really?*

The room phone rings, startling her out of the cold thoughts.

"Cheers. I'm ringing for a Miss Ava Marks. Is this Ava Marks?" The man has a comfortable West Coast Aussie accent, a mixture of old-school English with the West Coast pattern of nearly every sentence rising at the end as if asking a question.

"Who is this?" She shakes her head to dispel the ghosts. She is at once annoyed and reassured by the pungent bleach smell flowing from the hotel bathroom.

"Sorry, I should've said, I'm Clark Lewis. I work for an oil exploration company that does business with SpearCo. Mr. Dubbledon asked me to call . . . tumm . . ."

"Of course. He told me about you. Hey, I'm two days early. How did you know I was here?" She covers the receiver and snorts to expel the bleach and the ghosts. *Good timing for a distraction.*

"Good. I thought I wrote the days wrong. He was

adamant that I greet you as soon as you arrive. I must be lucky." He pauses as if awaiting a comment. "I just called to double-check your arrival, and the desk put me through to your room. I have plans this evening, but a meeting tomorrow afternoon would be spot-on, say about five? Mr. Dubbledon says it's your first time in Perth, and I should show you 'round and about."

"Great. I really appreciate it. We can meet in the bar here at the Orchard Hotel. I have long, blonde hair and . . . "

"I know who you are. We may be on the other side of the country, but we do get television out here," he says in a half-joking voice. "I'll be the one with two bottles of pink champagne."

Now Ava laughs. "That's a joke on me. Champagne is great or we can just order drinks in the bar. Thanks, again."

Pink champagne, an arranged escort, and he's shagging some Tahitian girl. Or maybe worse. Maybe it's Bev. Ava knows she should have told Skip about that fake.

"Stop it!" She says aloud to the empty room. *He just likes being your friend.*

Ava knows Skip doesn't have women friends. Doesn't desire women friends. Doesn't even understand having women friends.

He's as confused as I am, just for different reasons. Forget it. Call Patricia's room and tell her we have a tour guide tomorrow at five. Forget it. Forget it. Call Patricia. Ava grabs the Giorgio perfume bottle from the giant YSL bag. That cold little bottle is easily found without looking into the overstuffed directions of her life. Just touching it is like a peppermint rush. Three sprays through the bathroom doorway. "Take that!" Outrageously expensive flower extract champions her cause. She feels better, not because ten-dollars-worth of perfume wins, but because at least she did something.

PATRICIA AND AVA sit in the Orchard Hotel bar enjoying two coffees, real coffee, full-bodied, freshly ground Colombian, while Patricia talks about the casino in Perth. That's the only place Patricia cares to see. That is probably the only place Ava knows she shouldn't take her considering Patricia already called home for money twice because of gambling. Perth is called the most beautiful city in the world, and Patricia wants to see the casino! No need for a bicoastal losing streak, Ava decides. She likes Patricia. Tries to remember to call her Pat as requested, but Ava is not big on nicknames. Patricia does her job well and has few vices. When you're on the road, having only a few vices is a big plus. Besides, Patricia is a good source of amusement, with her Catholic school upbringing and constant angst about sex and fish on Fridays and all kinds of things a Methodist like Ava finds fascinating in an educated person. Ava caused a twenty-four-hour response to angst their first venture into the Southern Hemisphere when she asked Patricia if protocol demanded New York-time Friday fish or Sydney-time Friday fish, since Friday is a half-day apart. Patricia actually called home to talk to her mother about it.

This competent, professional woman who already feared hell because of missing church a couple of weeks was checking to see when she needed to watch her diet. *So, she can't have sex with a man she loves out of wedlock, but she better have sex with one in wedlock even if she doesn't love him, and she evidently has to eat fish on everybody's Friday, and may see hell anyway because work takes her to some desolate place with no Catholic church.* Ava ran this mental scenario again as Patricia talked up the casino brochure. *Evidently, gambling away all the money Patricia has on her and while in a foreign country—no problem.* In some ways, Ava surmises, the teachings of childhood really do keep us children our entire lives.

Clark Lewis is punctual and has a gym-fit, strawberry blond, male friend in tow. Ava recognizes Clark simply because he's the first man under forty entering the bar. She notices his brown-locked, teddy bear cuteness. He notices her, too, and throws up his hand, stopping his companion. Turning his back to the women, Clark appears to engage in a quick consult before proceeding to the table. The men perform unconscious, ceremonial tie straightening as they approach the young women.

"Don't look now, but I think our nervous escorts just arrived," Ava tells Patricia, who turns for a look.

"Nice! I get the one in front," Patricia says as the men cross the room toward them.

"You can have both. They're only here to—Gentlemen . . ." Ava rises with an outstretched hand.

"Miss Marks, we are—" the first one begins, shaking her hand as if greeting a lumberjack. That handshake is all she needs to cross him off the potentials list.

"*Ava*, please," she tells Clark in a patronizing voice. "This is my road manager, Patricia. I asked her to join us this evening. You must be Clark. Let's stick to first names. I'll have enough trouble just remembering those." She pulls free of the jack-hammer handshake and points toward bachelor number two. "Ava."

"Yes, Miss, um, Ava, this is . . . well, Edward," Clark says. "Just first names, right, old chap?" Clark turns to jack-hammer Patricia's hand.

Patricia's right shoulder is shaking. She pulls Clark down into the chair next to her. "So you chaps work for SpearCo?"

Ava has never heard Patricia say "chaps" and takes the newfound word as code for "old schoolboys, this is going to be fun!"

Motioning to Edward to take the opposite seat, Ava eases into her chair like a bored guest whose presence is demanded at the company cocktail party. "No, I think Clark said an exploration company," she tells Patricia. *Yeah*, Ava thought. *They want to explore us.*

Clark held up a left hand to the bartender. "That's right. Our company does some contract work for SpearCo. I was surprised when Mr. Dubbledon called me himself. I usually speak to one of the serfs." He laughs nervously. "Of course, we did get that call from him just a couple months back," he says to Edward. "Moving up in the world."

Patricia laughs and gives Ava that "Was I right or what?" look.

The foursome do the "What are you doing right now?" formalities with Patricia and Clark doing most of the talking. Ava's eyes drift toward Edward, mainly because she can feel his eyes on her. He's leaning back comfortably in his chair, Scotch neat barely touched on the table in front of him, and she detects a smile, more with his eyes than mouth, the kind you usually get from old acquaintances when they're smugly amused by something.

Edward takes a slow sip of the Scotch. "Now that we know one another's pets' names, would you ladies be interested in seeing our local casino?" Edward asks suddenly.

Ava couldn't tell if Patricia yelled "yes!" before or after jumping up and grabbing the blazer from the back of her chair. With a nod of defeat, Ava looks back at Edward. "I think she's interested. I need to run up to the room and get some cash."

"Not tonight. It's our shout," Edward says, as he drapes Ava's red cashmere cardigan over her suntanned arms. "Chilly out tonight."

"That's right," says Clark, bounding out of his chair. "The casino it is. We're on Skip tonight! Skip! I sound like I'm in the club now."

"Just so he doesn't hear you call him that or we'll be out of a contract," Edward says, a smile softening his firm tone.

THE BRASS AND glass and chandeliered casino is very elegant. All Australian casinos are elegant. The dress code helps. No track shoes, no T-shirts, no anything typically Yank. Ava feels underdressed in a white cotton shift and red-orange leather Bandolino sandals. But she decides that her golden suntan more than makes up for the lack of a cocktail dress. *I love the Southern Hemisphere summer*, she thinks as they cross the open gaming room. They attract attention as they loiter near the craps tables, while Clark exchanges money for chips. The roulette wheel catches her attention, and she watches three turns before Clark returns with a handful of chips.

"Fifty for everyone to get us started," he says, handing Patricia her portion.

Ava gives Patricia a hard look that she pretends not to see. "None for me. I'll just watch. I'm not much of a gambler," Ava says, still trying to catch Patricia's attention.

"I'll take hers," Patricia blurts, her eyes dancing around the room like a first-grader entering Disney World.

"No, no," Edward says as he intercepts the chips that Clark is about to give away. "You have to make at least one bet," he tells Ava. "For sport. So we won't feel guilty about lingering." He hands her five $10 chips.

Ava thinks there's no way Patricia will feel guilty about lingering. *At least our money is in the room safe, so I won't have to mother her in here.* "Okay, one bet." She walks over to the roulette table and places the five chips on a favorite number, black 11. The Italian man next to her at the roulette table is wearing Armani—and Aramis. She can't describe the scent except to say that pheromones come in second. Intoxicating. It's the scent a woman imagines will fill a room when she's snuggled under an aged quilt on down pillows in front of a crackling fire with her beloved with the snow falling on the quiet woods beyond the cabin. Squirrels and chipmunks munch the bowl of pecans left for them on the covered front porch, tiny footprints on the front stairs the only signs of a world beyond that plank-and-beam-ceiling room. "Well, hello," she says in a playful flirtation as he moves over to make room for her.

The thirty-something Italian with his dark hair just slightly too long and his tanned face just slightly too handsome looks over Ava, from her blonde locks to her clear polished toenails. He turns to the side and waves her up to the table.

Edward reaches for the chips, dividing Ava from the firelight stranger. "You can place them in a general category like . . ."

She catches his hand mid-air. "I know. They're where I want them."

The wheel spins, the ball bounces a couple of times, and she is the only winner at the table. Everyone bursts into applause as $400 in chips slide across the table toward her.

Patricia has just experienced the ruination of a gambler:

NATALIE NEWTON

seeing possibilities. "I can't believe it! I've never seen anyone do that!" She is much more excited than Ava, much too
excited. "I can't believe it! You don't even gamble."

"Place your bets . . ."

Patricia shakes Ava's arm. "Bet again," Patricia says too
loudly, eyes darting back and forth.

Ava returns one $50 chip to Edward and hands the rest
to Patricia. "You go have a great time. I just want to walk
around and see everything." She didn't have to suggest it
twice.

Patricia turns a few steps away, yelling to Clark, "Well,
come on."

He trots off in her direction. "See you in a bit!"

"Would you like a drink?" the Aramis stranger asks Ava.
"To celebrate?"

"Thank you. I'm with someone, but if I didn't have a
date, that Aramis would have grabbed me as easily as a but-
terfly net."

"Bad for me," he says in his deep-voiced Italian accent.
"Another time, yes?" He looks at Edward then turns back to
the table.

Edward drops his chip into the pocket of his suit coat.
"So you're apparently lucky and obviously not a gambler.
What would you like to do this evening?"

"I'm fine. I just enjoy walking around and seeing everything" . . . *and catching a whiff of Aramis*, Ava thinks.

"You don't strike me as someone on the sidelines," he
says as he lights a cigarette.

Ava is not a fan of smoking. Two of her grandparents died
from smoking. "Only in the casino. It's just not my thing,
but Patricia loves it, so I'm glad we're here. You should place
a bet." She can't help burning a glare at his cigarette.

"I'm a poker player, not a gambler," he says. He takes a few steps and squeaks his cigarette dead on a glass tray. "And I'm a little spent this evening. I just got in from two weeks on the road. Let's have a seat over here and watch the world pass." He heads for a circular gold velvet ottoman placed amidst the gaming tables.

A cocktail waitress, a slim French woman, no more than twenty-five but suspiciously well-endowed, walks over to get their order just as Edward turns to her. "Ah, bon-"

His back is to Ava, but she is quite certain that he taps his finger to his lips to interrupt the waitress's greeting. "A bottle of Moët & Chandon. Bring a stand, please. We want to sit for a while." He nods toward the ottoman as he drops a $10 chip on her tray. There seems an endless supply of them crunching together in his jacket pocket.

"Come here often?" Ava teases.

He looks a little surprised. "Often enough."

They sit. He interviews her with a deft hand. By the time they finish the Moët and Patricia finishes the chips, Ava knows she has said too much but has no idea about what. On the other hand, Ava ferrets out little more about him than he is the accountant for the exploration firm and lives in Perth and likes to surf, not much for nearly three hours!

The chatty Clark and suddenly quiet Edward drop Ava and Patricia at the entrance to the Orchard Hotel as they express their gratitude and promise to get together again, though Ava doubts it will happen. They take the elevator to their rooms at the opposite ends of the fourth floor. Patricia is quiet as she always is after winning-losing-winning-losing-losing. Ava is quiet as she seldom is after too much champagne. Waving goodbye in the hallway, Ava heads straight to the aspirin bottle in her room. It's already on the bathroom vanity awaiting her return. Champagne doesn't visit well with her. She lingers in the steaming shower, creamy suds slicking away the cigarette smoke from her hair. For the moment, all stressors reverse whirlpool down the drain. She is transported to a crackling fire with tiny squirrel footprints outside in the snow.

AFTER ANOTHER DAY of inane interviews about hulls and crews and club members and captains, Ava gladly returns to her room. Her mood quickly improves when she discovers a blinking red light on her phone. "Hi! It's Skip," the voice message says. "I hear you already met Clark and he took Townie with him. I'm back from Texas. Why didn't you call?"

"I did. You were shagging number 1,008 in Tahiti," she says to the phone. Ava takes a long shower before ringing him. She needs to steam away the chill.

"You met Townie," Skip half-yells over a cricket match on the television. "Aristocratic accents and big wallets can be very sexy."

"Who are you talking about?"

"Townie. Clark Lewis says he took Townie with him to meet you girls. That's funny. You show up with Pat, and he shows up with Townie. So what did you think?"

"They're very nice. We had fun. Too much champagne. A little gambling."

"How little? I bet they charged everything to me!"

"I wouldn't know about that, but they took good care of us."

"On my buck. So what about Townie? Clark's secretary told Fiona that Townie seems quite taken with you. I know he didn't get anywhere even though you could use a good roll in the hay."

"Is that a statement or a question?" She pauses for his comment but only hears him swearing at the cricket pitch. "It was just a night out. I haven't heard from him. Why are you so interested?" She wants to mention Tahiti, but not enough to lose her confidence with Fiona.

"I thought maybe he is taking you to the Ball. Clark is engaged and I heard his girl wouldn't let him meet you alone." Skip laughs lightly, "Don't blame her."

"Is that why Clark brought a friend? I thought it was odd since he didn't know Patricia would be with me. I guess I could ask Edward to the Ball. He gave me a card. It must be in my purse. I never looked at it."

"If you want to, go ahead. He doesn't impress me that much. Competent, I guess. I have a courier coming by tomorrow to pick up your jewelry. We have someone headed back in your direction, so he'll hand it off for delivery. You still at the Orchard?"

"Yes. Thank you. I really appreciate it. I wish you could bring it yourself. Too bad you'll miss the America's Cup Ball. It's quite the hot ticket in town."

"That's all right. I've seen my share of drunk millionaires. You just be careful." Knocking in the background. "Just a minute." Muffled female voice in the background. "I've got to go. One of my neighbors just came by. She gets lonely, you know. And you're not—I'm coming. You go on in and get comfortable! Gotta go!"

"Have fun, Skip." Ava hangs up before he can dig his hole deeper. Before she digs it for him.

She's insulted. He talks like he wants to be around her one minute and the next he's into Act III of a French farce. She doesn't know if he needs reining in or gelding. Both may not be enough. She wants to think this behavior is a reaction to his divorce. She also wants to think this is not why he got a divorce. *Maybe Fiona . . . no, no, no.*

Back in the elevator to meet Patricia and their local film crew in the lobby to do out-takes in Fremantle—or Freo to the party crowd. The Who's Who are jetting in as the Challenger races end. Ava welcomes the distraction. First interview, Dennis Connor of the *Stars and Stripes.* They meet at the crew dining hall, a warehouse where the crew eats daily. One table is devoted entirely to open tubs of ice cream. The giant bowls of spaghetti and meat sauce emit a tantalizing aroma of garlic and sautéed peppers.

A few of the crew chat outside the building with Ava. They don't know who she is, but from her Southern accent they probably think she's either a debutante here for a good time or a career girl working her way through middle management in Perth. They're young, which means they are more interested in talking about themselves than asking about her. The twenty-something captain of the *Betsy,* their tender boat, probably the largest tender in the history of tenders, is very flirtatious. She guesses that he assumes she is a debutante. She learns the crew's sign of the mushroom: arms forming a half-oval that meets in touching fingertips above the head. Meaning *they feed us shit and keep us in the dark.* When Mr. Connor arrives and approaches her for a handshake, the crew's faces drop as they realize they were talking to a reporter. They rush inside to the *shit.* She imagines they will eat for the next week without any complaints. The interview goes well. The next one down the "row" is more like a movie trailer starring Rodney Dangerfield. The European captain is too well-honed at interviews. He sounds like he's reading from a script. The monotony is occasionally punctuated by humorous relief when his assorted friends pass by to make comments, prompting all sorts of arm gestures and shouted words in Italian from him.

Ava is relieved when she heads down the row, but gladly takes the three passes to the *Stars and Stripes* private party tonight across from Freo's upscale hotel, The Esplanade. More *rah! rah!* interviews along the 12-meter warehouse row. It's fun and frivolous, an ostentatious display of wealth and playboy behavior, and she's more bored than at a cricket match. Everything smells like wet canvas. Her cheeks hurt from smiling. She hopes the camera interprets her look as excited and happy rather than frozen in a clownish terror. Ava invites Patricia along for the party tonight, hoping it will get her mind off the local casino. At least the party is exciting Ava. No better atmosphere for getting a dozen leads in a couple of hours. Loose lips may sink ships, but they've made her career.

Back at the hotel, the phone's red message light is flashing again. "The surf report is good for Margaret River. I'll pick you up Saturday morning. Oh, this is Edward Townsend. Give me a call."

Ava thinks about asking him to the party tonight, but she works better alone. Besides, that would leave Patricia to her own devices, which may not be so good. *That snit. He just assumed I kept his number . . . Good for him.* She searches through her bag for Edward's business card. She likes confidence.

A deep breath. She dials the number. "Edward, it's Ava. Have an extra board?"

"I can find one. I'll look for a wetsuit, too. You can't tame Margaret River without a suit. Did you have a good day?"

"We're in the middle of the tourism interviews. Spent

the day in Freo. You can imagine. I'm pooped," she adds in case he's going to suggest seeing her tonight.

"Get plenty of rest. Meet you in the lobby on Saturday at nine. You'll see what real surf is like."

"Not much rest tomorrow. Friday is gearing up to be a big day in Freo. Margaret River, is it far?"

"No, not too far. You don't have interviews scheduled for the weekend, do you?"

"No. It's that I just don't know this coast. Is Margaret River an hour away or ten hours away?"

"Not far. Pack a bag."

"A bag? I don't..."

He interrupts the objection he assumes is coming. "You'll want to change after your swim."

"Oh, right. Thanks. I look forward to it. See you Saturday."

"Right-o." Click.

Do people really say, "right-o?" She decides that if Saturday goes well, she'll ask Edward to the Ball. Then she can stop worrying about an escort. Surfing. Been a while. But she tackled Hatteras by age sixteen. *Not worried about some local thigh-swipers. I saw the waves along Freo and City Beach in Perth. A boogie board would better suit the waves.*

THE LINE WAITING to enter the *Stars and Stripes* party is about twenty people long. Two security men, both blond Aussies in their late twenties, are checking each pass and pausing to chat up every solo woman under age thirty-five.

"We'll have our turn at bat in a few minutes," Ava tells Patricia.

"The left one is cute, don't you think?" Patricia is standing on tip-toes for a better look as though her three-inch heels are not high enough. She's wearing her form-fitting purple dress that means she plans to party.

"What is here happening?" A Swedish or German accent startles Ava. The voice is behind her, just inches from her ear.

She turns. A grinning, well-dressed man, maybe in his sixties or seventies, is flanked by two stern gentlemen in their forties. The older man is dressed casually in a windbreaker, cotton dress shirt, and pleated trousers. The other two are in dark suits, looking out of place in this beach-resort town. Ava silently reprimands herself for her ignorance of many Western European accents.

"*Stars and Stripes* is having a party," she says, smiling politely at him while she feels the glare of his companions. Her cheeks turns hot in the night breeze.

He turns back to his companions. "A party. How fun. We go in."

They nod a yes without speaking.

"It's by invitation." Ava shows him her ticket. "I'm sorry. I only have one extra."

"Oh, unfortunate." He keeps staring at her.

For some reason, Ava feels patronized.

"We like to go." He turns around again. "Henrich, maybe you see what you can do."

As the line moves forward, it's Ava's turn to be ogled by the door security. "Give me a minute. I'll see if I can find someone. I know most of the crew." She approaches the entry.

Henrich says something in German, or maybe Swedish, while the older man ignores him. "Good. Good. Oh," he offers his hand, "I am Dieter Dietrich. We wait here."

Ava shakes Mr. Dietrich's hand only slightly. He holds her hand as if it's a small bird he might damage. "I'll see what I can do. I'll be right back. Here." She hands Henrich the extra ticket, a gesture that seems to startle him. "You are welcome to come in to look for someone you know." She notices a strange tattoo on his thumb. Something exotic. Still can't place the accent.

"What are you doing?" Patricia asks as they clear the door.

"They seem nice. He seems nice I should say. I'll try to find Dennis. Never hurts to do a good deed." She heads off into the crowd as Patricia spots a crew member beckoning them over to the bar. Ava asks a couple of people about Dennis, when one of the yacht club members overhears her.

"Mr. Dietrich is here?"

"Yes, he's at the door. He said he would like to come in. Oh, there's his friend Henrich."

"You left him at the door!" The man rushes through the crowd to the doorway. Within seconds he enters with Dieter and Henrich and the other one who, without a word, made Ava feel as though she was in the presence of a killer. Dieter is still smiling as she sees him scanning the crowd, basically ignoring the yacht club member. Then he spots her watching him and holds up his hand for her to wait. It looks like a Hitler salute. They all head toward Ava.

"Ava. Thank you." He turns to address the yacht club member as though he is the houseboy. "Might we have table? We need five seats. Yes?" He looks at Ava. "Five seats? You are alone?"

"Yes. Just my friend Patricia."

To Ava's surprise, instead of looking insulted, the club member says, "Oh, yes. Right away."

"I love Americans," Dieter says to her. "They always say they can do something and they do it. There is such confidence. In other countries I do not see this confidence or this friendliness. Do you think that is because of the schools? Is that how they teach you?"

"I certainly never thought about it that way. Maybe it's just because of whom you meet."

He laughs. "Maybe so." He starts to say something, but they are motioned over to a large round table being set up with six chairs. "Here we are. You please will sit with us?"

Ava hesitates. He seems interesting. The way he is being treated is certainly interesting. "Of course, thank you." She glances over at the dance floor. The DJ is spinning Michael Jackson and Madonna tunes, which seem out of place. "In Australia, shouldn't we be hearing Midnight Oil or even Mental as Anything?"

Dieter looks confused at the question. "You like to dance?" Dieter asks as he holds a chair for her. "Here, you sit by me. You make me happy." He takes her arm and guides her to her seat. "Very nice," he comments on the softness of her brown suede jumpsuit.

"Yes, I love to dance." She's glad she wore the suede jumpsuit. The brown leather self-belt cinches her waist and the suede is soft as a baby blanket. She knows she looks a million bucks in it.

"Then we dance. First we order." He leans over and says something overpowered by the blaring of Springsteen's "Born in the USA." The crowd roars.

Dieter jumps up and takes Ava's hand. "We dance to this, yes?"

They make their ways to the edge of the crowd. Everyone is laughing and singing along, so she sings along, too. Dieter seems very amused. He is a surprisingly good dancer. Had she expected him to hobble? Even sixty seems so old when you're under thirty. A couple more dances and she asks to sit. The jumpsuit is great for cool nights. Not so good for staying cool while dancing.

Ava is greeted by a tub of Moët & Chandon. The three men all have what looks like Scotch on the rocks. Patricia is sitting at the table talking to the Italian hull designer working on the *Stars and Stripes*. She's enjoying her champagne.

"Ava, there you are." The hull designer motions to the table and chairs, the only ones in the standing-room-only party. "You must know someone."

"Just these gentlemen."

"Are they with the network?"

"No. We just met at the door."

"Would you like to dance?"

Ava is breathing hard and feels flushed from the exercise and closeness of the room. "Maybe later. I need to sit for a minute."

"I'll dance," Patricia says, grabbing his hand and pulling him along behind her.

"Your friend?" Dieter asks.

The whisper is so close she feels his breath on her ear. Scotch. Definitely Scotch. "He's a hull designer for *Stars and Stripes*. Nice guy."

"You like him, yes?"

"I don't really know him. But he seems very nice."

"So he is not male friend . . . boyfriend." Dieter fills her glass with champagne.

"No. I don't really know him."

"And where is boyfriend?"

She hesitates. *Do I have a boyfriend? I guess I don't.*

"No boyfriend. How about you. Where is your family?"

"My boys are in Sweden. They are same years as you. Well, older than you maybe, yes?" He gives her a little wink, cute not lusty.

"And your wife?"

He smiles and hesitates. "I lost their mother in plane crash many years now with my one daughter."

"I'm sorry. That must be very hard."

"I had two other wives," he says, the sadness more subdued. "Removed them in divorces. Wrong choices."

"I'm sorry. It's hard. I'm divorced, too. I wouldn't want him back, but I kind of miss being married and just knowing someone is there. You know?"

Dieter stares distantly at her as though seeing right through her, or into her thoughts. He's no longer smiling and laughing. She can't interpret his look.

"I like being married, also," he says. "But love will never be the same as first love. Yes?"

"I don't guess it can ever be the same," she says. Ava tings her glass rim to his. "To first loves." She sips her champagne without looking at him, even though she feels his eyes on her as surely as if they were a soft blanket in the night. She needs to break the spell of the champagne. Of the sincerity. "That Moët is so nice, but I really need some ice water."

He whispers to Henrich, who leaves the table immediately as Ava rises.

"Henrich will get it for you. Let us talk about you. Let us talk of first loves."

More than two hours pass without her noticing. She even receives water with plenty of ice. They talk about her career and all the funny situations she found herself resolving. Talk about her pets and their stupid antics. He wants to know all about growing up in North Carolina. He can't visualize it, so she talks of the white sand beaches lapped by salty air and brackish back bays smelling of fish in the warm summer breeze. Homemade apple pie with melting vanilla ice cream in the afternoon shade of the front porch. Low laughter filtering through window sheers on cool days. Music in the living room every night while her parents dance to Frank Sinatra and Dean Martin. They don't talk about Skip. They don't talk about her ex. He tells her nothing about himself. Not having a man drone on about his life and accomplishments is fun and refreshing to her. He shows genuine interest in Americans and how they live.

He sits so close to Ava that they are nearly joined from shoulder to elbow. He seldom looks away. After a pause in the conversation, he lightly taps her hand with his index finger. "What do Americans want these days?"

"Well, I guess every guy wants a country club membership and a Porsche. Every girl wants a long string of pearls and a Porsche." She laughs her light-headed champagne giggle.

"Do you have what you want?" He is smiling broadly enough to laugh.

"I have the pearls. Still working on the Porsche." They ting glasses in another toast. Ava looks at her watch and realizes the late hour. "Uh-oh, I need to get going. We have an early shoot tomorrow."

"More mushrooms to interview?"

"I shouldn't have told you that. Don't tell Dennis. His crew were just joking around." She stands to go.

He motions to the other men who spent the evening talking among themselves in German, she thinks. They are a little too far away for certainty, trying more to give Dieter privacy than themselves. "We all go now. I walk you."

Ava asks Patricia if she's ready to go. She says her good-byes to the three people talking with her and they head for the door. Patricia is humming a tune Ava doesn't recognize. She is glad to see Patricia happy somewhere other than the casino. They stroll from the heady smell of expensive liquor into the coastal air softened by hundreds of flowers planted for the Cup.

They walk across the perfumed lawn toward the Esplanade. The clear evening sky is well lit by the fortune-teller's map above them. "You come to my room," Dieter says, taking Ava by surprise. He places his hand in the small of her back.

"No, we have to go." She gently pats his shoulder, trying to avoid conflict.

"You come. We make babies."

"Ava!" Patricia grabs Ava's hand and starts pulling her along.

"No. No. I am not bad man. I marry your friend. She will be my next wife." He turns to his two companions. "She will be my next wife."

Ava tells him, "I think we've all had a little too much to drink." She raises her hand to hail a cab.

"You don't have car? We take you home. Where are you staying?"

"The Orchard Hotel," Patricia says.

"That is in Perth?"

"We'll take the cab. Thank you for a fun evening. I had a very good time. I hope all of you enjoy your time here." Ava pulls the cab door closed behind her. As the cab drives away, she turns and sees the three of them standing in the same spot talking like conspirators. Someone with a slight limp approaches them. The Germans turn to shake hands with the new arrival.

Ava turns back around in the cab. "Well, already forgotten. Looks like their friends at the hotel found them."

"Just as well. So what was that?" Patricia asks.

"It was strange, that's what. I think I was just interviewed. For what I have no idea. I'm the journalist, and he's the one who found out everything. All I know is that the Italian designer that was so nice to us—you know, the one that does hull design—was excited to meet them. They are planning an entry for the next Cup."

FRIDAY MORNING'S SUN brightens the hotel room as Ava enjoys her Devonshire tea breakfast—a pot of tea with open-face scones smothered in strawberry jam and whipped cream. She takes each bite slowly as if savoring a sweetness long past. Already dressed in an ivory silk blouse and red linen suit, she is prepared for a day of interviewing. With a ring of the room phone, a front desk clerk tells her that she has a delivery.

Good. My jewelry is here. One thing about Skip, he has a fantastic network, she tells herself.

She squeezes into the crowded elevator. The stifling box opens to a noisy lobby crammed with tourists and businessmen. They mingle in a hectic fray, mellowed by the potted jasmine perfuming the room like a Neiman's cosmetic counter.

"Miss Marks—here." A male clerk in his early twenties waves her to the end of the front desk counter. He hands her a small black box with a note attached. For some reason, all the clerks stop working and turn to watch.

"To go with the pearls," the note says.

For a moment, she is totally confused. She opens the little box. A heavy, heart-shaped silver key ring the size of a fifty-cent piece is engraved "AVA." It looks and feels like real silver and holds three keys. She turns to the clerk. "What?"

All the clerks watch with amusement as he points to the front door. "Just outside, Miss. The black one."

"What?"

"Go outside, it's waiting for you."

"I didn't order a car." *I might as well see what it's about. I can't believe Skip would rent me a car,* she thinks as she zig-zags through the crowd.

A valet, no more than eighteen or nineteen, is waiting outside and eagerly opens the large, glass front door for her. "That's what I call a real Bob's yer uncle gift," he says, pointing to it. As she passes through the doorway, the valet runs to the driver's door of a new black Porsche 911 Carrera.

And there it is. Black mirror-polished paint. Black supple leather. Top down. She can almost hear a choir in the background. The sticker is removed from the window and neatly placed on the front passenger seat. The owner's manual is on the driver's seat beneath a single sterling rose. She is dumbfounded.

"Allow me," the valet says as he opens the driver's door.

Ava's mind freezes. She can't reason the situation. "This isn't mine. I didn't order a car."

The valet is oblivious to her distress. "The dealership dropped it off this morning. Me mate, Don, works the'. Let him deliver it, lucky bugge'. Says it's the only one in Puth. His boss had to work the phones last night to find it."

Ava waves her hands to-and-fro like living windshield wipers. "What? This isn't mine. There is some mistake."

"Oh, it's definitely yours. Bob's yer uncle, it's yours."

Something. Last night I said something about a Porsche—pearls and a Porsche. Can't be. It's not Skip at all. It's that German or was he Swedish? Oh God. What if he's European Mafia or something? Calm down. Of course, not. But those two other guys looked pretty scary. "Close the door."

"Don't you want to . . ."

Ava gives a stop signal with her right hand. "Close the door. Don't touch it!" She walks swiftly back to the front desk and plops the keys on the counter. "Send it back."

"What?!" The desk clerk is incredulous. "We can't send it back. We don't know where to send it."

"Oh, yes you do. The valet knows who delivered it."

"But we don't have the authority to do something like that. It's in your name. You—"

"You accepted the delivery. You return it. And I don't want a fingerprint on it. Call that Dan or Don or whatever his name is, and tell him to come get it."

She hurries upstairs and calls the Sydney office.

A woman with a heavy Irish brogue says, "No, Mr. Murray isn't in yet. I can tell him you called."

Ava doesn't want to leave her relocation to chance. "Could you please look and see if the network house in Perth is vacant?"

"Just a minute. . . . Well, yes and no."

"Yes and no?" Already flushed, Ava's hand quivers as she squeezes the receiver.

"Couple of the execs are using it for the Cup, but there's a granny flat attached. No one is in the granny flat, don't you know."

Ava calms herself in hopes of warding off gossip at the Sydney office. "Give me the address, please. Patricia and I are checking out of the Orchard. Just tell me where to pick up the keys to the granny flat."

AFTER THE MORNING shoot, Patricia begrudgingly checks out of the Orchard. She doesn't understand there are some gifts you don't keep. Ava decides you can grow up in New York and still be naive. She can't check-out fast enough. A faint but distinctive musky odor in her room sends her into a sneezing fit as she gathers her bags. Thankfully alone in the elevator. Then back to the front desk when the same clerk from this morning comes over with another box.

"I took care of everything, Miss Marks." He looks at her as if he's glad this obnoxious Yank is leaving. "Another delivery for you. I rang your room, but you must have been on your way here." He holds out a small package tied with twine.

"What is this?"

"I'm sure that I don't know." He places the box on the counter in front of her and leaves abruptly. The only writing says, "Miss Ava Marks, Orchard Hotel, Perth" She recognizes the curlicue handwriting immediately: Skip's secretary. Ava had forgotten about her jewelry in all the commotion. She hears a female voice down the counter whisper, "No, that one came from a SpearCo director. And I think he's married." Ava decides to open the box after she gets to the granny flat. The prying eyes make her face flush. She feels sorry for the local man Skip sent into the lion's den. Poor guy will probably be having dinner with the wife and five kids when her best friend rings up with the gossip. *I can only hope he told her about the errand.*

Eden

"SO *THAT* IS the story! I've heard the urban-legend version," says Iain as he lovingly adjusts his Akubra. The hats have been made in Australia since the early 1900s. They're at once a status symbol and tip to Aussie history. Women like them because of the swashbuckling swagger that comes at no extra charge.

"I didn't know there was an urban-legend version." Ava opens her purse, searching for her Oakley sunglasses: pink, an impulse buy. The sun is high and bearing down as they meander along the overgrown trail, stiff brush scratching her ankles. "So many things happened during the Cup that I hoped my gossip would be quickly upstaged by the next outrageous act." She tenderly rubs her stomach. "That breakfast was so good that I could eat another one right now."

"There was a legend, all right. Still makes the rounds at the club." Iain smooths his thick hair and replaces his hat. "Time for tea, I think. Been a good four hours since brekkie."

"Come on, Iain. You know the victim is the last to know."
Four hours? Her autopilot turned on after the eggs, and she has no idea where she walked the past four hours, but she knows where she has been—in Perth not seeing much that was before her.

He chuckles, that high-pitched kind that could be mistaken for a parrot cry. "Okay, Holy Roller." There's affection in his voice, an odd tone that seems to herald the erasure of decades from his face.

"Excuse me?"

"Holy Roller, the mates got the expression right, didn't they?" He looks at Ava with the wide eyes men get when they're little-boy naughty.

"I would hardly say that I'm the preachy kind."

"No, it came from the Rolls Royce. The story is that some high roller sent you a diamond after meeting you and Skip trumped with a Rolls Royce, and you returned both of them. So . . . holy roller."

"You just never realize how ridiculous gossip gets until you're on the receiving end. No one ever asked me about it. You mean the men at the club think that's what happened?" She raises her face to the sky mouthing obscenities.

Oh, it's not so bad. Makes you look apples, really. It's more a joke on the chaps than on you. Really. Me mates have all given a few gifts they wished later had been returned. You make Sheilas look good. Like maybe somebody besides me mum has a conscience!"

"If I didn't know better, I would take that as a compliment."

"Don't let it get out! Me mates will think I am going poofdah."

That comment will definitely be left alone. "Yes, tea time. I'm thinking more like 4X time. Let's really give them something to talk about. Oh god, now I'm being compared to mums!"

"The day you drink a 4X, actually, the day I see you drink any beer, is the day I quit women. Then I'll be certain I know nothing about any of you."

"Yeah. Yeah. A Roller, huh?" The fact is she seriously doubts Skip could have afforded a Rolls Royce, and besides, he never would have made that kind of gesture toward any woman. The quiet sea calms her noisy mind. A faint saltiness invigorates the dry breeze. She wonders if she had said "a string of pearls and a Rolls Royce" if . . . *I still wonder how one gets engraving done overnight.* "Iain, you know what I just realized?" Ava stops and turns to look at him. "Followers take 'no' as no. Leaders take 'no' as a challenge to try harder. When I said 'No' by returning the car, that man looked all over Freo for me—I heard he was at the Orchard, and the next week I learned he was on 12-meter row asking my location. So, when I told Skip 'no' about the cruise, he probably didn't think it was really a No. He thought I was trying to get more effort from him. My god, do you think he thought I was attention-seeking or that spoiled?"

"You're asking me, the chap with the worst record with Sheilas in Oz? Besides, that German or Dutch or Swedish or whatever chap probably blows more on dinner than I make in a year. And Skip, well, I don't have a yacht in the Sydney-to-Hobart. How the hell would I know the thoughts of people like that?" He looks out over the sea, breaking their eye contact. "You're a beautiful woman, Ava. Beautiful women make men mental. . . . Makes me wonder – about a woman saying 'no' – never mind."

"Well, thank you, Iain, but you seem sane enough." She pokes him in the side to break the moment.

Iain jumps away from her poking finger. "That's because you aren't my type."

"Oh, you mean a Yank."

"No, I mean smart with long legs. I have enough trouble with dumb and short legs."

"Good god, all of you are impossible." She leaves the trail and walks through the freshly cut grass outside the inn. *Cut grass always smells like summer.*

"So, I guess you spent the weekend dodging the chap?"

"Didn't need to. Saturday morning Edward picked me up to go surfing at Margaret River." Up the stairs to the empty front porch. She plops into the only chair with overstuffed pillows, flowered pillows, of course. "I gave him directions to the granny flat, and he was punctual as a prince."

"Well put. He must have loved the Porsche story." Iain takes the chair across from her. "I'm sure our host will be out any minute."

"I didn't tell him the Porsche story. We had just met, and well, who's going to believe that you talk to someone and have a couple of dances and they send you a Porsche?"

"Good point, Holy Roller." He winks as he tilts back in his chair. "So when did you find out that Margaret River was hours away? The whole story, now."

SIX

Margaret River,
Western Australia, AUS,
January 1987

EDWARD SPEEDS THE Toyota Celica down the two-lane highway. Even though it's a bright Saturday morning, the kind that tints everything yellow, Edward and Ava have not seen another car in the past fifteen minutes. She is comfortable on the brushed-cloth seat, watching the kilometers of sandy roadside disappear into gum-tree forests of wild scrub plants. The farther south they travel, the more lush the environment. Ava does not miss the starkness of the Outback, kilometers of sandy clay sparsely covered by windswept gum trees and scrub brush, but she does miss the herds of kangaroos. She even misses the thump-thump of their walking. It's an unnerving sound until you realize it's the sound of a 'roo and not some madman thumping a piece of heavy firewood against the clay. Edward and Ava sit quietly, no radio, no talking. She thought she was the only person who likes driving in silence. The noise of her mind often fights radio music for attention.

Her mind returns to the interior of the Celica. *I guess I should say something*, she decides. "So, are we almost there? You haven't said how far it is."

"We should be there in time for a late surf. Besides, only mad dogs and Englishmen go out in the midday sun."

"But you are an Englishman. How far is this place? Do we have time to surf and eat and still get back tonight?" She realizes now that this is not a day outing to the beach.

"Of course not, I have us booked at a small hotel for the night. You'll like it. All the surfers stay there. Well, the employed ones stay there. You'll likely see more young chaps sleeping in their vehicles and on the sand than at the hotel."

He keeps watching the road as if he has just told her that they're stopping at the shop for a cold drink.

Ava glares at him, irritated that he avoids looking at her. "I didn't know we're spending the night!"

"Don't be naive. It's too far for a day trip."

"I asked you how far it is and you never answered." She falls back into her seat. She is flushed with anger. One-night stands with virtual strangers is not her thing, and it's insulting that he would assume it is. "Turn back."

He blows out a full belly laugh, forcing the air from his lungs in one burst. "Don't you get fired up fast as a cricket pitch. I booked two rooms, all right? Besides, Mr. Dubbledon told Clark to show you a good time, but not too good. He said that is his domain."

"What do you mean, 'that is his domain?' Mr. . . . . Skip and I are just good friends."

"Tumm. Yes."

"'Umm. Yes.' What does that mean? We *are* just friends. I'm sure he wouldn't tell anyone otherwise."

"Are we talking about the same Philip Dubbledon?"

"We are good friends. Period." She says it with such conviction that Edward turns to look at her. "The relationship has not gone further than that."

"I'm impressed. I thought his mother was probably the only woman with whom he could be 'just friends.' " He pauses, then continues. "Look. I didn't mean to insult you or anything. We can turn around if you like."

"Do we really have two rooms booked?"

"Of course. You don't think I'm that easy, do you?" His playful tone puts her at ease.

"I guess it would be a shame to come this far just to turn around," Ava says. "Don't let me forget to call Patricia. She's expecting me back tonight."

Edward reaches for the radio, but she places her hand on his to stop it. "I like that we're comfortable in the quiet together," she says softly.

His eyes remain on the road, his hands now back on the steering wheel. "Me, too."

THEY DRIVE AND drive down a narrow dirt track. The shoulders are potholed by wayward tires dug deep into the orange-grey sand. Finally, she spots five cars parked on the side of the road. Edward pulls in beside the first car, a weather-beaten Holden, the only Australian-made car.

"The extra wet suit is in the back seat. You can change into your swimsuit in the car if you want. We walk from here." In a single motion he throws open the car door and leaps into the breezy, slightly balmy sea air.

Ava doesn't want to seem out of her element. Sure. She strips and puts on a swimsuit in the back seat of a car every day. She climbs into the back and opens her travel bag. Through the rear windshield she sees Edward pull off his shirt, wrap a towel around his waist, and up go the pants into the air. From the looks of it, he's done the towel-dressing-room routine for years. She climbs out of the car in a one-piece yellow swimsuit. She waits for him to notice her pinkish golden tan, fresh from the rooftop pool at the Orchard Hotel, before she starts wriggling into the wet suit.

"You may want to put that on after we get down to the water." He stands there in blue board shorts looking surprisingly fit. She is more used to suits hiding soft rolls.

He pulls the two boards from the car roof with ease and props them on the side of the car.

"They look a little wide."

"You have a good eye. It's a local shaper in Perth. You're going to love it. He was the first one to use triple fins. This one is yours," he points to the shiny, yellow-lettered board.

"Wow. You cleaned that up well." She could see what looked like months of semi-scraped wax all over his board.

"It's new. It's for you."

"Oh, I couldn't."

"Of course you can. Let's go."

He starts off down a well-worn sand trail leading to the right, but she still can't see the water. After five minutes hiking through soft sand, they crest the hill. A stiff breeze catches her off guard. Smells of seagrass and something, maybe wet stone. The trail stretches into the horizon in front of them and water level is a steep drop.

"How far?" she asks.

"Oh, it's a hike yet."

He wasn't exaggerating. Another fifteen minutes of trudging through deep sand flowing into the sides of her boat shoes and they were finally descending. Crashing waves semi-drowned the faint yells and laughter of a dozen or so people below them. Getting closer. A couple of girls were sunning topless on brightly colored towels. Two surf-boards lay just above the tide line. At least ten surfers were in various stages of catching waves. She gasped. Stopped in her tracks. Beside the last surfer, two huge dolphins rose and rode their powerful tails on the crest of the shared wave. In seconds, the dolphins flipped off of the wave and took a running leap out of the frothing water as they headed back to sea.

Her mouth agape; blowing sand stings her tongue. She spits out the sand without thinking. Pthhhht. "Did you see that?"

Edward turns back to her. "Welcome to Margaret River. Worth the trek, eh?"

"You bet it is."

After a quick rest and some direction on where to avoid dangerous coral and rocks, Ava dives into the needle-cold Indian Ocean. No wading in here. Just grab the board and jump from the shoreline. She knows that if she tests the water with a toe, her rational mind will scream, "Run!" She surfaces from the first wave dive with an "Ahh" and sits astride the board, hugging herself before diving under the next wave. Everyone in earshot laughs. Never had she immersed in melted ice water. Knew better than to hit the Hatteras waves in the winter. *No more bitching for more ice in my water. Remembering this misery will make tap water cool enough.* She is too frozen to shout back to Edward, who is two wave-crests ahead of her. Then she's bumped. Not hard. Just enough that she looks to her left. A playful dolphin splashes her face with his nose and leaps into the oncoming wave line. Flat on the board. Paddling. Dive. Paddling. Dive. Fantastic.

Three hours later her arms are shaky and she is limp

with exhaustion. Her eyes sting, nose stings, mouth tastes like seaweed saltwater. She is happy. Empty mind kind of happy. She wants to ride the board to the sand and hop onshore like a pro, but the strength isn't there. She takes a good roll as the wave breaks and knows she's through for the day. Dolphins are all around them. She didn't get the thrill of surfing alongside them, though. They seem to know she's the Margaret River rookie and stay a safe distance from her board, which launches like a missile as often as it rides the waves.

Edward rides in just behind her. "You hit some big surf today. I'm impressed! Ready to call it before *the doctor* gets here?"

"The doctor?" Her voice is as shaky as her arms.

"The sea breeze afternoon trade wind. We're sheltered here. Wait 'til we head for the car. You're going to feel peppered with flying sand."

"Oh, great. I'm too tired to walk ten feet right now. Give me a few minutes." She pulls the long zipper string to free herself from the wetsuit. It peels from her chill-bumped legs and falls to the green, cotton quilt he had spread. "Could you just get the valet to send over the car?"

"GOOD TO SEE you, Baron," the hotel owner gives a slight nod to Edward.

Everything smells of chips: fried-potato yard, fried-potato foyer, fried-potato owner. Actually, it's quite comforting to the exhausted surfers.

"We have ya rooms ready, t' be sure. Gave ya the adjoining ones on the side, we did. Yer own entrance." The middle-aged man is wearing a bright orange polo shirt and white linen trousers. He walks around the front desk with two keys. "This way, Miss." He bows to Ava slightly then leads the couple back out the front door and through a small garden gate to the rooms. "The Missus has everything ready for ya, t' be sure. Just give her a ring if you be needing anything." He unlocks the side-by-side doors and flings them open in unison. Turning to Ava and Edward, he hands each of them a key. "I'll be right back with yer bags, m' Lord, t' be sure."

"Ta, Miles. No need. I'll fetch them myself. You've taken care of everything as usual. Thank you."

"Yes, Sir. Nice t' have ya with us again, t' be sure." He nods to Ava without making eye contact. "Miss." He shuffles quickly towards the gate.

"So you did get two rooms. Good for you." Ava crosses the threshold with a ceremonious march, planting both feet just inside the doorway. Sun floods the room, making it as bright as the water was cold. Softly billowing curtains and sheers are pushed back, the fresh air intermingling with the cotton-candy scent of wildflowers in a vase. Or was that aroma room freshener? Her nose searches for the comforting chips. A layer of sand coats her face. She steps back outside the doorway and removes her shoes. Sand flies in all directions as she slaps the soles together. With a hand, she brushes her sandy feet. Edward is staring at her. "What? This is how Yanks do it."

"No. I just realized you might have stayed if we only had one room. I can go back."

"Ha, ha." Ava goes back into the room and throws herself onto the white bed. She is unconcerned about getting sand everywhere. The down-filled comforter greets her with a long pooof. *I love smooth sateen cotton!* "Yesss," she says, with a great exhale of sea air.

Edward walks through the open door dividing the two rooms. Ava hears a champagne cork pop. She sits up cross-legged.

Edward holds two flute glasses in one hand and a bottle of Moët & Chandon in the other. "For you, Miss, t' be sure," he says, mimicking their host.

"Why, thank you, Sir . . . m' Lord." She takes a glass and savors a long sip of the cold fizz as sweet as vanilla frosting. "Did he call you *Baron*?"

"And I thought you were being coy. You really don't know, do you?"

"That you are a baron?"

"I inherited three years ago after my father's passing. My sister's family lives on the estate. I'm over here making something of myself, as they say. Too young to settle down just yet."

"So that's what Skip . . ."

"What?"

"Oh, nothing."

He clinks his glass to hers. "To beautiful . . . Margaret River."

"To beautiful Margaret River," she echoes.

They take a sip. He leans toward her. She turns her face up to kiss him. She wants to kiss him. She's been thinking about it since he swam over to her after her first spill. She gets a kiss on the forehead. His lips are sun-warm.

"Okay, off to the showers with you. One hour and we are off to tea, or rather alcohol as it were." He leaves abruptly, closing their adjoining door behind him. His outside door clicks shut and she falls back on the bed. Beautiful Margaret River. *Oh, I need to call Patricia.*

NATALIE NEWTON

AVA AWAKENS UNSHOWERED. Her scalp itches of salt. Her hair is Medussa-styled. She thinks about getting up. Fast asleep again. She jolts from her dream about a pile of fried potatoes. Edward is sitting next to her on the bed, gently shaking her. "Wake up, Sleepyhead. Wake up, Sleepyhead. We need to eat. And we have the evening ahead. I brought your bags." Her dream of fried barramundi and smooshy, salty, steak fries—the Aussie version of fish and chips—is gone, but the oily scent lingers in her mind. She asks for fifteen minutes and takes thirty. Damp hair and quick makeup later, she and Edward are on their ways to the only local pub.

She keeps reminding herself that he saw her sopping wet in the ocean. *This has to look better than that*, she tells herself. *Besides, this is my periwinkle silk shift. Any woman would look great in this dress. Even if I only have pink flip-flops to wear with it.*

Edward opens the car door for her. If he had not, he never would have seen Ava again. He's supposed to be a well-mannered baron. Besides, men who don't open doors don't get second dates. Where Ava comes from, manners are the measure of a man and women expect better treatment, not equal.

Exiting the car, Ava pauses for an exaggerated stretch. "I need a drink."

"Sure, that's your door right there. I'll meet you at the outside tables in, oh, fifteen minutes." He starts down the walk toward another door.

"Wait a minute. Whaddya mean?" Ava rushes to catch him.

He stands with a half-cute and half-irksome grin. "That's the Ladies Bar. See the sign. Women go in that side. Men in the other side."

"You gotta be kidding me." She shakes her head to make sure she's awake. *An Aussie pub with Amish-like segregation?*

"That's the way it is here in the country pubs." He heads toward the door labeled *Men's Bar*.

He's joking, Ava thinks. *I'll get inside and he'll be there laughing at the bar.* She opens the Ladies Bar door to enter a room filled with chatting women. A couple of them are even holding babies. Women from sixteen to seventy-six sit around laughing and chatting. The scene is surreal. Through the double-sided bar she can see men watching cricket on the telly. Glasses clink over moans and roars. On the women's side, Dame Edna's comedy show is on the telly, but no one is watching. Nearly everyone greets Ava with "Cheers" or "G'day" as she approaches the bar. She says "Hi," and hears, "Hey, a Yank! Good on ya!" *So this is why men go to bars alone just to have a drink. Because they can. Women look like call girls waiting for a profitable evening, but men go to watch the game with the blokes and talk about male things like women, sports, money, work . . .* Ava wonders if a male/female segregated bar could ever happen in the States without ACLU intervention. She realizes that hanging with women like herself has its appeal. No one's flirting or fixing her hair or worried what her boyfriend is doing. *Hey, he's drinking a Swan Lager and watching cricket. That's what he's doing,* she muses.

When Ava meets Edward outside, he's at a picnic table with two dinner platters. "What happened to you?" His voice is light, frivolous, jolly.

"I was engrossed by Dame Edna," Ava says, adding, "well, not really. Don't worry. I just enjoyed meeting all the women. What fun. I wish we had this bar in the States."

"Now you're giving me a hard time." He takes a bite of his shepherd's pie.

"No, really. How refreshing to go out for a drink and not have everyone either hitting on you or thinking you want them to hit on you. You're a guy. You wouldn't understand."

He nods, agreeing that he probably doesn't. "This is so good. I can't tell what spice they use. Got you the lamb plate. Shepherd's pie can be an acquired taste. Tell me if you want something different."

They dawdled over the food and a pitcher of Margueritas. Ava is exhausted from surfing and still has a dry crust of salt in her nose. She is full from the butter-soft lamb, mint jelly, and roasted red potatoes. The gin and tonic inside the pub followed by Margueritas outside, make it a perfect day. Darkness sets in all at once like the flick of a switch. Her head is spinning with goofy tales as they drive back to the hotel. The air smells primordial and every few minutes sea water trickles from her nostrils.

Edward hands her his handkerchief, neatly pressed into a perfect square. "Just keep it," he says.

"Why isn't your nose running?" Ava asks as she stumbles along toward their private entrances.

"I didn't fall all the time."

She turns and lands a good punch in his abs. It's like punching plywood.

"Oh! So you're violent, too!"

Ava shakes her hand as if it's hurt. "I'm sorry. I didn't mean to land it quite that hard."

He unlocks her door, follows her into the adjoining rooms, and pours two glasses of the complimentary bottled water. Ava excuses herself to go to her bathroom. She is so very attracted to him and lightheaded with the spirit of the day. She thinks of Skip. Skip and all those women. She thinks of Edward. Skip. Edward. Edward. She touches up her makeup and slinks back into her bedroom—her empty bedroom. The adjoining door is closed and locked. The hotel notepad resting on her pillow says, "See you in the morning." *Gosh, did I look that bad tonight?* She walks over and taps on the locked door. "Edward?" She hears his shower running.

THE NEXT MORNING while brushing her teeth in a sticky-eyed daze, there's a knock on her outside door. "Yeth?" she says through the door.

"It's Edward. May I come in?"

What the hell. She opens the door and stands there in her white T-shirt and chartreuse boy-shorts, the only clothing she brought suitable for sleeping. Her hair is a mess. Her eyes are baggy from last night's alcohol. Flocks of parrots call good morning—way too loudly.

"Should I give you a few minutes?" he says.

"Come on in. I suppose coffee is only a dream out here in the country."

"Afraid so, but the owner's wife is bringing us Devonshire Tea. I told her extra cream." He tries to look away from her.

"I would kiss you," she says, "but as you can see my mouth is full of toothpaste. I'll be right out." In the bathroom she changes into a pair of black-and-white-striped tights and a fuschia silk blouse, her alternate drive-home clothes for yesterday. Half-dazed, she realizes she needs to close the door.

"You Yanks are shy, are you?"

She applies blusher, eye shadow, mascara. Hell with the

rest. "I obviously scared you off last night, so you may as well see the worst of it," she yells through the door. She walks out of the bathroom feeling and looking much improved.

"On the contrary. You were charming. And the story about misplacing your car . . ."

"Oh god, I told you that?"

"You don't even remember, do you? That's why I thought it best to go to my room. With a woman like you, one certainly wants to be remembered."

Ava thinks she should tell him what a nice thing that is to say and do, but breakfast arrives. It's turning out to be a whipped-cream day.

Eden

IAIN RISES FROM his chair and stretches like a big cat, bending back his neck and pushing fists high into the air. "Edward, Edward, Edward. Gotta give it to him. The chap knows how to woo a lady. So you asked him to escort you to the America's Cup Ball and the rest, as you Yanks like to say, is history."

The weather suddenly feels arid and hot, the kind of air that dries perspiration before you see it, leaving you feeling the gritty salt powdering your skin. Ava is flushed. She needs to walk out to the sea or at least off the front porch. She remembers everything. She smells Skip's Old Spice and her eyes momentarily refuse to focus.

"Actually, we made another trip to the beach. He surfed one of the more harrowing points at the River while I lazed in the sun. We had a quiet ride home. I couldn't read him as well then. Anyway, the next morning I am awakened by roses being delivered with a hand-written poem." The ghost scent grows heavier, making the air suddenly dense. *Then* I asked Edward to the Ball. Frankly, until then I didn't know if he even liked me that much as a friend. Edward plays his cards very close."

"Everyone says that about him. A poem, huh? So, he decided to take on the Skipper. That was bold. Never thought much about it. Guess bold gestures go a long way with the ladies."

"I don't know if it was that at all," Ava says. "Skip and I had never taken our relationship past friendship, so you could hardly say that Edward was vying for my hand."

"For a smart lady, you don't know much about men, do you?"

"Hah-hah. But this story isn't about my trip to Margaret River. You see, while we were away, Clark and Edward's executive offices were ransacked. Every door in the office was kicked open. Someone was in a hurry to find something."

"Now, that is news. I never saw a police report."

"I don't know that it was reported. Edward and Clark spent the next week trying to figure out what was taken. But as far as I know, they never discovered anything missing," Ava says. "Normally, Edward would pop in on the weekends to do his updates while it was quiet in the office. We think someone must have known that he and Clark were both out of town that weekend. They still have no clue what anyone would be looking for, and there wasn't another break-in before or after."

"What were they exploring at the time?"

"They had four or five projects going. You know what has always worried me? Well, not at the time. Not soon enough. The real stories of what was happening versus the appearances. Don't think I ever thought that I was the center of the universe, but it makes a pit in my stomach to think I may have been at the crux of wrong appearances. I guess we can call it 'Holy Roller Syndrome.'"

Iain motions toward another couple entering the porch. "Let's take a walk."

They head into the dry afternoon air. Parrots call one another behind the inn. A young couple in matching navy windbreakers—"Miles to Go" printed on the back—and matching olive cargo shorts are heading down the seaside path. More castaways. Their soft laughter chills Ava, she doesn't know why. Her breakfast is not settling well.

"Now explain what you mean about appearances. I totally get the Holy Roller implication." Iain is interested, looking through Ava as his mind calculates the odds of various felonies.

"This is where I need an outside view. To the outside world I'm a journalist having multiple meetings with the President of SpearCo, who's planning to bolt from the company and take with him some high-value oil leases. Then I cross the country and meet with two of the three top executives in an oil exploration company known to contract business with SpearCo. Then a Porsche is delivered to my hotel by a man I've been seen with the night before, and who, I discover later, is known to have holdings in a competing oil company. Then a SpearCo courier hand-delivers a brown paper package. Then I head off for the weekend with this man everyone thinks I hardly know, and who not only does exploration for SpearCo but also, it turns out, is in the Old Schoolboy network. Then . . ."

"Then someone goes through the files to discover what's happening."

"Do you really think so? Tell me I'm not the catalyst for

peaking suspicion."

"I can't tell you that." Iain gazes up across the garden at the flock of parrots gliding in for a landing—beautiful, pale grey down against a pale blue sky. "The obit said 'natural causes.' I assumed Skip had a heart attack. Right?"

"Wrong. Meningitis." She watches Iain for a reaction, for any sign that she is not some conspiracy theory nut.

"How the hell did he get meningitis? Why would that kill him, anyway? He looked healthy as a red 'roo." Iain removes his Akubra and scratches his head, waving away some black flies with a few flips of the brim.

She knows she's not crazy. Not paranoid. Can think things out. Call it intuition. Or just a gut feeling. There's more to Skip's death than meets the eye. The truth lies deep below the surface like the oil he drilled.

"Exactly. I am not some nut." The pale grey flock goes to ground.

"Lost our son to strep," Iain says in a soft voice. "They say it's harmless, too, something you get over." He stares off into the bush as if searching for a lurking animal.

"Your son?" She realizes her voice is almost whispering. She never knew Iain had a son. Never knew Iain to talk about himself. Ava stands very quietly, waiting to see if he needs to talk. An eternity passes.

"Annelisa and I had a son. She went to sheep country for her sister's wedding and Jack stayed with me. He was only two. . . . Bad age for a wedding and all. And I wasn't exactly the sister's favorite person anyway." Heaving a sigh long-buried, Iain presses his fingertips into his forehead. He looks as though he might collapse in paroxysms of despair. In a moment, he ages two decades. He sniffles.

Ava doesn't want to cope with his crying. She speaks up

to save him. "And Jack caught strep throat?"

"Just a sore throat I thought. Kids have sore throats all the time. He stopped complaining, so I thought it was better. One morning I can't . . . I can't wake him, so I think he's just tired because he feels bad again. The doc comes over to the house and says Jack . . . well, he says Jack has gone septic. So, I rush him to hospital. . . . The sister kept saying that he was too young." A tear escapes Iain's blinking eye, filling the dry riverbed on his left cheek and finally bringing rain to the waiting branches en route to his chin. "I kept asking what that meant, and she just kept saying that he was too young. Why didn't she just say he was dead? He wasn't too young. Too young isn't a disease. His problem was an asshole dad who didn't take him to hospital." The flood washes his eyes clear, bringing cleansing salt water to all the dry river beds. The drought is finished.

"Annelisa was on her way home. I had no way to reach her. I signed some papers, no idea what they were, and then I was home. I guess I drove. And I'm in the kitchen, somehow, and Annelisa walks in the front door with a bag of presents, all happy and smiling, yelling, 'Where's my Sweetie?' I couldn't speak. She was asking if Jack was sleeping or out back playing. It was like those dreams where you need to scream, but you can't make any sound. Then it came out. I heard myself telling her that Jack died at hospital from strep. She dropped the bag, and this little brown stuffed dog with a red satin collar rolled onto the floor. Jack wanted a dog. She ran to his room. She ran all over the house calling for him." Iain dries his face in the crook of his arm.

Hugging him seems appropriate, but Ava restrains herself, since they are not close friends. In her family, a first-degree relative requires no more than a half-air hug at holidays. "Iain, I am so sorry. I had no idea. It's not your fault. That could happen to any parent. Annelisa probably couldn't be comforted because she was in shock."

"No, that's just it. I didn't try to comfort her. I just left her there running through the house calling, 'Jack? Jack, come to Mummy!' . . . I took off for a month. Just went walkabout. Hell, I don't even know where I was most of that time. When I came home, she had moved to her mum's in the country."

"Oh, Iain, I don't know what to say." The image of Annelisa alone in that house, running room to room, pierced Ava's heart with an ancient arrow. And the funeral. Annelisa must have stood leaning on her mother at the funeral, no husband in sight, no father to say goodbye.

Ava's hand is on his back as she stands quietly with him. She can't tell him it's all right because it isn't. Can't tell him that he couldn't help it because he could. "You have to tell her you're sorry. You need to forgive yourself, and to do that, you have to tell her. All of us let people down. You were in shock, but that doesn't make it right. She may never forgive you, but she deserves to hear you tell her that you regret your behavior. She deserves that."

They walk up the front porch stairs, and he stubs his right toe, almost tumbling onto the porch. He catches himself with a loud thud, mumbles something Ava can't decipher, and manages to pass fairly unnoticed by the fellow travelers as he lumbers, head bowed, to his room.

Ava settles into the overstuffed, rose-and-yellow flowered sofa in the sitting room and mindlessly thumbs through last month's *Australian Cosmopolitan*. The pages keep turning, but she records nothing. There is a stinging scent, ever so faint, of musk. She sneezes three times, automatically saying "Excuse me" to the empty room. Outside, two couples talk over sailing adventures, oblivious to the storm inside. So often death strikes suddenly and leaves behind the fatal poison of regret. Dead ears never hear what we meant to say. Dead eyes never see what we meant to show. Dead hearts never feel what we meant to give. And in death, the puzzle piece of the person that resides in us festers with regret.

Ava is far away, a little girl sharing a box of raisins with her grandfather, who smells of Old Spice, when Iain returns and sits next to her on the sofa. The scent stays with her as she time-travels to the inn. "Okay?" she asks him.

"Tell me about the America's Cup Ball. I need a good tale about ostentatious displays of wealth." He tries to smile, but his bottom lip still trembles as though the earthquake within him will resurface any second.

SEVEN

Perth, January 1987 America's Cup Ball

FILMING INSIDE THE Ball is prohibited, so Ava's professional work is finished. Personal work, however, is only beginning. Edward was relegated to a footnote because of her schedule. Every time she thinks about it, she hears him say *shhhedyule* in her head. Skip is in China. His only goodbye was a quick call telling Ava to "have a rave" at the Ball and that he hopes Edward "doesn't turn into a pumpkin." Ava removes hot rollers from her hair for the second time, and her hair is limply straight for the second time. She powders her makeup.

The lack of air conditioning in the granny flat is usually fine, but today there's a hint of humidity, which unnerves every primping woman. She flips her head upside down and starts spraying. *There—instant bouncy hair.* Shooosh-shooosh-shooosh, the rose-scented hairspray semi-locks the ends of her hair into a flip. She'll pretend it's a fashion statement. She slides the emerald, satin top over her head. It has a deeply squared front and back, perfect for dressing *after* makeup, and cute puffy short sleeves topped by satin bows. Next are the full-length, black, raw silk gloves. Then the button-button-button of impossibly small silk-covered glove buttons until her frustration almost peaks. *A lady covers her arms when royalty is present. Damn, I look good,* she thinks as she swishes in front of the dresser mirror. Quarter-twirls back and forth lift the full satin skirt into a swing with that lovely swish-swish of light crinoline. Her cold glass Giorgio perfume bottle makes a swoosh sound as she sprays the crinoline. *Perfect.*

"Ava? Ava!" Edward calls from inside the front doorway. "Are you beautiful yet?"

She rounds the corner, swish-swish, clutching her black-sequin purse.

"You certainly are!"

He is handsome: sun-streaked hair perfectly groomed, pink nose from recent surfing, Armani black tuxedo, a real bow tie hanging untied around his neck handsome. And he is wearing Aramis. Has any woman in the world ever resisted Aramis? More importantly, he remembered. The first night they met there was a brief encounter with a handsome Italian at the roulette table, a handsome Italian wearing Aramis.

Edward remembers, she thinks. "You are beautiful, too."

"I can never get these things right," he says, tugging on one side of the loose bow tie. "I don't suppose you . . ."

She walks over, pushing away his fidgety fingers. "I'm a woman of many talents. Lift your chin." In a few seconds, he has a perfect bow tie despite the slipperiness of the silk gloves maneuvering the satin tie. She tightens the slide buckle on the side.

"I probably don't want to know how you do that so well." He admires himself in the convex wall mirror.

"Probably not." She steps through the open front door.

"A limo! You shouldn't have gone to the trouble, but I'm glad you did."

They slide easily onto the black leather seat. The driver closes the door behind them, not the wham of lesser cars but the muffled oomph of luxury.

Ava adjusts her three-person-wide skirt. "I could get used to this."

Edward pulls the open bottle of champagne from the built-in ice bucket. "Pink champagne, mademoiselle?"

They share a laugh as she playfully thumps his tummy with the back of her hand. It isn't really pink champagne, and he is no pumpkin. He remembered that, too.

Entering the Ball is like walking the red carpet.

"I'll be seeing flashbulbs for an hour," Ava exclaims as they near the entrance.

They don't stop to pose for photos. In the rumble of "there's so-and-so" and pop-pop-pop-pop "oh there's so-and-so," she hears a man yell, "Baron, are you and Miss Marks an item?" Edward shows their invitations to the door security as he gently but firmly pushes Ava inside by the small of her back.

"What is the next gauntlet?" he asks, fingering his bow tie.

She playfully pops his fidgeting hand. "Don't mess with a masterpiece.

A huge chart on a table indicates they are sitting at the banksia-tree table. Ava turns to enjoy the beauty of the scene. She is one to take note of a moment.

"I've never seen so much taffeta in one place."

Happiness in a box: smiling, laughing, hands shaking, air kissing, and back patting everywhere she looks. Even this anteroom is heavily decorated with bouquets of hothouse flowers and potted indigenous trees. A grinder for the *Stars and Stripes* team, sun-bleached blond hair combed for the first time she's seen it, stops to greet them. This Cup is his third, and he has confided to Ava that it will probably be his last.

"Hello, Steven." She offers her hand in greeting.

"Miss Marks, you look lovely this evening. We all clean up well, don't we?" He gives her the firm handshake of an equal while looking toward Edward.

"*Ava*, Steven... Yes we do! You look quite dapper in that tux." She frees her hand and adjusts her black, silk glove. "Edward, this is Steven ... I'm sorry I don't ..."

"Wheeler, Steven Wheeler," he says, offering his hand to Edward.

As they shake hands, Ava continues, "Yes, I'm sorry. Steven, my escort, Baron Townsend." She notices Steven's expression change as he drops Edward's hand. "Um, yes, nice to meet you. Good to see you, Miss Marks—Ava. Have a great time." He smiles nervously and disappears back into the crowd.

She has introduced Edward as "Baron" for the first time and is surprised at the reaction—surprised at Steven's apparent intimidation and at her hesitation, as if telling a great secret.

Edward reads her mind. "He seems like a nice chap. Tumm, Ava, I am the Baron of ..." he stops, seeing the horror on her face. "In social conversation, just refer to me as Lord Shropley."

"Lord Shropley, how nice to see you here," greets a rather stout gentleman with that mouth-of-marbles accent peculiar to upper-crust Brits.

He's older, maybe in his sixties, wearing a tuxedo

obviously purchased in his trimmer years. He seems to avoid eye contact, which Ava notices immediately, because she's used to men heaping an excess of eye contact on all parts of her.

The man turns to the woman next to him, looking more at her waistline than her face. "Dear, look who is here." His eye finally rests on Edward's face. "You remember Lady Ketchum."

His petite wife is of the same age, with beauty-parlor brunette hair pulled into an elaborate up do of twists and curls. Yards of eggplant taffeta ruffle around her shoulders and hemline. She is pleasant and aloof.

"Sir Ernest and Lady Ketchum, please allow me to introduce Miss Ava Marks."

Ava offers her hand, which is either ignored or not noticed in the fray of the packed crowd. She searches Edward for guidance, but his look changes from cavalier to serious. She sees that Lady Ketchum is busy nosing the air, apparently sniffing out anyone worthy of her attention.

Sir Ernest nods Edward aside for a few private words. Now Edward is the one staring into the distance. Handshake. Edward returns to Ava's side, but he avoids looking at her as the Ketchums move along to the next acquaintance as quickly as they arrived.

Ava wiggles her shoulders, trying not to be obvious about her physical or social discomfort. She adjusts her five-pound satin weight by grabbing yards of skirt. *A hundred years ago, the clothes alone should have kept upper-class women thin,* she thinks. Her black, raw silk gloves are so beautiful that she stops to admire them: *all those tiny buttons. I thought I would never get the darn things fastened. Impulse buys are always the best.*

The pebbled softness comforts her, like pressing fingers into a well-worn teddy bear. She hopes that Edward knows she wore the gloves because Prince Albert and other royals are here tonight. *Wow! I guess my date falls into that category, too,* she realizes. Perhaps Edward will be impressed that she knows etiquette requires her arms be covered by sleeves or gloves at a formal dinner or ball with royalty. *Must be a way to work it into the conversation so he'll know I'm not just another coarse Yank who doesn't even know how to properly introduce him. Yes, that's embarrassing . . . and he did see horror on my face. I should've asked about introductions before we arrived.*

Edward scans the room, nodding occasionally and pretending not to notice Ava's squirming. "He and father were chums at Eton College. Sir Ernest spent a good thirty years in service to Her Majesty on the financial staff. You'll be the topic of conversation tonight, no doubt. Better call my sister tomorrow. . . . You look very beautiful. Thank you for inviting me to escort you."

"Thank you for coming. A girl doesn't go to a ball with a baron, uh, lord, every day!"

"Eva, *lord* is used in social conversation when—forget it. We'll do the crash course sometime over a bottle of Moët." He stops because they're being called in to dinner, and because *that* look is on her face again.

Sighs of delight can be heard from way up in the front of the crowd.

"Why do you need to call your sister?" She waits patiently for their turn to move forward.

"Ah, here we go. Oh, Sarah, I'll have to call Sarah because I know someone will be calling her tomorrow. I want to be the one to tell her that I've met a wonderful woman."

He walks forward, reaching to take Ava's hand without looking at her. He is already on auto-pilot without noticing the transition.

Ava reaches up and slides her right hand into the crook of his elbow. *A wonderful woman,* she repeats to herself.

Edward turns for a second and slides her hand down to his, intertwining their fingers.

"I knew Prince Albert would be here, so I wore the gloves. Aren't they soft?" she whispers.

He gives her fingers a little squeeze.

Ava can't see his face and doesn't know if he is amused or reassured. Either way, she glides along in a fairytale daze. Her ten compressed toes in three-inch, black, silk heels seem suddenly numbed by the joy. The beauty of the room fills her like a Thanksgiving meal: white linen covers round tables seating twelve people. Each table is centered with a six-foot flowering tree native to Australia. The scent is heady, like a jasmine grower's greenhouse. Lights twinkle all over the ceiling, imitating a desert night sky, and the live band is playing *Waltzing Matilda.* No one in this room ever went walkabout with a matilda, a hobo-style knapsack, but people are humming along all the same.

Edward spots the banksia tree indicating their assigned table. He leads them there and makes all the introductions.

Thank you, God, Ava thinks, wondering if she said it aloud. *I have the invitations yet we end up at a table full of his acquaintances.* Seems nearly everyone is Lord and Lady Somebody, meaning Fill-in-Title-of-Some-Estate Somebody, or Sir Somebody, so she decides to go with *My Lord* for the night, which she figures will be proper for the lords and flattering to Sir What's-His-Name. She tries to remember that if it is Sir – fill in first name, then it is Lady

— fill in last name. Of course, there are exceptions to every rule. One couple is Lord Somebody but his wife is Lady—fill in the guy's first name. Ava gathers from conversation his father is a duke. *Are you kidding me?* She decides to just go with Ma'am and hope that works. If not, she can always pretend it's a Southern thing. *Aristocrats are amused by colloquialisms,* she reminds herself. *Actually, this title stuff is pretty great because I am the world's worst with names.*

Fortunately, her evening is filled with the naïve joy of nonjudgmental company. Only under-the-table toe tapping indicates the party's amusement of a Yank saying Ma'am to anyone other than the Queen.

After all the introductions, Ava says, "*Ava,* please. Everyone please call me Ava" which has the unfortunate consequence of everyone then spurting out nicknames with way too much information about how Lord So-and-So came to be called "Hitchy" and so forth. Buckets of champagne appear by the table, followed by clinking glasses and the toasting of every nickname story. Between the accents and laughing and protesting and storytelling and clinking, she can't understand a fourth of it anyway.

Edward's look tells her that he knows she needs a drink—a real drink. "I guess shots are out of the question," she whispers to him. The waiter tips her off that Edward left a cache of the "really good stuff" here this afternoon—twelve bottles of her favorite Shiraz. *Twelve bottles! The essence of romance is forethought, and, now that I think about it, the wallet to carry through with it.*

The waiter places two open bottles with each couple. Another round of toasting ensues, of course.

Maybe such occasions are the only times when these people can really let down their hair – though I am the only woman whose hair is actually down, she thinks.

They enjoy the small talk and music and dancing. She doesn't know if Edward can waltz because there's not enough room on the dance floor to maneuver. Then she hears Jimmy Buffett.

"The band must be on break," she tells Edward.

"No, it's really Jimmy Buffett." He points to the stage behind her.

She turns to see Jimmy Buffett singing *Margueritaville* from the stage, tuxedo jacket open and bow tie hanging from his chest pocket. He finishes and takes a bow as the crowd whistles and shouts "Bravo!" Leaping from the stage onto the dance floor, Buffett disappears into the sea of dancers. She remembers the Hawaiian-shirt partiers at the two Jimmy Buffett concerts she attended: yuppies pretending their sixty-hour work weeks will lead to a beach-bum life. Hearing 'Wasting away in . . .' while seeing an audience in black tie is surreal.

"I love it," she shouts to no one in particular. This moment is one of those times she'll always remember: *a duke's son drinking wine with me and my baron date in black tie as we listen to Jimmy Buffett offer a slightly intoxicated rendition of the Yank dream.* "Great night, this is a great night," she leans over telling Edward.

The four-course meal comes and goes in seconds. All too soon the night ends, and they re-enter their black steel carriage. No pumpkin.

"Did you have a nice time?" Edward shouts; he's been talking over the roar of the ball for hours.

She pats down the pouf of emerald skirt in her lap. "Gotta give it to the Aussies. They know how to throw a party. Thank you for coming with me. This is one of the most fun nights of my life."

Edward leans in to kiss her. Not the friendship peck she received a couple of times, but a soft pressing that exchanges warm breath and departs ever so gently. "This is one of the best nights of my life, too," he says.

She is intoxicated by the richness of the evening, the champagne, the Shiraz, and the Port. Lord Somebody can't travel without his Tawny Port, so the entire table sampled a private cache of his liquid hunting lodge. Unfortunately, she is a Chatty Cathy when she's tipsy. She's droning on about every funny event of the evening, and Edward listens as though these tales are State secrets. Reaching into her beaded clutch, she fishes out his invitation as a memento. The ten-karat gold sailboat pin is still attached. He slides it into his inside pocket without a word. Chat, chat, Chatty Cathy all the way to the door. Then another of *those* kisses.

Edward turns to leave, but she keeps holding his hand. "Why don't you stay?"

He hesitates. "It's a perfect night already." He lights a cigarette, his first of the evening, as he walks to the limo while she watches from her open doorway. The limo drives away, but Edward does not wave goodbye.

She is half-undressed before her fuzzy mind wonders what she did wrong. She wants to care about it, but the alcohol won't let her. *Should have skipped the Port. I'll hang up the satin in the morning. Oh, that pillow is sooo soft,* she thinks as she sinks into the double bed. *Too bad Patricia had to leave early, she would have . . .*

"RING! RING! . . . RING! RING!"

Daylight streams through the window. Ava knocks the phone to the floor trying to pick up the receiver. *Oh god, I*

♦ 154 ♦

forgot the mandatory aspirin before bed. She bounces up, receiver in hand. "Ooooh," she groans.

"Miss Maaaks? Am I speaking with Miss Ava Maaaks?" the soft aristocratic voice asks with the unmistakable marbles accent.

"Sarah hea. Is this Miss Maaaks?"

"Umm, yes." *Did I meet a Sarah last night,* she wonders as she rubs her forehead.

"Forgive me. I had to ring you right away."

"Umm, yes."

"I do apologize. Lady Sarah Hampstead hea', Edward's sister. Just had to ring you."

Now, Ava is awake. She sits on the edge of the bed with her right leg still entwined in the ivory sheet. "Oh, hello, Sarah, um, Lady Sarah, Lady Hampstead." Ava hears a gushing laugh.

"*Sarah,* Dea'. May I call you Ava?"

Ava pushes her right foot through the sheet to the floor. *Need both feet on the floor for this one.* "Of course, Sarah. Is Edward all right?"

"I would say he is more than all right. I believe, Dea', Edward is in love for the first time in his life. I just had to call and talk to the girl who is finally halting his days of bachelor debauchery."

"What? Oh, Edward and I have only been out a few times. I'm sure you misunderstood—"

"Dea', I don't think I misunderstood anything. I spoke to Edward just an hour ago. It took me that long to track a number to ring you. My advice is that you put on a pretty frock—he loves yellow, tumm, and periwinkle—and see if you can close the deal before he turns back into *commitment-phobic bachelor.* Bully on you for passing the test!"

"We don't have plans for today. I'm sure you don't—"

"Wouldn't you know it would be the one with no clue about men who finally tames him. I know Edward. You *are* going to see him. See him soon. And I do know what I'm talking about."

"Sarah, it was nice of you to call. I'll tell Edward you made the gesture. I'm sure he'll find it hilarious that you think there is something between us."

"Oh Dea', don't you know anything? You will *not* tell him I called. If you like him, and calls from Lady Chatsworth and Lady Ellen say you do, you will powder that nose because he will be—"

Ding-dong. . . Ding-dong.

Ava turns quickly toward the front door in the adjoining room. "Ohhh," she grabs her forehead. "I'm sorry. Someone is at the door."

"Go get him. I'll ring another time."

Ava runs to the bathroom to quickly gargle and brush through the sticky hairspray. *The test? I guess I did something right.*

Ding-dong. Ding-dong.

"Just a minute!" She pulls on her red cashmere robe and stumbles to the door. "Ed—"

"G'day, Muss." A young man of maybe eighteen holds a vase of two dozen sterling roses, still that palest of lavender from just opening their beauty, a few drops of florist's water kissing their leaves. "Muss Ovo Mocks?"

"I think so," she says as she tries to decipher the accent.

"Ta. Roses for ya." He hands her the heavy, green-glass vase.

It's very cold and damp in her hands. "Let me get you—"

"No need, Muss." He walks back to the white panel truck.

"Show it with flowers" is painted on the side in red.

The small, white envelope peeking through the baby's-breath holds a note card:

> Just learned I am competing with a single sterling rose--inside a Porsche! Pick you up for lunch at 11:30. Casual.
>
> Edward

Ava inhales the roses' sweet perfume. Sterling roses have always been her favorite: like lavender silk seen though the white haze of purity. *Wait a minute! How could Sarah get my number from England? How could anybody track down this number?*

RING! RING!

Edward has good timing. "Hello there," she greets him.

"Ava? The connection's not so good. Can you hear me?"

"Skip? Yes, there's a lot of static, but I can hear you. Everything all right?"

"Flying out of Beijing in a few minutes," he shouts over the airport intercom noise. "Called to see how last night went."

"The Aussies know how to throw a party! Everything was beautiful!"

"And Townie?"

"Yes, he was beautiful, too!"

"That dog. I knew he would make his move. Well, you needed a good—"

"No. No move. He was a perfect gentleman." She hesitates. "He did send me roses this morning."

"Too gentlemanly. A man doesn't get anywhere by holding back. Red roses. Cliché, Townie!"

"No, sterling."

"Silver roses! What do you do with those?"

"Sterling is the color. Never mind. How's the trip?"

"Nothing concrete, but several interesting options. Got to go. See ya." And with that he was gone.

Ava glares at the phone as she bangs down the receiver. *Skip knows me nearly two years and doesn't even know what sterling roses are, and Edward knows me, what, days?*

RING! RING!

"Yes?"

Edward's voice is low, soft as a sterling rose. "That was quick. Good morning."

"Edward! Thank you for the sterling roses. They are just beautiful!"

"I would send a hundred, but property taxes to Mother England and that."

"Two dozen is the perfect number. I had a wonderful time last night."

"Me, too, Ava. Me, too. So I'll see you in thirty minutes."

"Thirty minutes? I thought you said eleven thirty."

"Ava, it is eleven o'clock. Did you just wake up?"

"Uh-oh. Can we make it noon?"

"Noon it is. And Ava . . ."

"Yes?"

"I had a wonderful time, too." No goodbye. Just a click.

One hour to remove the sticky wonderland hanging from her head. One hour to look into his eyes and see if she agrees with Lady Sarah's summation. *I haven't seen that look in so very long.* She thinks about Skip's call and realizes he telephoned to find out if she was alone. He confuses her, and she hates that she is intrigued by confusion. Her nose smells smoke and hairspray and tingles into a sneeze. *Looong shower. I need a long shower.* She pauses in the hallway, returning to the sitting room for one more lingering inhalation of fresh rose perfume. She buries her face in the silken petals.

EDWARD ARRIVES AT noon, not 11:59, not 12:01, noon. After three hairstyles, Ava has decided to go with straight hair pushed back with a white hair band—seventies style— because, one, there's no time for hot rollers, and two, she officially gave up trying to force her hair to be something it is not. This is the moment of enlightenment . . . or surrender, depending on her perspective minute to minute. From the tiny closet she tugs out the A-line linen shift, lemon yellow to match her mood—and Sarah's recommendation. White ballet flats welcome tender feet. She snips a sterling rose and pins it to the side of her hair band, a trick she learned on assignment to the Paris Spring Fashion Show. *Hmmm. At least the America's Cup crowd knows they aren't curing cancer,* she thinks, remembering some haughty encounters with her designer interviewees.

Edward walks right through the door and gives her a full *on-the-lips, eleven-hours-without-you-is-unbearable* kiss. Her pinkish lavender lipstick is all over his mouth. Luckily, she is holding his handkerchief from their surfing expedition. She wipes his mouth gently.

"Keep it," she mocks as she hands it to him. He remembers and smiles.

He remembers. "Should I apply more lipstick now or is this foreplay?" she jokes.

He is only a couple of inches taller than she, but his strength is surprising as he grabs her in his arms, has her down the hallway to the bedroom before her eyes can focus. He falls with her into the unmade bed.

"I have been really good, haven't I?" he asks, sounding almost apologetic. "On the way here, I told myself not to tell you how I feel. I know the thing to do is wait forever and make you wonder. I don't care. I need to know how you—"

"I didn't know myself until right now," she tells him as she rolls over on top of him and inhales a soft kiss. "I think lunch can wait."

Eden

AVA IS STANDING on the porch facing south toward Antarctica, but the breeze is not cold. She doesn't know if she is flushed from the memory of making love to Edward or because the breeze is suddenly blowing hot. Skip's Antarctic breeze is blowing hot. Screech! Screech! A maid at the inn opens the sitting-room windows onto the porch.

Iain is beside Ava watching the same empty sky, void of even the slightest shade of blue. "So that's what I've been doing wrong with women. I need *two* dozen roses." His try at levity is even less convincing to him than to her. "Who am I kidding? A shop full wouldn't do it. . . Funny that what you were pulling on Skip, worked on you."

"What? What do you mean?" she is distracted as 'Winding road that leads to your door . . .' wafts softly from the sitting-room radio.

Music is universal. So is love. So are the many forms of cowardice.

"Ah, Roller, the whole coy game of keeping the other person waiting. You and Edward played the same chess strategy." Iain looks at her for a reaction.

She is glad for Iain. He is lost in her story, and sometimes the best that one can desire is being lost in another's story. "You're right. I never thought about it like that. You just wait until I see him."

The screech of a rusting front door hinge announces the innkeeper's wife.

"Baroness, a telegram for ya." Smelling of frying fish and chips, the mistress of the house hands Ava a folded note. The stocky woman hurries back through the door as if biscuits are burning in the kitchen.

```
DOCKED IN HOBART STOP OZ IS A BEAUT STOP
GLAD WE GET TO BRING HER HOME STOP OPENED
YOUR LETTER STOP TA FOR THE PARTY CASH AND
WORDS FROM SKIP STOP HOPE HE KNOWS THE OZ
DID HIM PROUD STOP SET SAIL TWO JANUARY
STOP SEE YOU IN SYDNEY STOP PATRICK AND
CHRIS STOP
```

"They've arrived! Patrick and Chris made it to Hobart." Ava is more ecstatic than she expected that two of Skip's geologists were up to the task. Seems fitting they are the ones to conquer one last challenge for him.

She hands Iain the telegram. His face is like a gentle brook after the flood waters recede: rocky, quiet life beneath a rippling surface.

"Lucky buggers," he says as he reads the note. "They'll be shaggin' for years off this story. Hell, right now I bet they're havin' a go."

Ava playfully snatches the note from his hand. "That's your problem, Iain. You are too much of a romantic. I have to work on a way to get back to Sydney. Seems even I can forget a detail." She raises her eyebrows, obviously awaiting an offer of assistance. She is fishing to get more time with Iain.

"I can help you with that. I'm taking the AP chopper tomorrow if you need a lift." His voice is pleasant, a comforting babble from the brook.

"I thought you'd never ask." She winks, eliciting a smile.

They are forever bound by sharing their shortcomings and secrets, candor and confessions, and they are both the better for it.

Ava re-reads the note. "I'll call Edward later and tell him no need to drive here."

"Yep, I should have bought Annelisa two dozen roses. When I came to my senses, I mean. And I should have carried them on my knees."

"Was she your first love?"

"No, Mate. First wife. Last love." He is staring at the past again. . . "Only love," he adds in a whisper.

"I'm sorry, Iain." Ava knows he feels vulnerable. His tone is not that of an innocent. Rather, it is the whisper of a jaded crusader when the battles finally end, and it is apparent that his motivations and goals never matched his actions. "I'm sure you did what you could at the time. As long as we live, we have chances to make things better. Maybe not right, but better."

"I missed that chance. Instead of going to her mum's, I took the easy shag while I was on assignment in Bangkok, and Annelisa found out. That's how *I* made it better. Never knew who on the crew betrayed me."

"Oh, Iain, they probably told wives and girlfriends who then told—you know how it goes."

"You know, I bet that's right. Maybe they didn't mean

to knife me . . . but even before . . . before Jack I should've bought the roses and opened the doors and—hell, doesn't matter now. So how did ol' Skipper take the news he was beat to the starting post?"

"I waited and told him in Sydney, but someone got to him before I did. He didn't react at all the way I expected. . . And Iain, it does matter now."

"She never remarried. Annelisa, she never remarried. Think I might have a chance? A chance to make it better, I mean?"

Ava puts her hand on his shoulder and gives it a gentle squeeze. "Life is about taking chances."

EIGHT

Sydney, New South Wales, AUS,
February 1987

AVA TURNS TO Skip as he waves her through the hallway door of his condo. She checks her watch. She wants to hurry more than she needs to hurry.

"Sorry to rush through our visit." She walks into the living room but doesn't sit. "It's great to see you." She gives Skip a bear hug. "I have so much to tell you. Sorry I couldn't make lunch today. Maybe tomorrow? My rental car is outside loaded with junk." Nervous, she talks non-stop. "You know, electrical adapter boxes and crap that you don't want to haul half-way 'round the world."

Skip sits on the forest-green, leather sofa, easing himself into the plump seat cushion as though easing his mind into the realization that Ava is distancing herself.

Ava re-checks her watch. "Thought I'd drop the stuff off at a storage center since I'll be back next year for the Westfield Run. And you know my job. No doubt I'll be back in thirty days for who knows what!"

"Sit, Ava. I want to talk to you." Skip flips on the television as if she'll be staying. He lowers the audio to whispers and pats the seat next to him on the couch. "The adapter box can wait."

"I'm afraid you'll have to wait. I only have an hour before the storage center closes."

"Screw the storage center. Why didn't you just call me? I could've had someone move all that shit for you. Just leave it here."

"Skip, that's so nice, but I wouldn't want it to be in the way." She is purposely not sitting.

"It won't be in the way. Besides, I'm leaving in two days for Jakarta. Sit. We need to talk."

She still doesn't sit. If she does, he is likely to talk her into anything. He is an addiction she needs to break. "Skip, there's something I need to discuss with you. It's about Edward Townsend. You see—"

He pops the leather seat loudly with his hand. "I know. Heard the whole story. I'm sure Townie can be very charming."

Ava looks up at the popcorn ceiling. "I can't believe he told you."

"Oh, Townie is a gentleman—the Old School Boy type you have to watch. He didn't tell me or probably anyone else. My project manager Mick went to the granny flat the day after the Ball to give you a message from me. Seems he overheard some stimulating activities." Skip turns off the television in the midst of some tire advertisement.

Tires—petroleum product, she thinks.

A bowl of partially eaten chocolate ice cream is sitting on the coffee table. She remembers buying chocolate ice cream and leaving it in his freezer.

"Oh, god, Skip. I'm so embarrassed. You shouldn't have found out like that. I'm so embarrassed."

"Sit, Ava. We need to talk."

She reluctantly sits on the opposite end of the sofa. Skip slides to the middle. Not close enough to touch, just close enough to make real eye contact. They are quiet for a minute that lasts an hour. Ava waits him out. They keep glancing at the melting ice cream to avoid glancing at one another.

"Okay. So here it is." He clears his throat as if to address SpearCo board members. "I don't think you should be making any rash decision. How would it work with Townie, anyway? You move here? He moves there? You both move to England and then no one has a job?"

"What are you talking about?"

This conversation makes her uneasy. She certainly doesn't have any agreement with Edward. Doesn't even know when or if she'll ever see him again. With location shoots, everyone becomes like family, but not really family. Bonds are forgotten as geography and time separates the players only to release them into the next makeshift *family*. Just like stocking Skip's kitchen—the happy feeling of the warm gesture, but time made it seem like a scene from a movie.

Skip props his arm behind her on the sofa back. "Look. I'm not saying what I mean to say. What I mean to say is that I like you. I mean, we are good friends, aren't we? I think we are. And we might want to spend more time together. Or a lot more time together. And you aren't seeing Townie again any time soon anyway, right? I mean with you flying to the States. So, I'm planning to be in the States in three months to visit my mother. I thought we might get together."

"*Now* you're interested? I have sex with another man and that makes you interested. I don't know what we are. I thought we were friends. I thought all you wanted to be is friends. Believe me, I thought and thought about it." Her cheeks flush with anxiety.

"I thought all *you* wanted to be is friends."

"This is probably a novel idea to you, but what I wanted is *first* to be friends."

"Like Townie." Skip stares at the melted ice cream.

"Well, I guess so. Like Townie—Edward. Now, I don't know what to say."

Skip reaches over and puts his hand on her thigh. "Well, you could give me a shot at the title. I might surprise you."

"Oh, Skip. Really!"

He pulls his hand away. "Let's get the stuff out of your car before it gets dark. You'll stay here in the guest room. I have several loose ends that need attention tomorrow. We can have dinner. Talk some more, maybe. I have a red-eye out of here to Jakarta the next morning. You can just hang out here until your flight. I had a key made for you." He stands and takes a gold SpearCo logo key ring with two keys from his trouser pocket and hands it to her.

She instinctively takes the keys. *Forethought,* she notes to herself. *He already had the keys made. Or was it assumption?* "Jakarta? I thought you were headed out to camp with the Aborigines. . . .Skip, I don't think—"

"Your problem is you think too much. Come on. We'll get your stuff. Last-minute changes are a way of life in this business. Aborigines today. Jakarta tomorrow. You get the call and better go or someone else will beat you to the table." He heads for the door. The conversation is over and settled. He is used to getting his way.

Without further discussion, they grab a luggage cart in the lobby and load it up. Skip pushes the cart back to the elevator. Quiet all the way up to his floor. Quiet to the door. Quiet as he unloads everything into an empty hall closet.

She slides the heavy metal electrical adapter box to the edge of the shelf so it's sitting on the bracing. "I don't want to break your shelf."

"Everything else where you want it?" he asks with a tinge of sarcasm.

She nods and gives a thumbs up.

He closes the closet door. "Okay then, everything will be right there whenever you need it."

He carries her suitcase to the guest room and sets it on the floor.

She follows behind him. "I'll get the sheets."

"No need. Made the bed when you called to say you were on your way over." He stands with his side to her, looking away.

Ava notices his nervous demeanor. *Either he doesn't think it's the right time to consummate our relationship or he thought I wouldn't think so. Either way, he's trying to do the right thing. I like that he's trying.* "Thank you, Skip, for everything." Her voice is low and sincere.

"Well, don't stand there talking. You have thirty minutes. I'm hungry, and we're going out for real steaks before I head to Jakarta." He walks out, closing the bedroom door behind him.

"Thirty minutes it is," she says loudly through the door.

THEY DRIVE QUIETLY to one of Skip's favorite Sydney haunts, a bustling pub where you grill your own steak on a huge iron grill inside the restaurant. The parking lot smells of sizzling steak as he pulls Ava along by the hand. The hostess takes them straight to *his* table.

We sat here last time we ate here . . . and the time before that, Ava remembers. She wonders if he eats here so often that they just hold the table for him. *He must have called ahead while I was changing.*

They order immediately. Skip says he'll grill her steak. It's the first time he has spoken to her since they left the condo. "I'll do it, you turned it to ashes last time. Medium-rare, right?" He talks inches from her ear to be heard over the restaurant din.

At least she thinks that's why he's so close. His breath still smells of chocolate ice cream.

"Yes." Before she can say more, he is off to the grill.

The forty-something redheaded waitress from their previous visits brings a bottle of Shiraz and, with a nod from Ava, pours both glasses. She finishes her first glass just as a proud executive sets a steak before her.

"Now *that* is how you cook a steak."

"That smells sooo good, Skip. Thank you." Ava has to yell over the restaurant noise. She cuts through the blackened crust to the butter-soft red meat, steam wafting an aroma of campfire richness.

They enjoy the meal wordlessly, sharing the joy of good flavors in each other's presence. Ava knows he loves this restaurant. She also knows he picked it to avoid talking. The faint scent of Giorgio in his BMW told her another woman was the passenger not long ago. Probably had lunch with the *singer*. The mixed roar of fusion jazz and tipsy crowds makes it hard to hear the waitress. They're both glad for the intrusion.

They ride home listening to his Patsy Cline tape. Ava enjoys the satisfaction of a filling meal and the comfort of his quiet company. Quiet. He enjoys it, too. Like a tenth-anniversary meal with a couple who skipped the marriage. Now, they can mentally decompress. Tonight, neither will try to talk about anything serious and both are grateful for that. They go to separate bedrooms after pleasant good-nights.

Skip is already gone when she awakens the next morning. A note in the kitchen reads:

By some miracle, there is real coffee.
Help yourself to whatever you like.
See you about 4 p.m., Skip

The day gets away from her between stops at the network office, the endless wrap-up calls, and returning the rental car. At 4:20 Ava takes a taxi back to the condo, using her own key to go inside. It feels strange, as if she's doing something wrong. She doesn't snoop. Skip isn't here, so she enjoys a relaxing, steamy shower. By the time she dresses, she hears him in his shower. She stands quietly at the large window overlooking the Sydney skyline. Her head is pleasantly warm from the blow-dryer that took forever to remove the cold dampness from her fly-away hair.

I don't know when I'll see the Sydney skyline again, she thinks with a tinge of sadness. Being here is comfortable and familiar. Edgy and strange. She likes a plan for everything. Actually, she likes two back-up plans for everything.

Skip isn't big on personal plans. He emerges in his dock shoes, jeans, and a blue-and-black-striped rugby shirt. Even at forty and jaded by life, he has college jock all over him.

Ava wears a red, silk cocktail dress with a deep V-scoop in the back. "Oh, I assumed we were going to dinner. I'll change." She walks away from the window toward the guest room.

"Stop!" He stares as she turns toward him and waits. "Okay, I just wanted to enjoy the view. Put on jeans. We're having a picnic on the *Oz*."

WHEN THEY ARRIVE at the marina, a cool breeze is whipping through Sydney Harbour. Skip takes his khaki windbreaker from the back seat of the car and wraps it around her bare shoulders. "It will be warmer in the cabin." They walk swiftly to *Oz* and board—he first, then helping her. *I don't need help,* she protests silently. "You forget that I'm a Carolina girl who grew up on a diet of salt water."

But she takes his help. In her mind, it's no different than opening a door for a lady. Of course, she *could* open her own door. Once inside the cabin, she sees why he was late getting home. An entire buffet of pasta salads and cold cuts and petit fours crowd the galley's mahogany table.

Forethought. "Wow. I'm impressed. And you even remembered I like petit fours."

"Like what?"

"Petit fours." She picks up a little chocolate iced cake decorated with a red, sugar rose. She holds it aloft like a toast then pops the crisp chocolate-covered yellow cake into her mouth. "Mmmm," she hums as she bites through the sweet vanilla pudding layered in the center.

"Oh, is that what they're called?" he asks. "Okay, so Fiona picked up everything for me, but it was my idea. And I brought it over here."

"It's great. Truly. Sit." She motions to the opposite galley bench. "What a wonderful way to spend our last night in Sydney."

He pops the cork from a bottle of Moët & Chandon and pours her glass first. "A toast," he says. They lift their crystal flutes. "To the Sydney-to-Hobart." His look is schoolmaster stern. Clinking glasses. "You haven't forgotten your promise."

"I haven't forgotten. Skip, I want you to know—"

He holds his right forefinger to his lips. "Not tonight. There will be plenty of nights for that. Tonight we don't talk about anything serious. I just want to relax and enjoy being here. . . . Enjoy being here with you in my favorite place."

"Sounds great." She means it. Ava fills a plate with deli meats and peppers and cheeses and two large spoonsful of pasta salads.

"Don't be shy," he teases. "Didn't that red dress look a little tight earlier?"

"Skip, you know I'm just using you for your cold cuts."

He takes a bite of cheese, but doesn't react for several seconds. "I like having to listen to keep up," he says, nodding slightly and laughing.

They are numbed and warmed by the champagne, followed by white wine. Rich meats and creamy cheeses. Too many chocolate delights smooshing the dark cocoa flavor into mixtures of vanilla pudding and yellow cake. Two old friends. Comfortable just lingering on the deck and staring at the midnight blue twinkling sky. Hours pass. Finally, Skip breaks the silence by reminding her that he has a very early call. They go inside and toss the remains of the feast into a plastic bag that is dumped in a metal can at the end of the dock. How easily they clean up memories.

The ride home is quiet—no Patsy Cline. Skip reaches over and holds her hand. He has never done that in the car. She worries this affectionate touch means he intends to press the sex issue when they enter the condo. She's wrong. He gives her a long kiss in the living room followed by a bear hug. Without a word, he turns and goes to his room.

"Goodnight," she says in a raised girlish voice.

Relief. Disappointment. She knows he must hear her because she doesn't hear his bedroom door close. He didn't eat much food at dinner. He isn't attempting sex. He is quiet.

Ava walks over to Skip's bedroom doorway and watches him packing a carry-on that is open on his bed. "Everything all right?" She tries not to sound concerned.

"You startled me." He places a rolled shirt into the bag. "Just packing my carry-on. I had everything ready for a trip to the outback. Planning to check out some intriguing exploration finds near that Aboriginal tribe I told you about, until this Jakarta trip moved up." Skip grabs a handful of papers from the bed. He tosses them into the bottom dresser drawer, which is full of documents and typed pages and receipts haphazardly overstuffing the small compartment.

Ava leans against the doorframe. "Something is wrong, isn't it?"

He turns toward her. "Are you psychic or something? Okay. I had lunch yesterday with the singer—you know, the one from the band. My stomach felt off later and now it is hurting a little. Must have been something I ate. That's all."

Ava counts to five, then to ten, then to five again. "You seem to have a lot of stomach aches after you see that woman." She can't resist the comment and knows it sounds catty.

He gives a short, gutteral "*ha.*" "I think you're jealous. "I picked you, you know. She called yesterday and asked to stay over. I told her I have company and have to leave tomorrow. So, she suggested lunch. No big deal. Met her at that little diner off the third Sky Rail stop. You know the one. Must have been something wrong with that Rueben sandwich." He looks around the bedroom as if checking his packing list.

She picks up a pair of rolled argyle socks that slipped off the bed onto to the floor and tosses them into the open bag. "I'm surprised she didn't want to tag along to Jakarta?"

"Oh, didn't tell her about the change of plans. She doesn't

care about that stuff."

"Did you leave the table? While you were eating, did you leave the table?"

Skip stops searching and looks at her. "Most women would want to know what we said, and you want to know if I left the table? I don't have time for this." He slams shut the carry-on. "I left the table to go wash my hands like I always do. Okay? The sandwich and beer had just arrived, so I left to wash my hands. No, I didn't leave for a long time and let my food go bad. We talked about some funny incident she had in Adelaide, something with a costume, I don't know. You are the one here—and you're in the *guest* room. She wouldn't be in the guest room!" He presses his abdomen.

Ava walks over and puts her hand on his shoulder. "You should see a doctor. Do you want to go tonight? I can drive you."

"You're not my mother. I'm fine." He shrugs away from her hand. "I don't have time to see a doctor. It's just some bad food."

"Have you noticed that—"

"What? Have I noticed that you fuss over me too much? Yes. I need to get some sleep . . . unless you plan to give me a reason to stay up a while." He drops the carry-on bag to the floor and pulls down the beige comforter on his double bed.

"Have a good trip. I hope you feel better in the morning." She turns to leave.

"Yeah. You, too. Look, I'm sorry. I just have a lot on my mind."

She turns back to look at him; their eyes lock for several seconds that seem like minutes. "You take care of yourself, Skip. Thank you for everything. It was a lovely night. . . . I expect you to call me in North Carolina when you get back from Jakarta. My parents' phone number is on the kitchen counter. I should be visiting them by the time you're back in Sydney. No excuses. Just call me." She turns to go, but stops. An invisible force holds her in place. She wants to part on a light air. Wants him to miss her. Just wants him. "And take your vitamins and see a doctor and remember to be careful about what you eat in Jakarta and whatever else your mother would tell you." She walks away before he can comment. Chuckling coming from his room makes her smile. *Good. If he is chuckling, his stomach must not be that bad. Maybe I am just a worrier.*

THE NEXT MORNING Ava awakens to bright sunlight streaming through the uncovered window. *I forgot to pull the damn curtains.* A quick check in the hallway confirms Skip is gone. She wanted to say goodbye this morning, but knows he left well before dawn. The same note still rests on the kitchen counter. Across the bottom is scribbled: "Sydney to Hobart" She smiles and makes herself a cup of coffee. *He's on a plane to Jakarta right now.* She wonders if he is thinking about her. *I better stop thinking about him and get my stuff together. Airport in two hours.* This time she is booked the Sydney-Hawaii-San Francisco-Dallas-New York-Raleigh route. *Thank God San Fran has showers in the international terminal.* She packs a special carry-on for that welcoming, tiny, overpriced airport shower room that means she is back in the States.

Eden

"SO THAT WAS the last time you saw him?" Iain leans forward, elbows on his knees.

"That was the last time. I think I need to take a walk alone. See you for dinner about eight?" Ava stands and looks out toward the sea as if she can see all the way to Hobart, all the way to the promise.

"See you in the dining room at eight." Iain is steady and calm, in voice and demeanor, as though he, too, has reached a destination.

She doesn't see what Iain is doing as she leaves him on the porch. She is walking with Skip and remembering. She smells coffee, the dark-roast Brazilian in his kitchen, and tastes the crusty steak, hot from the restaurant grill. Her shoulders give under the pressure of that signature bear hug. "*Oz* made it, Skip. You build a good boat." She thinks about Edward, who should have landed in Sydney by now. He is returning from London and will be full of tales about everyone.

Losing a friend, wondering if you should have said more or done something differently, trying to let go with so many questions unanswered, imprisons joy. The questions cast a shadow large enough to eclipse any happy memories of the one lost, leaving their only presence in the ring of backlight surrounding the shadow. Better to allow the questions passage, releasing the caged joy so it may again fly free in memory. The memories of Skip are a red and orange and green and yellow tropical parrot waiting to sing again and lift to a high branch bearing fruit, the fruit of love that grows within as such memories are created. She wishes she could help Iain experience that joy, help him let go of the eclipsing guilt and the weight of cowardice. If only he could think of his son Jack and remember the high-pitched laughter of a two year-old boy chasing squawking parrots in the garden. If only he could remember Annelisa calling them for tea instead of her calling for a ghost. So many ghosts haunt decisions. The air should seem heavy with them, heavy with the scent of them, with the laughter of them, with the breezing touch of them, but only the faint salt of the sea comes to her now. It is an ancient scent in her blood, and it, too, is comforting.

A wombat rustles through the bushes, startling her. She can't remember if a wombat is a good omen or a bad one.

NINE

Outer Banks, North Carolina, USA,
March 1987

"SO I'LL SEE you there," Edward says over the crackling telephone line. "I'm going to stop at that shop in Hatteras and pick up a board."

"I'm telling you, it's too cold."

"I come from a long line of warriors. And I have my wetsuit with me. See you by tonight."

Ava sits in the worn recliner of a rented beach house in Duck and wonders if inviting Edward was the right thing to do. He called her parent's home and learned she was out here alone for some R&R. The Outer Banks are her hiding place. Whenever she finishes a big assignment, she rents a little beach-bum cottage and spends a few days cycling along Highway 12 and walking the beaches. Except for the summer, it's very quiet. The bustle of summer is fun, but she needs quiet to rejuvenate. Each time she stays on the Outer Banks, the "OBX" the locals are starting to call it, she tries a new little community: Cape Hatteras or Kitty Hawk or Duck or wherever. Always takes the Cedar Island Ferry. And every time she drives off the ferry, she stops and climbs out of her car to inhale the heavy salted-fish smell of the shushing

Atlantic. Her family has sailed this blue ghost for hundreds of years, and it haunts her soul.

We don't bleed blue because we're royalty, we bleed blue because we're watermen. And Edward is about to discover how cold that water gets, she tells herself as she puts sheets on the double bed in the second bedroom.

By five o'clock darkness is floating across the water. She worries Edward will have trouble locating the little beach house down the sandy side road. She turns on all the outside lights. After a quick check down the road, she runs back inside the cottage. The wind is brisk. Her signature pasta dish, Tazzie Pasta, is warming on the avocado 1970s stove: bow-tie pasta with hot Italian sausage and Gouda cheese mixed with mustard and butter and sour cream and garlic. Yummm. The woodsy aroma of burning seasoned oak drifts in from the living room fireplace and mingles with the sizzling garlic butter and sausage smells of the kitchen. Wind buffets the shingles of the 1950s cottage and whistles through the shutters. Nothing is cozier. She pours the rich sausage cheese sauce over the steaming pasta and stirs with a giant spoon. One wooden spoonful for a test. "Mmm." Sudden knocking bangs against the screen door, interrupting her reverie with anticipation.

"Whew! That temperature drops when you lose the sun." Edward bang-bangs through the front door with a new surfboard under his left arm and a black-leather hang-up bag over his right shoulder. He walks hurriedly to the crackling fire, drops both board and bag to the floor, and rubs his hands in front of the flickering yellow warmth. "This place isn't going to fall down on us, is it?" he asks as another gust bangs the shutters outside."

"I told you it's cold. Do you want to freshen up? The

extra room is down here." She points toward the hallway.

He inhales deeply and looks toward the kitchen. "Something smells very, very good. Can you cook, too?" He walks straight into the kitchen, lifts the lid of the pasta pot, and grabs a buttery bow-tie pasta with his fingers. "It's official. I'm in love."

She playfully pops his hand and replaces the pot lid. "You go wash up, and I'll get us each a bowl. We can eat in front of the fireplace."

"Oh, eating in the sitting room. How naughty." He winks at her, trots over for his hang-up bag and disappears down the hallway.

She pours two wine glasses of a Napa Valley Syrah, heaps two soup bowls with pasta, and grabs some cloth napkins and forks from the kitchen drawers. Edward returns just as she sets the glasses on the coffee table. He sits next to her on the couch and picks up the two glasses, handing her one with a slight bow of his head. Clink! go the glasses.

"To us. To life, love, very rich pasta, and wherever the hell we are on the North Carolina Outer Banks," he says, rubbing his left hand on his leg to warm it.

"To Blue Ghost tides and windswept dunes."

Clink! They silently savor the pasta and Syrah.

"Now this is the way to end a business trip to New York. Who wants Broadway and limos and room service?"

She playfully punches him in the ribs. "I was very surprised when you called."

"Not as surprised as your parents. They asked about twenty questions before giving me the number out here. I told them I'm the chap with whom you had the passionate affair in Perth and promised more great sex if I came to see you." He says it as if he's giving the weather report.

"Edward! No, really? Edward!"

He laughs, coughing with a full mouth. "No, they sound very nice. Your mum did all the quizzing. You know, 'Do you make lots of money?' and the like, then your father came on the line with your phone number, oh, and said for you to call him when I get here."

She jumps up and goes to the wall phone in the kitchen. "Hi Mom. . . Yes, he's here. . . No, he's alone . . . surfing . . . yeah, I know. . . That's right, he was my escort to the America's Cup Ball. . . . I don't know. He had business in New York and wanted to see the Outer Banks. A couple of days, I guess. . . Okay, I'll call tomorrow. Bye." She goes back to the living room, where Edward is opening a second bottle of wine. "Okay, so now my parents think I'm shacked up out here with some Aussie who flew over to go surfing. Thanks, Edward."

"I could call and tell them my intentions."

"No, thanks . . . What are your intentions?"

"Just some surfing and a good shag and slowly convincing you to let me take you away from all of this. I am truly a good catch." He puts his arm around her shoulder.

"I wasn't fishing."

"I know. Silly little girl. I actually had to come after you. By the way, Sarah, my sister, says hello and that she hopes she'll get to talk to you sometime. She's very curious about you."

She takes a sip of the cool Syrah. "I bet she is."

Edward doesn't stay in the guest room. Two days disappear in an instant. Long days are spent walking on the beach and sharing childhood stories and tales of crazy uni days. Late afternoons they cozy in front of the fire: he reads aloud from *Black Beauty,* the only book in the house, and they enjoy Syrah, stopping regularly to talk about the plight of animals. Edward is a quick study. He soon knows to pause for commentary on the wonderfulness of horses and the evilness of man, showing he empathizes with her.

On day two, Edward decides a surf is overdue. The wind is right and the temperature is a moderate sixty degrees.

Ava pulls the car into a parking lot next to the shoreline. "I'm telling you that you don't want to do this. I'm the local."

"You are such a girl sometimes." Edward hops out of the car and steps into his full-body wetsuit. Zzziiiip up the back. He drags the double-fin short board from the back seat and tucks it under his arm. Now the surfer stance: survey of the break, Zen-like stare into the distance, chin slightly lifts for air gauge. Off he runs into the tideline.

"It's a mistake!" Ava yells after him as she stands next to her open car door.

He pretends not to hear her as he affixes the Velcro leash. Quick wave toward the car without looking back. Hurtling into the water and SPLASH. He nose-dives his board under the first break line.

She reaches into the car for the folded wool throw she grabbed on the way out of the cottage. She bumps up the car heater to eighty degrees, walks around the car closing all the doors, and trots toward the shoreline. *Won't be long now,* she thinks.

Up pops the popsicle and the board. Frantic paddling to turn around. Edward tries to yell something but he's out of breath. A wave breaks over him, driving him mercifully towards shore.

She laughs and holds open the flapping plaid throw for him to see.

More frantic paddling. Failed attempt to stand in the

water. Numb feet start working and he runs, board under arm, into the wool warmth. The board falls, still attached to its master.

"Ittt'ss c-c-col-l-ld." He pulls the throw over his dripping head and wraps it around his neck and shoulders.

"U-huh," she says, smiling.

"Rrrreally c-c-cold!"

"You'll live. C'mon. Heat's on in the car." She bends down and yanks the leash from his ankle with a quick "Crunch!" She picks up the board and pops it to knock off some sand. Before she is half-way to the car, he is out of the wetsuit and sitting on the seat trying to dry himself.

She opens his car door. Heat pours onto her cold, wet hand. "Surrender the towel, Big Guy. Gotta get the sand off this board."

He reluctantly pulls the towel from behind his back and tosses it to her as he pulls shut his door.

The drive to the cottage is quiet except for the low chattering of Edward's teeth. She doesn't need to say "I told you so." Waiting for him to admit it to her is reward enough. A couple of miles of empty highway later they pull up the sand drive to the cottage.

She leaves the car running. "I'll unlock the door then come back and turn off the car. You wait here."

"T-t-t-taaa."

She unlocks the door and remembers to grab an oversized sweatshirt she has just inside the door. "Better put this on before you get out," she tells him as she cuts the engine.

"I know what you want to say." His voice is steady as he pulls the double-thick softness over his head. His chest now reads "Surfer Babe."

"No need. Just get straight into the hot shower, Surfer

Babe." She laughs lightly as he double-times to the shower.

The surf shop is a quick ten minute drive this time of year—no traffic and no traffic cops. She decides to take a quick drive and get Edward his own sweatshirt. The already tanned twenty-year-old behind the counter appears very glad to have company in the empty shop.

"How about Surfer Dude? Second rack over," he says.

"Good. Surfer Idiot would be better. He tried the waves today." She laughs as she picks the fluffiest sweatshirt."

"That hadda hurt! Guess those Aussies only have warm surf."

"Nope. And he's English. Lives in Oz, but definitely English."

"Never thought this little shop would go international. German guy and English-Aussie in the same week."

"Really. German? Here visiting family?" She took cash from her wallet to pay the clerk.

"Said he was sight-seeing. Asked about your friend." The clerk hands her change.

"You're sure? He asked about Edward? What did he say?"

"Something about had I seen any other tourists. Asked me if we had any great surfers out here, like from Australia. Told him our local boys are as good as any Aussie."

Ava takes her bag. "Did he ask you or did you mention us first?"

"Don't know. Maybe I mentioned it first. Dude looked intimidating. Didn't seem in the mood for visiting. Had this knarly tattoo on his thumb. Some kind of Egyptian writing over a cross or something."

She takes the keys from her pocket. "Thanks. Probably won't see you again. May be leaving this afternoon."

"Have a good one."

She had no intention of leaving this afternoon. Couldn't place any Germans. Sure it was nothing. Still, doesn't hurt to tell the town crier they are leaving.

AFTER A HOT shower, Edward volunteers to build a fire. He pours wine and chops the smoky Gouda and Havarti cheeses into little chunks and serves in a pie plate with Ritz crackers. "All I could find," he says as he places the plate on the coffee table.

"Nice to see you going native." And in her heart he is. The North Atlantic has calmed the pride of another arrogant foreigner. "Got you something comfy." She hands him the plastic bag from the surf shop.

"A jumper." He pulls the sweatshirt over his head and hugs himself with the fluffy arms. "Surfer Dude. Perfect."

"The clerk was very chatty."

"I know that. Surprised you aren't still there."

"Mentioned something about a German tourist."

"Yeah? Probably get all kinds of tourists out here. Everyone has heard of the Outer Banks."

"You're right. The cheese looks good."

She ate lightly and thought no more about the surfer dude clerk. More important things took priority—like napping in the crook of Edward's arm only now with total comfort. Australia seems far, far away. Her normal life seems far, far away.

RING! RING! RING!

"Oh, I forgot to call Mom." Ava jumps off the couch and runs to the kitchen phone.

"I was just going . . . Fiona? Hello. This is really a surprise. . . When? . . . Where is he now? Just a minute. Let me get a pen. Okay . . . So what do the doctors say? . . . Okay. Thank you for calling. . . No, really. Thank you." Ava hangs up, standing silently for a moment. Then she picks up the receiver and dials. The tone of her voice draws Edward into the kitchen. He is quiet.

"Hello. This is Ava Marks. I am calling for a patient, Skip—Mr. Philip Dubbledon. He was admitted with meningitis. . . Um, yes. I am his sister in the States. . . Okay . . . I understand. I would like to send him some flowers. What is the room number? . . . Thank you." She hangs up and looks at Edward. "Skip is in the Sydney hospital with meningitis. He passed out at a meeting in Jakarta. Somehow he was flown to Sydney. He's sleeping now. Sydney is a good hospital, right? Who gets meningitis? I thought that was a disease of babies and overcrowded people in poor populations. You don't die from that, right?"

Edward gives her a gentle hug—not the bear hug she is missing. She pulls away, because it only reminds her of Skip's hugs.

He steps back. "He'll be all right. Sydney has a good hospital. Odd timing," he says matter-of-factly. "Some meningitis was reported among the Aboriginal communities in central Australia. Saw the report just before I left for New York. Our company was exploring in that area last month, but I don't think Skip ever came out there. Don't worry. I've never known anyone to die from it if they get early treatment."

"Okay. Okay. I need to call in something for him tomorrow. No flowers. He is in intensive care. A dog. A stuffed dog. He's always saying he misses not having a dog, but doesn't have time to take care of one. Maybe when he goes out on his own . . . A stuffed dog. He'll like that." Her eyes tear as she strains not to cry.

"Out on his own? Did he tell you about our exploration in Indonesia? I thought it was a secret. Paid cash and told us to keep our mouths shut."

She catches herself. "Oh, I don't know what I'm saying. I mean out of the hospital."

"Ava, do you want me to leave?" he asks softly. He is looking at his sock feet on the floor.

"No, Edward. I'm glad you're here."

"I can sleep in the guest room. I didn't know he confides in you. I mean, I didn't know you and Skip are—"

"We aren't anything more than friends, Edward. For Skip, being *real* friends is a stretch. I need to sit down. He just told me about some plans he has. That's all. What did you say about the Aborigines? Did you say Indonesia?"

"Nothing important. Aborigines, yes. Some outbreak of an odd strain of meningitis, type A or group A or something."

He follows a dazed Ava to the couch. She quickly falls asleep snuggled into his shoulder. Sometime later, five minutes or five hours, she hears Edward on the phone, explaining to her parents what is happening. She tries to stay awake and hear the conversation, but the exhaustion of conflicting emotions pulls her back into the subconscious.

The next day she calls the hospital gift shop and has a stuffed dog sent to Skip's room. The third and final version of the note reads:

My name is Eve. I am your best friend who requires no mainte-nance. Ava

Version one was signed "love, Ava." Version two said "best wishes, Ava."

She can't call Skip in intensive care, so she calls Fiona who promises to keep Ava apprised of the situation. For now, Fiona is being told that Skip is stable and was moved to a private room a few hours ago. Ava calls his room immediately, but no answer. She decides she'll wait for Fiona's call tomorrow. No need to wake Skip when he needs his sleep. Ava is impressed that Edward is being supportive. He even calls Clark in Perth and tells him about Skip. Clark promises to have a company geologist stop by and check on Skip after meetings in Canberra. So, they wait. Ava imagines Black Beauty, in his aged and tormented body, running along the fence, whinnying to the boy now aged to manhood. Beauty recognizes the voice from his young, carefree years. Oh, to know such happiness again. It's worth bursting one's heart.

Ava contemplates her mortality, as people often do when illness confronts them. She feels as vulnerable as a hatchling sea turtle—just the beach to cross, the beach of monster bird shadows. She remembers lost love, the only time she ever knew the feeling of being *in love*. Wasted on her impulsive youth. Now, she has no fence to run along in hopes of regaining it. *I only have now,* she thinks. *Now.* She only has the hope of logical, grown-up love. Less passionate. More likely to last. *I have a friend with meningitis still trying to define love and a friend in lust who thinks I define love. Is it better to love or be loved?*

RING! RING!

Ava awakens on the blanketed couch in the Duck cottage. Darkness shrouds the room with only shades of red sky filtering through the curtains. *Red sky in the morning, sailor take warning.* The wall clock in the kitchen reads 5:15. *Edward must have left me sleeping on the couch last night.*

"Hello . . . Hi Fiona. Is Skip doing well? . . . Oh, good. . . He did! . . . Really . . . Oh, that's funny. . . Yes, I'll try him later. Thank you, Fiona."

Edward enters the room in grey sweatpants with "Surf Hatteras" printed up the right leg. "Good news?"

"Yes! Skip is awake and asked for a cheeseburger and a beer."

"So the Skipper is himself again." Edward takes the glass pitcher from the coffee machine.

"Go put on some shoes and a shirt before we have you at the hospital. I'll make the coffee." She takes the glass pot from him and points to the hallway.

"Okay, Mum," he says, bare feet slapping against the cold linoleum.

The reference sends a chill down her arms, causing her to shake the coffee pitcher. . . "and whatever else your mother would tell you," she whispers.

Edward is gone. He doesn't hear her. She didn't say it for him to hear.

Just as the Colombian dark-roast coffee aroma warms the room, Edward returns with added UGG boots and a white sweatshirt with green print reading "Ha'vud." He sees Ava staring at it. "A gift from a friend."

"The coffee is ready. Oh, there's more to the story. Just as Fiona was arriving at Skip's hospital room, she saw his ex-wife leaving the room. Skip opens his eyes when Fiona greets him and asks for the cheeseburger and beer."

"Yeah, you told me."

"When Fiona tells him that cheeseburgers and beer aren't going to happen, Skip's ex walks back into the room carrying a cup of tea. Fiona said Skip must have been asleep earlier because he sees his ex and says, 'What the hell is she doing here?'"

Edward laughs as he pours a cup. "You go, Skip."

"So, the ex ignores the comment and says 'I was so worried. Fiona, you should let him rest. The doctors say he is very weak.' And Skip says, 'Fiona is welcome. You get the hell out.' Fiona says the ex put on a poor act of crying and ran out of the room."

"So, Skip is well."

"Looks like it. I wonder if I should go to Sydney?"

"Ava, don't confuse fear of losing a friend with being in love."

"I don't confuse anything with being in love," she snips. She wonders if Edward is in love or just in lust. Wonders if he knows the difference. "The drugstore will open in a couple of hours. I want to get Skip a card, a funny card. He'll like that."

"Ava . . . nothing. So, what else would you like to do today?"

"I don't know. When do you have to leave? You never told me."

"Are you ready for me to go?"

"No. I love having you here, but I have to get back to New York in three days."

"Do you want me to drive back to Morehead City with you?"

"No need for that."

"I could meet your parents."

"No need for that."

"I see. Well, I guess I'll be leaving tomorrow."

He looks hurt as he busies himself making toast. One part of her is saying *don't throw it away again* while the other part is saying *I need to see Skip*. A couple of weeks ago she was aboard the *Oz* with Skip and not even thinking about Edward. A couple of days ago she was walking the beach with Edward and not even thinking about Skip. The smell of burning toast interrupts her thoughts. "How do you burn toast in a toaster? Go sit down. I'll make us breakfast."

She hears the television news coming from the living room: more cold weather; a convenience-store robbery; house fire in Cape Hatteras; chance for love—*no, that can't be right.*

"I FEEL BETTER." Ava gets in the car after mailing Skip a silly card about pinching nurses. "He'll get it in ten days. I guess it goes by sea turtle." They head up the Banks toward a seafood restaurant, one of the few open this early in the season. Edward says he's in the mood for fried shrimp, but she thinks he just doesn't want to be alone with her. They fill the silence with philosophical musings about everything from Kitty Hawk to space travel. The awkward conversation jerks forward and stops at erratic intervals like a bad transmission. Their road less traveled is becoming bumpier by the hour.

Finally back at the cottage, they both busy themselves packing. She distracts herself by thinking through her agenda. She needs to get to Morehead and go through her mail before heading off to meetings in New York. Edward is due back in Perth in a week. Says he plans on taking the New York–London route so he can see Lady Sarah. Ava remembers Sarah's marbled voice, full of excitement. She stops packing. *I need to talk to Edward. What am I doing?* She wants him to leave and doesn't want him to leave. Her mind is full of contradictions so loud she feels disoriented. *Now is the time. I only have now.*

RING! RING! RING!

She runs to the kitchen for the phone. "Hello. . . Oh, hello Fiona." Ava gives a little *It's ok* wave to Edward as he enters the kitchen. "Yes. . . What?! But I thought he was recovering! . . . Then why did they move him to a private room? . . . Let me speak to his doctor. . . Oh, that's right. I forgot it's the middle of the night there. . . Yes. Yes. . . No, you did the right thing. Thank you for calling me. . . I don't know. I'm supposed to go to New York. I don't know. . . Yes. I'll let you know. . . Oh, his mother. Did someone call his mother? . . . You mean his ex-wife? What has she got to do with anything? . . . No, I understand. You're not a relative. . . No, I understand. I'll call you, okay? . . . You take care, too. Bye." She slides down to the floor, sitting with her back resting on the pine cabinets. She doesn't even realize she is sitting on the floor. The linoleum is so cold that she can feel it through her jeans.

"Ava. What is it? Ava?" Edward takes the receiver from her and hangs up.

"Skip is dead. Passed away. Why do people say *passed away*? He is dead! How can he want a cheeseburger and then be dead?" She doesn't cry. She wants to cry. Her neck feels like it's in a noose. She reaches to pull away the noose but only feels warm skin. She feels Edward holding her: a bear-hug squeeze trapping her arms against her body. He is kneeling on the floor next to her.

"Ava? . . . Let's get you off this cold floor." He squats and gently lifts her with him. Somehow they end up on the couch. "I'll get you a glass of wine. I think this calls for a drink. I'll get us both one."

He is gone a second and then there is a glass of Syrah in her hand. She sips the cool liquid. Her neck relaxes.

He pats her leg. "I'll be right back."

She hears him making calls, talking to someone. There are bits of a conversation about the rental car and bits of a conversation about a geology study meeting and bits of a conversation telling Sarah he won't be seeing her. He comes back in the room.

She forces a smile. "I'm all right. Just a bit of a shock, but I'm all right now."

With his thumb, he wipes away a tear winding down the side of her nose. The touch is gentle. "No you aren't. Jeff at the surf shop is taking care of the rental car for me. I'm driving you home. Then we'll decide what to do."

"I have to fly to Sydney. Oh gosh. My stuff is in Skip's closet. I have to get it."

"We'll talk about it on the way to Morehead City. I wanted to meet your parents, anyway. If you decide to go on to Sydney, we can travel together."

She agrees because she can't think clearly enough to develop an argument or even figure out how to get back home. *New York.* "I need to call New York."

He pats her hand. "I left Patricia a message. I think it's her apartment. Found the number in your address book by the phone."

"My parents. I have to call them."

"Already rang your parents. They're expecting us. They didn't seem to know who Skip is. I just assumed—doesn't matter. I'll finish packing for us." He disappears.

She tries to focus on what she needs to do, but her mind instant-replays her last supper on the *Oz*. All those stars. Petit fours and Shiraz. That huge hand holding hers. Distant voices on the dock. She is paralyzed in the flashback. She feels the cool Sydney Harbour breeze on her face. "Edward!"

He runs back into the room. "I'm here, Darling."

He kisses her on top of the head, the way her father used to do when she was a child. She feels like a child. And so old. She feels so old.

"Let me get everything in the car. I'll be right back."

Eden

EVERYONE IN EDEN appears crammed into the inn's small dining room for dinner at eight. Fortunately, the crowd noise drowns Ava's conversation with Iain enough to keep it private. She is refreshed and ready to face sea monsters. She took a long bubbles-to-her-chin bath before dinner, soaking in warm water that slowly cooled its temperature and her nerves. Even Iain seems brighter as if the eclipse is passing and allowing light to brighten his soul. Neither of them mentions Annelisa or Jack. The two journos are here for Skip's story, and Ava knows that asking about anything else would be more invasive than nurturing.

Iain stabs his fork into the rich mutton on his plate and vigorously saws back and forth with his knife. "So you're telling me that Skip is sitting up and talking and then relapses and dies. In the hospital. In the hospital, he suddenly dies."

Iain has a squinted look Ava's never seen before, as if he's watching bacteria through a microscope. She is trying to focus on the conversation but is distracted by his poor table manners. *Skip would never saw meat like that*, she thinks.

He talks while chewing a chunk of the savory meat. "That outbreak, it was meningococcal serogroup A. I remember the report coming in. The outbreak was highly unusual. Seemed to spring out of nowhere. Think it claimed several lives. That would've been the same time Skip was planning to go to the area. But he didn't go. Right? Did he have the same strain?" Iain looks behind his chair, checking for eavesdroppers.

Most of the diners receded to the parlor and porch well over fifteen minutes ago. On the far side of the room, a table of four young men toasts over bachelor party tales.

She slides her fork and knife from four o'clock to six o'clock on her plate, the correct sign in Oz that she finished her meal. *When in Rome . . .* "I don't know. I never saw the hospital records. The nurse told me meningitis was diagnosed in Jakarta. That was about all I gleaned before a doctor came along and she stopped talking. I wasn't the next of kin, so I couldn't get any information. Fiona said she heard that SpearCo was able to get the records, but she never saw them."

"What about the autopsy? Were you in Sydney for the autopsy report?"

TEN

AVA AND EDWARD approach Skip's condo building. The air is windy cold, as autumn announces the Aussie winter approaching. "It's all right, Edward. I have a key."

"Why do you have a key? I thought—" Edward catches himself. Not the time.

"No, we weren't living together. I left my travel stuff in his closet, and he gave me a key to come get it whenever I needed it."

Ting!

The elevator door opens on Skip's floor. The walk down the brown, mottled-wool carpet is eerily familiar to Ava. The key works. They are inside the tiny foyer. She feels a cold breeze when they enter. "Is the balcony door open?"

They walk across the room, but everything appears closed.

"Let's just get your things. I feel odd about this." Edward stands in the middle of the room, twirling in a slow circle. "He is neat for a man living alone."

She walks into the kitchen. "The note from Skip. Here is the note from Skip. Edward, I must be the last one here.

I flew out later the same day. Look, here is my coffee cup in the sink. The maid. She comes once a week. I wonder why she didn't come in three weeks."

"Oh, Skip probably just canceled because he was out of town. Let's get your things." Edward paces the room as if they're burglars about to be discovered.

"Just a minute." She walks to Skip's bedroom. The bed is still unmade, just as he left it. The closet is as neat as ever. She walks to his dresser and hesitates.

"What are you doing?" Edward looks in the bedroom doorway. "I don't think we should touch anything."

She pulls open the top dresser drawer: boxer shorts are folded neatly in rows. Pulls open the next drawer: handkerchiefs on the left and socks folded and on the right. The next drawer: folded deck shorts. The bottom drawer: empty. She sits on the messy bed and collects her thoughts.

"What are you looking for?" Edward crosses the room and pushes all the drawers tightly shut, covering his hand with a handkerchief.

"Mess. I'm looking for mess. And papers. I know there were papers. Someone has been here." She goes to the hall closet and opens the door to see all her belongings. They are neatly placed on the shelves, but not exactly as she had placed them. The heavy electrical adapter box is in the center of the shelf. Ava sneezes softly then lets out a huge a-CHOOO. "Excuse me. Something is tickling my nose. Do you smell that?"

"Just smells like a musty closet not opened in a while. Is this what we need?" Edward reaches into the closet, but she holds up her hand to stop him.

Ava tugs the back of his dress shirt. "Don't touch anything. We need to get out of here."

"I'm sorry I was so nervous. You're just upset. Let's just get your things."

She clutches his arm. "Someone has been here. Don't touch anything. Come on. We're going to see Fiona."

She tries explaining about messy drawers and the moved adapter box. Edward is glancing at her as if she's crazy, so she stops. He maneuvers through the Sydney traffic to the SpearCo offices.

Fiona's desk sits at the end of the entrance hallway. She sees Ava step out of the elevator and half-runs to meet her. No hug. Just Fiona's hand on Ava's left shoulder.

"Ava, I'm so sorry. Crickey, it's bloody awful. I'm trying to get everything together, but it's all such a mess. And some man keeps calling from an oil-rig site in Egypt. We aren't drilling in Egypt, and I can't find his name in the company directory. I don't know what to tell all these people."

Ava takes a deep breath. *Don't lose it here.* "He's a friend of Skip."

"What?" Fiona looks puzzled as they walk to her desk.

"The man in Egypt. I think that is Skip's friend. You need to call him and tell him what has happened. Everything. Tell him everything."

Fiona scoots her chair back under her desk. "I have his number here somewhere." She thumbs through her message pad.

Ava notices the name of a funeral home as Fiona flips through the pages. "Wait. Is that Skip's funeral home? When is the funeral? Didn't they have it already? Do you know where he's buried?"

Fiona stops looking through the pad and stares at Edward. "I thought you told her."

"I couldn't," Edward says.

"Told me what? Edward?"

Fiona clears her throat. "Skip was cremated two days ago."

"But what about the funeral? What about the autopsy?"

"The hospital listed meningitis as the cause of death. Then Mrs. . . . Skip's ex-wife decided to cremate."

"*She* decided? What does she have to do with anything?"

"Well, as his heir—"

Ava slams her hand on the desk much harder than she meant. "She's not his heir. Skip changed his will to leave everything to his mother."

Fiona looks surprised. "How did you know that?"

"Because we talked about it. He was going to leave his daughters money for college and the *Oz* and leave his mother everything else." She feels Edward take her left hand in his with a gentle squeeze.

"You're right, well almost right. He was leaving the *Oz* to you. He had me type up the changes. He was supposed to drop them off at his attorney's office to get the Last Will and Testament updated by his return, but he left me a message that he forgot and left the papers at the condo. He told me not to worry about it. That he would . . . that he would . . ." Fiona is sniffling back tears.

"It's all right, Fiona. I know. I know. I think you should know that Skip would brag about what a great job you do and how well you look—looked after him. So Mrs. Dubbledon and her daughters get everything." Ava feels a gruesome numbness as if the dentist injected her entire body.

"No, the daughters don't get anything. The old will was from before they had the twins."

"Fiona, Skip says you do everything in triplicate. Do you have a copy of changes to the will?"

"No. It wasn't company business, so I didn't bother. It was just something I whipped together over lunch. I never thought I needed it. I'm so sorry. I never thought I needed it."

"It's not your fault. Does anyone else know about the changes?"

"Well, I may have mentioned something about it to a sister at the hospital. You know, before Skip woke up. We were just talking about how you never know what will happen."

"Was that the same time you saw Mrs. Dubbledon there?"

"Maybe. Yes, I think so. But she wasn't in the room yet. I don't think she was."

"I need her address."

"Is everything all right? Did I do something wrong?" Fiona looks as though she's trying to rub away a headache through her forehead.

"No, Fiona, Skip always thought you did everything right. He really cared about you in his own way."

Fiona nods as she pulls a large address book from her desk drawer, thumbs through it for a moment, and writes down the address of the ex-Mrs. Dubbledon. "I'm sorry. Losing Mr. Dubbledon. Mr. Schultz leaving. Today is just a bit . . ."

"Mr. Schultz?" Ava asks.

"Yes. Mr. Dubbledon wouldn't like that. Said he did a good job with the Aborigines. We thought he would stay. And now everything is changing."

"When did Mr. Schultz leave?"

"He's back there now packing up his desk."

Ava glances at Edward. "You stay here. I'll go say goodbye."

"Miss . . . Ava . . . You aren't supposed to go—"

Ava turned the corner to enter the side offices. Past Skip's door. Past the board room. Two more doors. Mr. Schultz seemed to be running his hand along the bottom of his middle desk drawer. "I heard you are leaving. Just wanted to say goodbye."

Mr. Schultz looks startled. "Tumm . . . I was just—"

"Don't get up. Just wanted to tell you that Mr. Dubbledon spoke highly of you. I'm sure he would've wanted you to stay."

"He spoke about me?"

"You don't remember, but we saw you one night at that restaurant where all the men take their, well, mistresses, for lack of a better word."

Mr. Schultz laughs nervously. "Of course. I remember now. Nice of you to stop by." His hand is still below the desk drawer.

Ava crosses the office and offers a handshake. She is curious what he is holding beneath the drawer. "Best of luck."

He pulls his right hand from below the drawer. "Yes, thank you. And to you." His hand shake is quick as if touching her will give an electric shock.

She notices something on his thumb. It passes so quickly that it could be an ink smudge. "Well, goodbye then."

"Goodbye. Good of you to stop." He sits back in his chair.

Ava walks slowly down the corridor to the front desk. Something she can't define is troubling her. "Thank you, Fiona. Just had to say goodbye to Mr. Schultz. We'll talk later." She takes the address and walks quickly to the elevator, tugging Edward along by his hand.

When they are alone in the elevator, he looks anxious again. "Ava, I think you should leave this alone."

"I have to pay my respects to the grieving widow—or is she called ex-widow or ex-wife widow?" She is angry and that feeling of strength banishes all vulnerability.

He drives them to the two-story home perched on the hillside overlooking Sydney Harbour. All the way there he tries to talk her out of seeing the woman. Ava confides she's never met Skip's ex, but knows what to expect from Skip's stories. Edward protests one last time before saying he will wait in the car.

No cars are parked at the house. Gemma, Skip's brunette daughter, answers the door. Skip used to call them "darkness and light," since the twins were a brunette and a blonde with personalities to match. Ava recognizes the girl from a photo in Skip's living room. Gemma's face is puffy. *Such regrets. She must be crying.*

"Gemma, I'm Ava Marks, a friend of your father. Is your mother home?"

"No. She went shopping with Mrs. Kindle. They'll be back in a couple of hours. Did you work for my dad?"

"No, we were good friends. He has a lovely photo of you in his living room. I would know you anywhere. You have the same eyes and stubborn chin."

Gemma smiles a little. "Would you like to come in and wait?"

"I would like to leave your mother a note, if that's all right."

Gemma moves away from the door and allows Ava inside the modern home. The living room is very formal with white carpet and white, damask-covered chairs. She could never imagine Skip in this room.

"I'll get some paper." Gemma exits for a moment and returns with a gold SpearCo Cross pen and small notepad.

The pen is unusually cold in Ava's hand. "Thank you."
She writes:

> *Mr. Dubbledon's secretary and I are the witnesses to Mr.
> Dubbledon's new Will. The one that leaves his property to your
> daughters and his mother.*
>
> *Please contact me immediately to discuss this issue. Fiona
> knows how to reach me.*
>
> *Ava Marks*

Ava knows the teenager will read the note the moment
she's alone. Adding that the girls are Skip's heirs will insure
the message is immediately given to the ex. Ava knows teenage girls. "Your father talked about you and your sister very
lovingly," she tells Gemma as she hands her the note. *White
lies are sometimes good.*

"He was always working," she sniffles. "And I . . . I was
so horrible the last time . . ."

"He loved you very much. Your father's new Last Will
and Testament provides handsomely for your college. Please
give this to your mother." Ava knows it's terrible to involve
a grieving girl in this situation, but she also knows Gemma
is likely to tell everything she knows to everyone who'll listen. There is no better way to address the controversy. *Skip
wants his mother taken care of and by God . . .* Ava walks to
the car without looking back.

"Good. I'm glad that's over," Edward says as he opens
her door.

She doesn't tell him that it's nowhere near over. "Help
me remember to call Fiona in three hours."

"Are we going to the police station?" Edward checks his
watch.

"And tell them what? That my friend died in the hospital and his drawers are too neat. No, I am just going to do what I can at this point."

"Well, our office intruders could learn from Skip's. It's much harder to prove an issue when everything is left in its place. I guess if you're looking for something, you need the ransacking crew *and* the cleanup crew."

"You're right. There have to be extra people. Otherwise, the ones cleaning would know how it looked to start with. There have to be extra people." From the moment she heard Fiona talk about the will, Ava assumed Mrs. Ex had taken her daughters' key and gone through Skip's condo looking for it. But then she would have known how the drawers looked. She may have taken the changes, but she was not the last one in that condo. "Edward, you're so good to help me with all this. I don't want to cause problems for you. If you need to get to Perth or if it could hurt your career to get involved, I'll understand if you need to go."

Without a word, he pulls the car over to the curb and puts it in park. He looks her in the eye, "Ava, I'm going to marry you. You may not know it yet, but you want to marry me, too. When all of this mess is over, however long it takes, we are flying to London and getting married. Don't say anything. I'm not asking if you want to. I'm telling you that I know we both want it, and I am looking after things from this moment forward. And I'm telling everyone we're engaged, because that way, if nothing else, no one will harm you. I'm too much of a public figure for anyone to harm me." He holds his finger to her lips in anticipation of a protest. "We're going to get something to eat because neither of us has eaten today. Then we're going to see Fiona. Then we're going back to the Westin and get over our jet lag." He holds up his finger again. "Ah-uh. We'll discuss it later."

"So that's going to be my proposal story," she says sarcastically, lightening the mood. She hates bossy men. But this feeling of being taken care of, of feeling safe, is a good feeling, a comforting feeling. She hasn't felt this way since she left for college at age eighteen. *Maybe I like bossy men. Maybe I love this one. A grown-up love.* She doesn't protest.

FIONA STANDS AS she spots Edward and Ava entering the hallway to her desk. "I didn't know where to reach you. A solicitor called for Mrs. Dubbledon. He says he needs to see us today."

Ava motions for Fiona to take her seat. "It's all right, Fiona. I left a note for *ex* Mrs. Dubbledown. I'll take care of this. Did you tell him anything?" Ava inhales deeply through her nose, making a slight whistle. Something, a scent of something . . .

"Well, no. I was so stunned. I just said I was expecting to hear from you this afternoon." Fiona notices Ava sniffing the air. "It's Old Spice. I took it from Mr. Dubbledon's office and put some on my notepad." She opens the top desk drawer, revealing the white bottle of Old Spice. "I'm so silly."

"No, you're not silly at all . . . It's a nice memory, isn't it? Fiona, I decided to stop by instead of calling because I need to check for something. Would it be all right for me to go into Skip's office?"

Fiona looks surprised. She takes a key from her center desk drawer and walks Edward and Ava to Skip's office door. "I've kept it locked. I don't know why. I just thought, well, it's too soon to be in here." Fiona steps back from the open door, letting them pass.

Edward is staring at the huge, L-shaped desk as Ava

looks behind it. "Ava, what are you looking for?"

"I don't know. Something." She opens a drawer. Neat. She opens another drawer. Neat. She pulls open one of the filing-cabinet drawers. Papers are neatly in their folders.

Fiona steps into the office. "I don't think you should be in here."

"Fiona, did you straighten Skip's office for him?"

Fiona laughs heartily, as if she's been suppressing it for days. "No one straightened Mr. Dubbledon's office. He got very testy if he couldn't find something."

"Come over here." Ava pulls open the file drawer again for Fiona to see. "Look."

Fiona looks surprised. "It's so orderly."

Ava crosses the room to Skip's desk. She starts pulling open drawers and leaving them open. "Look."

Fiona walks to the desk and gently closes all the drawers as if lowering a coffin lid. "Someone has been in here. I locked the office door after he left for tea on the sailboat. I didn't forget. I locked the door. Mr. Dubbledon picked up the take-away bags from behind my desk. He was late. He didn't even come back in here. So, I locked the door as soon as he left. And I'm sure I locked them after I went inside for the Old Spice. Positive. I started to cry as I was turning the key."

"Do you always leave the key in your desk?"

"Yes, but I lock my desk when I leave the office." Fiona looks at the office-door key in her hand as if it holds a secret.

"Where are the tapes for the security cameras in the office?" Edward is looking at a camera mounted outside Skip's office door.

"Normally, they're kept in the break room."

"Normally?" Edward is suddenly very interested.

"Well, yes. There was some wiring problem a couple of weeks ago. Then there was a mix-up in getting it fixed. The company thought we canceled or something. They're coming this Wednesday." Fiona is slowly realizing something. "But I'm sure it was over a month ago, now that I think about it. Mr. Dubbledon was just getting ready for his trip. It was right after the trip to Jakarta moved up, and we had to cancel everything planned for that site visit in the Outback."

Edward looks at Ava and nods toward the door. "I'm sure it's nothing. Ava, we need to be going. Oh, and Fiona, I want you to be the first one here to know, Ava and I are engaged."

Fiona's jaw drops.

For someone with great timing, Edward must be the one losing it. Ava is not sure how to comment, so she doesn't. "Fiona, do you have the number for Mrs. Dubbledon's solicitor?"

"MS. MAAAKS, THANK you for coming so quickly. Joanne, bring tea . . . ta. Ms. Maaaks, please have a seat." Mr. Foxley is sixty-something, with a sharp nose and bald except for a band of closely clipped reddish-grey hair circling his head in a horseshoe from ear to ear. He motions to one of the two chairs facing his desk.

At the other end of the room, Ava takes the seat at the head of the boardroom table. "Thank you."

"Tumm . . . yes." Hesitantly pulling out the chair next to Ava, Foxley runs his right hand across his scalp. His stern look signals that he knows she feels in control of the situation, and he doesn't like it. He takes the chair to her side, instead of sitting at the table like an employee.

"Mrs. Dubbledon has brought to our attention that her

husband may have written a new Will recently. You see, any Last Will and Testament would not be recognized until it is witnessed and filed. The latest one of recaaad is from fifteen yaaas ago." He pulls at his suit jacket from the hem, a sign that he is either uneasy or angry . . . or maybe both.

"It was nice of you to take the time to clear that up for me." Ava tries hard to stay calm.

"Of caaas, one knows this is a difficult time for everyone. We want to help howava one may." Mr. Foxley lures her like prey.

"Of course. So, if Mr. Dubbledon's secretary has the new Last Will andTestament signed by Skip—Mr. Dubbledon and his secretary and me, then it wouldn't be valid until it is filed somewhere? May I use your phone? I'm not sure that is correct."

A heavy silence fills the room as Joanne brings tea and sets it on the boardroom table.

"Ta. That will be all," Foxley says in an effort to quickly dismiss her. "But the updated Last Will and Testament isn't signed. I mean there isn't one on record that is signed." He rubs that bald scalp again.

"And how does the *ex*-Mrs. Dubbledon know the new will was never signed?"

"Ms. Maaaks—" The solicitor stops talking while Joanne takes her time closing the office door. "Ms. Maaaks, if this is about you getting the *Oz*—"

"How does his ex know the new will gives me the Oz? Mr. Foxley, I didn't even know that until Fiona told me." Ava locks her gaze on his eyes.

"If you signed it, you would know he was leaving you the *Oz*." He glares her down.

I was too sure of myself, and I have said too much. "Mr.

Foxley, this is all just too distressing for me. Edward, Lord Shropley, is waiting for me in the lobby. Perhaps I should have him call the police for me. I'm sure they can sort out all of this better than I."

"The Baron of Shropley? One wasn't aware...let me make a call. I'm sure we can saaat this out." Mr. Foxley forces a smile and leaves his office to make the call. He is gone for several minutes—long enough to check and see that Edward is indeed in the lobby.

"Thank you for waiting, Ms. Maaaks. Mrs. Dubbledon, umm, the ex Mrs. Dubbledon says she is just too distressed to come to the office. She understands that you must be grieving as well and wants everyone to be happy. She authorized me to sign over the *Oz Rox* ketch to you. She says that is only fair if it was promised to you."

Not too distressed to go shopping, but too distressed to see me, Ava thinks. She has what she came for. She knows that the ex was in Skip's condo and took Fiona's typed document for Skip's updated Last Will and Testament. That is one person down. But it doesn't help Skip's mother. "Okay, here's what we're going to do," Ava continues. "You are going to get *Oz Rox* put in a trust or whatever you people do here. The *Oz* is mine for one year. Then your office will oversee her sale, without commission, and send one hundred percent of the proceeds to Mr. Dubbledon's mother." Ava reaches into her purse and gets the piece of paper with Skip's mother's address and telephone number. Mrs. Dubbledon, Skip's ex-wife *not* his mother, will pay all expenses for the docking fees and insurance and sale of the *Oz.* Here is Lord Shropley's solicitor in London. He will determine if the sale price is fair, and he will need to see all of the documents before I sign anything." Digging in her purse, she finds Edward's business card with the solicitor informa-tion written on the back.

"Well, one doubts—"

"In exchange for these terms, I walk away. I don't tell the police that the ex Mrs. Dubbledon has broken into Skip's condo and stolen property. I don't go to the tabloids and tell them that you and she are trying to cheat an elderly woman in Texas out of her son's estate. I am *not* negotiating. It's a yes right now or I'm getting one of Murdoch's vampires on the line. You know I mean it." Ava keeps her hands in her lap so Mr. Foxley won't see them shaking. She's not sure if this is extortion. She just knows it's as close to fairness as this situation is likely to get.

Mr. Foxley stands and gives Ava the lascivious look that men whose wives are watching usually reserve for street-walkers. He extends his hand to shake. "One is certain we can handle it as you say and make everyone satisfied."

Ava doesn't shake his hand. Instead, she places Edward's card with his solicitor's name on the back into Foxley's paw. "We'll expect to hear from you within forty-eight hours." She leaves the room without looking back.

"But why do you want the *Oz* for a year?" Edward nearly backs the rental car into a passing van in the parking lot.

"Because she is going to sail in the Sydney-to-Hobart. Let's go to the hotel. I need a drink. I'll explain it all to you there."

Eden

EVEN THOUGH AVA savored her last bite over a half-hour ago, the creamy gaminess of the roast-duck pasta still engages her senses, reducing her final glass of the second bottle of Shiraz to a pale accompaniment. Iain is leaning on his back chair legs, accepting of life the way one becomes after a good meal or a great tale. Wild game elicits some hunter-gatherer fire in men that mesmerizes them as surely as a deep-woods campfire lighting the night. The smokiness of the duck strengthens so that Ava nearly smells the campfire.

"So that's how the *Oz* got to this race." Iain is finger-combing his thick hair. "Sheilas. I tell you. No offense."

"None taken." They are alone in the dining room. The hostess impatiently comes and goes through the doorway. "I think she's ready for us to leave. What time do we meet for the chopper?"

"Oh, not until one. Time for tea, then back to the real world. . . . I called Annelisa." Iain leans forward, squaring his chair legs as he grounds himself. "I have to tell you. Tell someone. She took the call. She . . . She . . ." His glassy eyes squint back tears. "She thought I blamed her. All these years, she thought I left because I blamed her because she didn't mention Jack's sore throat." His voice breaks, and he stops before losing control.

The dining room is as quiet as woods invaded by camping hunters. A couple of minutes pass—long enough for one's life to flash in the campfire.

"Nightcap on the veranda?" Iain stands and bends at the waist a moment to stretch his back. "Getting old," he explains.

Ava laughs lightly. "Maybe just some fresh evening air."

They walk quietly to the front porch. The evening air is still and slightly cool. Two other watermen sit at a far table enjoying cigars. Iain and Ava settle at their regular table as easily as if they flowed there with the current.

He pulls a cigarette from his pack then replaces it. "I told her the truth. All of it. . . . The bloody cowardice of it all. We cried. . . . I'm going to see her at the airport. We're going to go see Jack. See him at his resting place. It's time." He pulls the cigarette and lights it. "And I sent her roses. They'll be there tomorrow morning."

"You what?" Now, Ava is lost in his rending tale of mis-interpretations, lack of action, and cowardly inability to ex-press feelings. His story of love lost, fatherly love, romantic love, familial love. All lost. *He has time to right his story—or at least make it better.* She reaches across the table and squeezes his hand.

"Yellow. Annelisa likes yellow roses. I sent two dozen." Iain is glassy-eyed, but he shows her a full smile of tobacco-stained teeth.

The moment is broken by the whoop-whoop-whoop of a helicopter landing somewhere behind the inn. Many of the pastel-hearted seafarers are taking the easy way home. The sound is a familiar one today.

She leans closer to Iain so he will hear her over the noise. "Good for you, Iain. We don't have forever. Good for you."

ELEVEN

Shire of Shropley, ENG,
October 1987

LADY SARAH HAMPSTEAD enters Edward's suite with two full champagne glasses. "How beautiful," she says sincerely. At a petite five-five, she is a ball of lightning in rose taffeta. Her sandy blonde Rapunzel hair is pulled up into loose ringlets fastened by white rosebuds. In the South, Ava would say Lady Sarah has *gumption*. Here, one just refers to Lady Sarah as having the ability to *be the making of*, well, anything: this wedding, her husband, social acquaintances, children's charities, what have you.

Lady Sarah circles Ava at racehorse pace. "I knew Grandmahmah's gown would be perfect."

The English put the accent on "mah-mah" instead of "grand" and the outcome is that the name becomes grand in the saying of it.

"That underlay of bridal satin is the perfect length. Grandmahmah was the Right Honourable Countess Exmund, not the Countess *of estate x* . . . not a title from a land grant. No, a countess in her own right. There aren't many of those titles remaining from unbroken lines. . . . You favor her very much. Edward was her favorite. Well, Edward is everyone's favorite, now tisn't he? This gown will be a wonderful surprise for him. He'll recognize it straight away from the pahtrait." She lifts the end of the eight-foot train, heavy with hand sewn seed pearls. "Such beauty. Nothing is as beautiful any more. Don't you agree?" She finally hands Ava her glass of champagne.

"Thank you so much. It is truly beautiful. I'm almost afraid to wear it."

Ava is really thinking that she doesn't know how she's going to hold up under a good twenty pounds of beading for . . . how many hours? There are layered yards and yards of ivory bridal satin with seed-pearl patterns of small to large roses haphazardly cascading from her shoulders to the bottom of the gown, as if grown in Tiffany's and tossed into the satin wind.

She sips the sweet bubbles. "I've never seen anything like it."

Two Italian women, both in their forties and obviously sisters, rush about in matching pink Chanel suits. Ava gathers that Lady Sarah hired them to do the bridal hair and makeup and wonders what kind of hairdressers can afford Chanel suits. The women abruptly leave then re-enter the room carrying the veil. They've been working feverishly on Ava for two hours, but she hasn't been allowed to see the result.

She notes that the ivory Venice lace veil has no beading. *Thank goodness*, she thinks. *Maybe I won't break my neck.*

One of the women holds the top of the veil just inches above her coifed hair, pulled loosely into a bun nearly on top of her head.

She tries to hold her head still as she squats low enough for the woman to attach the veil. *What do I know? I thought hair buns are worn on the back of the head.*

"Perfect! I'll be right back." Lady Sarah disappears through the French doors.

Ava admires the delicate lace. Her champagne disappears like a liquid lace confection.

"Such a wonderful day, Baroness," says the older of the two women.

"I'm not a baroness yet," Ava jokes, realizing immediately that the woman is worried she may have offended. "But it does sound very nice."

"Here we are," the ball of lightening glides across the marble floor, her three-inch heels as quiet against the polished stone as on the deep carpet. Lady Sarah holds a coronet of pearls and diamonds set in real silver that is shaped like a quarter moon. She gently hands it to the older woman, who gingerly takes the jewels with a sigh as if touching a shroud. "Grandmahmah's coronet. You must wear her coronet. I wore it at my wedding, and one day our daughters will wear it."

It is surprisingly heavy. This entire day is surprisingly heavy to Ava. Now, she *is* afraid to leave the house. The Chanel sisters pin the veil to the coronet while she tries to balance on bended knees. *I am so glad that I talked Sarah out of a St. Andrews wedding and opted for the small, local chapel built by her great grandfather.*

The hundred guests were narrowed to family and the closest friends. Of course, Sarah outsmarted Ava in that the "country house," as Sarah likes to call it, can hold hundreds more. So, Ava gets the small ceremony and Sarah gets the reception party which, from the number of catering trucks in and out of there the past three days, Ava is assuming will feed the entire county plus the British armed services.

Edward and Ava never discussed finances. She knows that he has an executive position in Australia, so that told her something. The extravagance of the wedding is unexpected, and she wonders if Sarah's husband is somehow paying for it. In rolls the Queen Anne full-length mirror. Faloomph. The antique mirror thumps onto the huge Oriental rug. Ava makes a whooshing sound as she sucks in a chest full of air. It's the sound one makes when startled. It's the same sound made after *being the making of* Sarah's magic.

"*I* want to marry me," Ava exclaims when she sees her reflection. *The only thing missing is a choir in the background, and that will be supplied soon enough,* she thinks.

"Welcome to the family." Sarah is smiling at the two women, who are standing side-by-side, hands clasped as if praying. "Now, the challenge is the carriage without wrinkling her."

Ava is still staring at the gorgeous siren in the mirror. "I thought we settled on your father's Bentley."

"For moors weather, Dear. For a beautiful afternoon such as this one, we must use the carriage. And it's Edward's Bentley, now." Sarah glides out of the room as the Italians start scooping and chattering in Italian.

The carriage is decorated in the wedding colors of rose and white. The sterling roses in Ava's bouquet are the only lavender. A bridal bouquet that practically fills the racing-red, velvet seat. Ava gingerly gets situated on the plush seat, the Chanel sisters still chattering in Italian, and Sarah directing with only a motion here and there of her hand. The whole pouf ball of the bride is finally piled perfectly, like a giant white cupcake. Ava feels the carriage lean to the left and turns to see her father in white tie. The family kept her parents so busy with activities that their only time to talk together was over formal dinners.

"How did I have such a beautiful daughter?" He pushes slightly on her icing to make room for a seat.

She inhales the heavy perfume of damp roses. "Your little girl is about to become a baroness, Dad."

"You are already my princess. It's not too late to change your mind." He's not smiling.

"Okay. . ." She isn't sure what to say. "I'm sure. We're happy together."

He gives her a slight smile and takes her left hand between his bear paws. She sees his formal gloves peeking out of his jacket pocket. The carriage jerks forward with the clip-clop, clip-clop of the matched white horses.

"If you're happy, I'm happy." He looks around as they pull away from the huge stone house that looks more like a magnate's mountain hotel than any country home she ever visited. The horses follow along the low stone wall as they head down the dirt lane to the road. "I always saw myself like this," he says sarcastically.

She knows he is trying to joke with her to ease his tension. She wants to talk about nonsense and life lessons, about sorrows and great happiness, but she can't speak. As they enter the roadway to the village, she hears clapping ahead. A small boy yells out, "Congratulations, Milady!" The townspeople have turned out to see the new baroness and have dressed for the occasion. "Oh, Dad!" Ava squeezes his warm hand. "And they dressed for it, too!"

"They're coming," he whispers.

"What?"

"They're coming to the reception. Lord Hampstead explained it to me: villagers on the lawn and invited guests in the ballroom. It's tradition."

"Sir Richard, Dad."

"What?"

"Sarah's husband is Sir Richard Hampstead. You call him Sir Richard. Sarah is . . . never mind . . . I'll get you a cheat chart."

They laugh and smile at one another. She is his daughter: his looks, his expressions, his talents, but not his temperament. He is much more patient, though he claims that comes with age.

She tries to capture the elusive moments of the ceremony, but she's in a fog as if dreaming the entire event. Her cheeks hurt from smiling. The world smells of roses. Rings exchange. Edward. She did capture the snapshot of Edward's face when he first saw her. He caught his breath, too. They promise . . . something. A simple kiss, not the passionate one of black-and-white movies. Dragging the twenty pounds of seed pearls and satin down the aisle. Cheering. Jerking forward.

Clip-clop. *I am a baroness*, she thinks.

Then, *the* kiss.

Clip-clop. Clip-clop.

"Congratulations!" Schoolchildren and townspeople smile and wave at the passing carriage.

Clip-clop. Clip-clop. Clip-clop.

His warm lips press hers, gently, firmly, pausing as the sides of their noses gently touch. His breath smells of peppermint tea. And there it is, "I love you, Ava. I love you."

The receiving line goes on for over an hour before she pays real attention to anyone. But then there is a familiar face—not a relative, not a close friend, not a business acquaintance. It was the face from the *Stars and Stripes* party.

Lord and Lady Shropley, Mr. Henrich Savauge," says

Sir Ernest, who is assigned for introductions to the wedding party.

Henrich clicks his heels and gives Ava a slight bow. He barely touches her outreached hand as he quickly passes. She notices the tattoo on his thumb that she had forgotten. A type of cross covered in hieroglyphics.

Sir Ernest continues his duties. "Lady Sarah, Mr. Henrich Savauge."

Lady Sarah offers her hand for Henrich to air-kiss. "We regret Dieter could not make it. Perhaps he can visit in two weeks when in London for Edward's meeting."

Ava's mind is racing. *It is him. He has to know that I'm staring.*

Mr. Savauge moves forward in the line without even a glance back at the bride.

"Lady Shropley, Lady Jane . . . Lady Shropley, Lady Jane . . . Lady Shropley . . ." Sir Ernest places himself in Ava's gaze.

Oh, that's me. "Lady Jane, so nice to meet you."

The teenage girl smiles demurely, but her eyes are fixed on the coronet. Sir Ernest moves her along.

Ava turns back to Edward, who is talking to an old friend standing behind them. "Edward that was Henrich, from the *Stars and Stripes* party. You know, Dieter and Henrich."

Edward laughs quietly at something his friend is saying, too low for Ava to hear.

She is not amused that Edward ignores her. "*Edward . . .*"

"Yes, Dear. Dieter and Henrich are long-time family friends. Dieter and father would hunt together. You've seen the trophy room. Remember? You asked if we could give the animals a decent burial. You are so cute, sometimes."

"But you never told me that . . ."

Sir Ernest is back. "Lord Shropley, Sir Richard and Lady Meadowood."

Edward coolly re-enters his role as bridegroom. "Sir Richard, Dabbie, so wonderful of you to make the journey."

She doesn't think she says anything, but she isn't sure. She remembers shaking hands. Meeting in two weeks? Old hunting buddies? Did Dieter already know who I was? Did Edward know I met Dieter that night? Did Edward already know about the Porsche when we went to the Ball . . . to Margaret River? Ava doesn't like coincidences. Doesn't really believe in coincidences. Not really. But she wants to believe. Right now she really wants to believe in them.

Edward leads her by the arm to the ballroom. "Duty is done for the moment. Shall we join the party?"

The orchestra is playing a waltz, but no one is dancing.

Edward crosses her to the center of the room. "We get the first dance. Tradition. A little different from the States. Yes?" He nods to the orchestra conductor.

Tap! Tap! on the music stand. Schubert's *Serenade* begins as Edward glides her across the floor in slow motion. Dum de la dum dum . . . The music sounds odd, and she can't decide if it's an odd choice for the first dance or if she feels dissociated from the scene.

The first dance on my wedding day, she thinks. She accidentally steps on Edward's foot, but he acts as if he doesn't notice. *My first dance as the Baroness of Shropley. I need to be in the moment, I'm just not sure how to do it.*

The muffled clapping of hundreds of gloved hands. They pause. The eerie whisperings of a hundred lowered voices. A waltz begins as couples flow onto the floor. She doesn't recognize the melody. No correct order of dance partners listed here. Nothing as crass as imposed formality.

"You are the most beautiful woman I have ever seen," Edward enunciates each word as she follows his lead.

The beaded train is heavy on her wrist. She longs for the cool night air. Her shoulders are heavy with the weight. Fifty bobby pins pull tiny hairs on her head. She looks around at the beautiful scene as he skillfully glides her to the edge of the crowd.

Edward scans the room as he leads her off the floor. "Let's retire to the library. I think we need a moment."

He nods to her parents, who dance past them, her father obviously trying to follow some recent lessons as her mother whispers directions in his ear. The newlyweds weave through the crowded anteroom and down the marble hallway. The click-click-click-click of her heels is only slightly muffled by the well-wishers.

How does Sarah walk these halls without a sound, Ava wonders. She hears voices and strains to make out the words. *English accent.*

". . . a Yank! Fun way to take one for the team, if you ask me. Anyway, good of you to bring the report," a man says in the library just ahead.

"Not a choice really. I know the rights are worth millions, maybe billions. Don't know how I'll explain the information leaking."

Edward looks quickly at her, but she shows no signs of overhearing the conversation. He speaks over the voices coming from the library. "We can step outside if you prefer," he says, suddenly stopping in the hallway.

She is curious about the voices. "No, no. A quiet sit-down is a good idea." She walks on before he responds. She still hears the English accent. Easier to understand at this distance.

"...daft. An office break-in is always good for ... Edward, oh and the beautiful bride," says Sir Ernest.

The library doorway frames the couple. Three men stand next to an antique Atlas opened on the center reading table. A couple of loose maps lie outside the book, a tome at least two-feet square. She's never seen it open and marvels at the detail on the yellowed pages. She is trying to forget the Yank comment. The room smells of cigar smoke, parchment, and old leather. The Oriental carpet of deep reds and browns is the thickest she has ever felt underfoot, like walking on foam rubber. It's a man's room. She feels very comfortable ... and safe. As the men turn, she realizes that one of them is Henrich. He is talking with Sir Ernest and someone she doesn't know.

Something about break-ins, she remembers. The day is too overwhelming and exhausting to muster curiosity.

"We'll take our leave," Sir Ernest says as the newlyweds enter the room. "I'm sure you would like a moment alone." Sir Ernest and the stranger walk toward the door.

Henrich carefully replaces the two individual maps into the Atlas, gently closing the large book, and pushing it to the far corner of the table, where it usually resides. "Lord Shropley," he says with a nod as he exits the room.

"Tea, m' Lord?" A young maid is standing in the doorway.

"Champagne, Elsa. Tonight we live on champagne."

The maid curtseys slightly and disappears, closing the eight-foot mahogany door behind her.

"What is the meeting in two weeks?" Ava can no longer wait.

"What, Dear?"

She lowers herself onto a brown leather couch, rubbing her sore wrist as the weight of the skirt is lifted from her wrist strap. "I overheard Sarah mention a meeting in two weeks. She was talking to Henrich. We'll just be back from our trip to Austria."

"I was hoping to save it for another time . . . Are you ready to live here, to close up shop in the States and Australia and move to Shropley?" He lifts the heavy train to help her sit more comfortably on the glove-leather sofa. The room is so quiet that she can hear the fire crackle as a log dislodges itself from the stack. "There we are." He examines her chafing wrist. "Not good, that."

She enjoys his gentle touch. "I thought we would be in Perth for a while. I mean with your job and—"

"That position was to get the proper training. One cannot make shrewd investments when one doesn't understand the industry. Things have changed so much since father's time. I have a responsibility to the family and the estate."

He sits beside her and takes a cigar from the jarrah box with brass corners. Tap! Tap! A brass Churchill snips the end. Twoop! The match strikes and soon the room fills with the earthy scent of Cuban tobacco.

"I didn't know you smoke cigars."

"Only on special occasions. Does it bother you?"

"Smoking bothers me, but I actually enjoy the scent of a good cigar—sort of like a good fire with cedar kindling." Ahchoo. She sneezes at the smoke.

"Bless you. . . . Well put, but this move situation. You won't need to do anything, of course. The staff can handle whatever you need."

"Can we afford to do that? I mean the taxes on this place and everything."

He coughs a laugh that sends a smoke cloud, reflected in the baroque mirror hanging nearby. "You let me worry about that. A group of us are putting together a consortium."

"Edward, just how chummy are you with Henrich? . . . Lady Sarah called me before our trip to Margaret River. She said something about passing a test. What did she mean?"

"Darling, one rarely knows what Sarah means. Let's not talk about all of that now. And it's Sarah, not Lady Sarah. You're family now. Tomorrow, Vienna! You're going to love it. Much better than some old cruise to Antarctica or somewhere." He puffs three little smoke rings into the air, watching them waltz to the twelve-foot ceiling before colliding with coffered moldings.

"True. Funny, I don't remember ever telling you about that."

"About what?" Edward looks at the cigar he is twirling between his right thumb and forefinger.

"Skip buying tickets to Antarctica."

"He did? What a funny coincidence. Just a touristy place to mention, I guess." He taps the end of his cigar in the crystal tray. "Up we go. We must keep up appearances with the guests." He pulls her up from the deep couch as her toes slide back into their vices.

TWELVE

Eden

THE LATE EVENING air is chilly on the front porch. Another whoop-whoop-whoop interrupts the muffled thumps of kangaroos passing near the inn.

"That must be our cue," Iain says as he stands. "Good to have the fairytale ending. Wish everyone's story could end that way. . . . Never one for coincidences myself. You'll sort it out."

Edward bounds onto the front porch of the inn. "Dahling, I wanted to surprise you." He kisses Ava firmly on the top of her head before she has a chance to stand. "And what's this? I find you holed up here with ol' Feenie."

Iain chuckles and offers his hand. "Good to see ya, Mate. Guess you caught us."

Edward drops his black overnight bag on the plank floor and pulls a chair from the neighboring table. "So what are you two conspirators getting up to? Not telling the family secrets I hope, Dahling."

Ava self-consciously smooths her hair. If she had known he was arriving, she could have at least brushed it. "All of your escapades, but Iain says they are too boring to print."

"On that note," Iain says, gathering his things from the

table, "I'll leave you to it. Have some last-minute, *interesting* blokes to talk to before everyone heads out. See you tomorrow, Ava, tumm, baroness. Baron." With a slight nod he heads upstream.

"Let's go up," Edward says. "Bushed from the travels. And haven't seen you since the great sea adventure. Come on. I want to hear all about it." He takes her hand.

"How did you manage a ride?"

"I have my charms. And some cash. Rode in on the supply chopper with some bloke with a bum knee. Had to help him aboard, poor bastard. Left him to the pilot. No worries. Let's get out of here. I missed you."

They pass the remaining nightcap revelers in the parlor. Usual suspects. The preppy foursome with matching yellow slickers on chair backs at the card table, loner with the baseball cap reading a newspaper in the corner, bachelor-party gang with a couple of local twenty-year-old Sheilas. Ava always notices. The young Irish girl is watching the front desk. A middle-aged man with a Sydney accent chats her up, as Iain would say, while she files index cards.

Edward stops briefly at the desk. "We're together," he says. "Just in on the supply chopper. Message the *Tazzie Devil* crew that their part arrived. Pilot will be needing accommodation. Put it on my tab. He's staying over to take me back tomorrow. Oh, and some other chap. He'll be in any time."

"I'll need the pilot himself to sign a card, ta." She places a blank index card and pen in front of him on the desk.

"No worries. I can do it for him." Edward signs "Lord Shropley" and walks off holding Ava's hand.

"Ta, m' Lord, tumm, Lord Shropley," the girl yells after him.

The bed is turned down with a lofty, white comforter added. The evening air slightly breezes through the sheers. The room is redolent of sea air and lingering mutton fat being burned off the barbeque pit in the back yard.

Ava busies herself closing the two half-open windows. She pulls down the vinyl blinds. A-choo. Ahhh-chooo!

"Now don't go getting allergic to me," he jokes as he grabs her waist and they poooof into the bed. "I need a proper kiss, Lady Shropley."

She jokingly presses hard into his lips, but quickly turns her head for another ahhh-ahhh-choooo! "I'm so sorry. Excuse me. Something in the room. Must be the night air."

"Looks like I arrived just in time to care for you." He gives her a quick kiss on the cheek.

"Yes. Just in time."

THE MIDDAY CHOPPER circles the inn twice as Iain and Ava gather their bags on the front porch. They lose sight of it as it circles to the open field behind the inn, but the whoom-whoom-whoom . . . whoom . . . whoom indicates a landing.

"So Edward is in the consortium. I've heard the rumors, but nothing concrete about their intentions." Iain checks the contents of his bag a final time. "So where is the lucky bugger?"

"Inside on a call. Some message this morning. Let me say goodbye." Ava drops her bag on the ground next to Iain and enters the inn. Her party seems the last of the guests, and she imagines the innkeepers will be glad for the rest. Edward's raised voice, emanating from the office door, catches her attention.

The Irish maid catches Ava as she nears the office behind the front desk. "I'll beg your pardon. We'll be needing a signatory for the pilot. On the Lord's bill, don't you know. Oh, and the other mister never checked in."

"Here, I'll sign for the pilot." Ava walks to the desk and takes the pen.

"And t'other?"

"Lord Shropley doesn't know him. Must have boarded one of the yachts in the harbor."

"Yes, m' Lady."

"No, he's out. Tisn't negotiable. *My* call. . . . That's right. . . . *No*. . . . Ava? Just a minute, Dahling . . . I have to go. . . . No, there's nothing else to discuss." Edward hangs up the phone.

Ava knows better than to pry about particulars. Edward doesn't react well to snooping. "Everything all right?"

He is flushed. "No worries. Just business. Let's get you on that chopper. Mine leaves in about twenty minutes."

Before they can head outside, Iain walks into the parlor. He is carrying his bag and Ava's bag. "Don't hurry. Pilot says he noticed a leak. Could be a good two or three hours."

She turns to Edward. "Looks like you'll beat us to Sydney after all. Even though you have to fly as cargo!" She notices baseball-cap guy passing by the side window. She thought he left early this morning. "Only a few of us still here. Should have no problem getting early tea." She waves them toward the dining room.

Iain pops his fist into his hand. "Damn! Annelisa is meeting me at the airport. Hope she didn't leave home already."

Ava looks at Edward. "Maybe he could . . ."

"I'll be right back." Edward leaves the dining room and she can hear him taking the stairs two at a time.

The pudgy mistress of the house places three cups with saucers and three pots of tea on their table without a word.

She leaves the large carrying tray on the next table and disappears back into the kitchen. Iain and Ava are her sole customers.

Iain squirms nervously in his chair. "I called this morning. Annelisa liked the roses and poem. We're having dinner tonight in Sydney."

Ava's eyebrows raise. "Poem? Iain, you wrote a poem?"

"Nope. Took it from the Yeats book in the sitting room." He winks. "She'll never know. I feel great! How do you feel?"

"Safe . . . and like I'll never know." She didn't need to explain what she would never know. Not to Iain.

Edward rushes back into the room. "You're all set, ol' chap. Pilot says you can take my spot. Be in the garden in fifteen minutes. May as well enjoy your tea."

"Are you sure?" Iain's stress is leaving his face.

"Absolutely. I'll wait with Ava. Give us time for a walkabout."

The three pass the time speaking of trivialities: the weather, the cricket season, radio reports of raging crews drinking Hobart dry. They are all preoccupied with their own agendas, their own duties awaiting in Sydney and beyond. They can't live in the moment like the pod. There is always tomorrow. Always something in the coming tide.

The young pilot waves through the dining room doorway as he passes.

"That's you," Edward tells Iain.

"Love awaits," Iain says smiling, lightening the emotion with a sarcastic tone. "Lady Shropley, my pleasure. Be in touch?"

"Have to hear your story . . . and end the one haunting us." She stands and hugs Iain. "Go get her, Feenie."

He smiles at her using his nickname. "Later, Mates."

She settles back into her seat. "May as well request tea sandwiches or something. Looks like we're here for a while."

Edward walks over to the kitchen entrance. "Pardon?"

Whoop . . . whoop . . . whoop-whoop-whoop-whoop . . . whoop . . . . . whoop . . BOOM!

Edward runs to the window as Ava instinctively crouches and covers her head.

She yells through her knees. "What the hell was that?"

"Stay down!" Edward runs away from the window as pieces of metal shatter the glass.

CRAAACK! BOOM!

"What the . . ." she looks pleadingly at Edward.

He runs to the other window. "Stay here," he shouts. "I mean it, Ava. Stay here." He disappears through the dining room doorway.

She can hear two women screaming in the kitchen. Outside a man is yelling something she can't decipher.

"Lady Shropley!"

She looks up to see the network pilot enter the dining room. For a second, baseball-cap guy pauses in the doorway then disappears.

"The cargo chopper," the man in the pilot uniform is yelling. "The cargo chopper. Lord Shropley!"

"Lord Shropley is outside." She is confused. She can't think. Can't focus.

"No. His cargo chopper exploded!"

"What? No, Lord Shropley is coming with me." She is finally in the moment. Not Sydney. Not tomorrow. Not agendas. "Iain! Iain Miller!" She knocks her chair to the floor jumping up and running past the network pilot.

Edward is standing in the garden with the innkeeper. Fifty yards away a fireball erupts from a stand of gum trees. Pieces of hot metal scatter everywhere, causing small smoke signals to rise in memoriam. The innkeeper runs to the water spigot and drags the large hose around to the small fires beginning to ignite.

She runs to Edward, standing still as an obelisk. "Edward, what happened? Is it Iain? Did his helicopter blow up? Edward?"

He isn't thinking ahead, either. But he is also not in the now. He is thinking backwards. Considering past decisions. Weighing past assumptions. He can hear Ava crying, but his mind is too full. Recognition. No reaction.

"Ed . . . Edward!" her face soaks with tears. She shakes her husband back to the living.

"Come on," he says suddenly. "Need to get inside. Tisn't safe out here. I need to make a call."

They run back inside the inn as if more death may rain from the sky.

"Stay here," he tells Ava as he sits her in the parlor. "I mean it, Ava. Stay here." He runs to the office and slams the door behind him.

Her mind races. She needs to call Annelisa. Someone has to call Annelisa. But maybe it wasn't the helicopter. Maybe it was something else. Edward will find out. He'll find out what it really was. . . . "Edward!"

Edward emerges from the office in a few minutes. His face is as pale as dried coral. "Don't worry, Dahling. The authorities are en route. I have a car coming. No chopper. We'll wait for the car. Now, I have some calls I must make. I need you to wait here. Can I get you anything?"

"Does that mean it was the chopper?" She feels drugged.

Edward's demeanor suddenly changes from stress to concern. "Yes, Ava. It was the chopper. Iain is dead. Do you understand?"

"I have to call Annelisa."

"Later. I'll get the airport authorities to track her down. You can call later."

"But Edward, you were supposed to be on that chopper. It could have been you."

"Stay here. Okay, Dahling? Stay here."

He doesn't need to tell her to stay because she couldn't move if the inn caught fire. A few people rush past her. She doesn't notice who they are. There is shouting. Can't decipher the words. Time passes. So much time. The pounding of her heart sounds an overwhelming whoop-whoop-whoop-whoop in her ears. The world goes black as the deep sea.

Edward is talking in a low voice. "Yes. Check on that. Good chap. . . . Ava? Ava?" Edward shakes Ava to awaken her. "Let me help you to the room."

She is groggy but too dazed to recognize the man walking away—the man in the navy jacket and at the Kirribilli apartment.

"Who is that, Edward? Do you know that man?"

"Who? You're still in the riptide. Bloody awful day. Let me help you."

Somehow they make it up the stairs, but she sneezes as the door opens. Ahh-choo! "Not this room. We can't stay here."

"This is our room, Sweetie. It's all right."

"No." She pulls her arm away from him. "I want another room."

"Of course, whatever you want. I'll go ask . . ."

"Don't leave me, Edward." She grabs his arm.

"We'll go together, all right?"

They go back downstairs. The young Irish girl is crying and crouching behind the desk. Can't even respond to

Edward, just hands him another key. Ava clutches his sleeve with both hands.

TAP, TAP, TAP. Tap, tap, tap. The gentle knocking at the door makes Edward and Ava sit up on the bed in full alert. Laying on top of the bed fully clothed for two, four, six hours, they are both stiff and anxious. Hard to determine the passing of time. Both pretending to be asleep to avoid talking. Neither slept. The sun lowers in the sky. There is an eerie quiet.

Edward checks his watch. "Half past four," he tells Ava. He crosses the room but does not remove the chair she placed under the doorknob. "Yes?"

The Irish maid speaks in a jittery voice. "M' Lord, your driver says come now. M' Lord?"

"Yes. Ta. Tell him we are coming. Ava, let's go. Our car is here." He picks up two leather bags from beside the bed. "Ava?"

"Is it all right?" She doesn't move from the bed. "Maybe you should check first."

"All right." He puts on his jacket and moves the chair away from the door.

"No. Wait. Don't leave me alone. I'm coming." She grabs her extra bag and runs across the room. She holds the back of his jacket all the way down the stairs.

"Charles," Edward says as he nears the bottom of the stairs. "Good to see a familiar face. We'll catch up in the ca'. Ava, this is Charles Spencer. We were at Oxford together. Charles, my wife, Ava. Charles did an honors degree at Murdoch University. Haven't seen him in years."

"How fortunate you turn up now," Ava says. "I'm sure you're no professional driver."

Charles shakes her hand when she offers it. "Tapped for Her Majesty's Service, Lady Shropley. We're going to get you home and sort out this business. Edward, we have you booked out of Melbourne, Ol' Boy. You'll be at the manor house before you know it."

"I have business in Hong Kong—" Edwards starts.

"Maybe you *had* business in Hong Kong, but my orders are to get you home. Whatever you're mixed up in, you're coming under wing. Some business about the opening of oil leases. It's all greed on deck. Above my pay grade." Charles takes the bag she is carrying and one of the bags Edward is carrying. "We're off, then." He motions to a woman leaning on the front of the car finishing a cigarette. "Lord and Lady Shropley, may I introduce Emma Stoneford. She'll be travelling with you all the way home."

Emma drops her cigarette and grinds it into the grass with her three-inch black heel. She opens a back door of the car. "Lady Shropley," Emma motions for Ava to sit in the back seat.

She sits without a word. Something about the woman bothers her. Emma is very attractive with waist-length auburn hair flowing down the back of her Diane von Furstenberg black and white wrap dress. The stretchy material is revealing enough to accentuate her . . . her *bumper tits—isn't that what the bartended said?*

"Nice escort," Edward says, joking with Charles as they round the car.

Charles reaches the back door first and opens it for Edwards. "Don't let the cover fool you. She's a chemist with a black belt. Higher pay grade than mine. *Cold,*" Charles whispers.

Ava turns to Edward as he sits next to her. "And she

knows Patsy Cline songs."

Emma pulls down the sun visor and looks at Ava in the vanity mirror. "I see why Skip liked you. They should've sent me to Jakarta. He'd still be here." She calmly checks her lipstick and closes the visor. "We needed him in play. Now it's a bloody mess with the Europeans teaming up. You played it well. Picked the right side this time. Just stay in the shallow end, Dear."

Ava is silent.

Edward looks at her. "Do you know her? Did Skip know her?"

"I'm sure Miss Stoneford knew me much better than I knew her. It was a long time ago. I'm sure she will take good care of us. She is *very* dedicated to her job. Charles, I never forget a face. Have we met?" Ava thinks for a moment as Charles silently adjusts the car for the trip. She doesn't miss the nervous gesture. "Have you ever been to Yalata?"

Emma snickers and turns to Charles. "*That's* why you are below my pay grade."

Charles stiffens. "Sure I must've been through there a few times."

Edward shifts in his seat to get comfortable. "So good. We all know one another. Charles, you'll have to fill me in on the issue here. At a better time, I mean. I'm sure it will all sort out."

"Always does for your kind," Emma says matter-of-factly.

Edward ignores the comment.

"Shall we go?" Charles asks nervously, pulling away from the inn before anyone responds.

"So Emma, are you saying something happened to Skip in Jakarta?" Ava asks.

"Goodness no! His geo hit him way before that trip.

Good timing I must say. To infect someone with meningitis and have it bloom in a third world country. We should recruit that shit if we can find him."

"You mean Schultz?"

"Of course, Dear, though not his real name. No idea of his real name. Watching him for weeks. Missed that one. Too busy following our bunny—that would be you. So Lord Shropley, you can thank your new wife for leading us to the oil exploration papers regarding Indonesia. Smart of ol' Skip to pay in cash. Good thing you keep such tidy records. Of course, if *we* found out about it . . ."

Ava stares at Edward. "You did an exploration for Skip? Off the record? The deal with the prince? Edward, did you tell Dieter and Henrich?"

"Dahling, of course not." He pretends to struggle with his seat belt. "And you already knew so the word was obviously out there. You mentioned it at Margaret River." He looks at Emma. "So you broke into our offices?" he asks her.

"Not *me*. I don't get my hands dirty with trivia." She smooths her long hair and adjusts it behind her back. "Seems there's quite a list of people interested in that deal."

Edward takes Ava's hand from her lap and gives it a little squeeze as he forces a smile. "I'm sure. We'll sort it out later. . . . So, all set. How do you feel, Ava?"

She gently removes her hand and puts it back in her lap. Moments in silence. She watches passing native wildflowers sprinkling yellow and purple and red into the ocean breeze. A lone 'roo and two-foot Joey munch the colorful dessert. Pop! goes the roof of the car as a minor bird swoops the Mercedes passing too close to its nest. She turns. Can't see the ocean. She hopes for calm seas. *Oz Rox* is under sail to Sydney. She imagines Skip at the helm. Her promise kept.

Evening onset blazes the left horizon in rose and orange. *Red sky at night, sailor's delight.* "Shielded by ancient earth . . . and like I'll never know," she says, staring at the sunset. Edward looks through business cards in his wallet. "Know what, Dear?"

No response. Her watermen ancestors hoist ghost canvases. Time to release sunken ships and appreciate the value of a yare tender.

www.ingramcontent.com/pod-product-compliance
Lightning Source LLC
Chambersburg PA
CBHW061104100525
26447CB00075B/53/J

·